# WHITE SPIRIT

# WHITE SPIRIT

## RESTLESS SPIRITS BOOK 1

### AMY RAVENEL

Charlotte, NC

FALSTAFF
BOOKS
WWW.FALSTAFFBOOKS.COM

*To Mom and Dad for letting me follow them around the house, asking how to spell different words, and for reading (or trying to read) my first efforts. Thank you, and I love you!*

The suitcase flew out of nowhere. Tristan Johnson ducked as it sailed across the hallway, missing his head by inches. When he didn't hear it crash into the wall behind him, he turned. The suitcase vanished without making a sound.

"I told you to leave." A young, blonde woman with pale skin gripped the open doorway. She glared at him, her anger permeating the air. Her voice echoed throughout the building.

Tristan straightened, his heart beating a mile a minute. His hands tightened on the heavy box in his arms. "I'm sorry. I must have the wrong…"

Her light brown eyes flashed before she, like the suitcase, disappeared into nothing.

A cold chill slid down Tristan's spine. He sucked in a breath as his whole body shook. The box wobbled, but he kept it from toppling to the hardwood floor.

"Damn it. Not again," he muttered under his breath.

He jumped when someone yelled at the other end of the

hall. The box wobbled again. A young man with a head full of dark hair raced towards him, determination on his face.

"I'm going to kill you, man!"

He picked up speed and charged. Tristan braced for the impact, but the man ran straight though him. He whirled around to see nothing but the window at the end of the hallway. He set the box on the floor before he dropped it for good. Gritting his teeth, he sat and slowly breathed in and out.

*Every. Damn. Time.*

Closing his eyes, he took a deep breath. *Stay calm. Focus on the here and now.* His father's advice rang in his ears. *"Picture a high wall built with bricks. Surround yourself with it. It's your shield, your sanity. Wrap yourself in it."*

"Shut them out. They're not real," he whispered.

Voices from the past overlapped each other in a cacophony of noise, each one vying for his attention. It surrounded him, squeezed in, and left his ears ringing.

Tristan imagined his inner wall strengthening around him. He mentally placed red bricks on top of each other, building the structure layer by layer. As each piece settled into place, the buzzing in his brain died down. A few sounds from the past whispered in his ears, but the majority drained away.

He opened his eyes. No one was standing in the doorway of the apartment. No one ran down the hall. No echoes, no shadows. Tristan was alone.

Blessed, blessed silence.

"Is the box too heavy for you, Johnson?"

Tristan stood and nodded to the white, blond man walking towards him. At least he was real and solid. Zack Beckett sauntered down the hall, his arms full of two medium-sized boxes.

Tension eased off Tristan's shoulders. The corner of his

mouth quirked in a half-smile. "Shut up, Beckett." He lifted his box off the floor, thankful that nothing breakable was in it. He entered the open apartment, now clear of angry women from the past.

"I'm only saying if you need help, you should let me know." Zack followed him and set the boxes on the bar separating the living room and the kitchen. He ran a hand through his damp, sweaty hair.

Tristan rolled his eyes. "Is that why you're carrying the smaller boxes, Shorty?"

"Conserving my strength, Jolly Green Giant." Zack rolled his shoulders.

"Tristan slacking again?" Drew Keane walked into the apartment after them. He deposited his boxes in the back corner of the living room with a loud grunt. The grunt turned into a groan that increased in pitch as he stretched and popped his back.

"Man, I carried most of this up here without you." Tristan punched Drew in the lightly tanned arm.

"You were sitting in front of the door with your eyes closed," Zack pointed out.

Tristan shifted his weight from foot to foot. "I was getting used to the place." He tapped his temple.

All the joking left Zack's face. "You okay, man?"

Tristan waved him off. "I will be."

Drew wiggled his blondish-brown eyebrows. "See anything interesting?"

"A pissed off woman who threw her luggage at me, and a guy who wanted to kick my ass. Nothing special."

Drew dropped down on the fluffy beige couch. His shoes landed on the coffee table with a thud. "You always get the boring visions. No hidden treasures? No major make-out sessions? No..." He paused for emphasis and lowered his voice, drawing out the word. "Muuurdeeer?"

Tristan rolled his eyes. "I hope there's no murder. Those are the worst."

Every place had a different psychic energy, and Tristan never knew how it would affect his ability to see the past. Sometimes the past nudged against his mind, presenting transparent images, like the woman in the doorway. Sometimes it charged through like an elephant, knocking him back against the wall. In those, he not only saw but also touched and felt the movie playing out in his mind. In the worst moments, the vision took him over. When that happened, he had no idea what was real and what wasn't. It took days or months to get used to a new place.

"What is this? Are you guys taking a break on me?" Kayla Collins pushed into the room, sweat glistening on her dark brown skin. Her gaze swept over them, a smile on her face. "Am I the only one around here who can handle the work?" She placed her boxes on the kitchen table.

"Why do you think I want to marry you?" Zack moved behind her. He wrapped his arms around her waist, lifting her off the ground. "Man enough for you?"

She smacked his arm. "You're crazy, you know that?" She laughed as he set her down. Her dark brown eyes sparkled. "Alright, guys. Let's keep moving. The rest of that junk isn't going to move itself." She jerked a thumb at the door.

"Aw, come on, Kayla. One break. We've been moving all morning." Drew pulled up the bill of his Duke cap and scratched his damp hair. "And some of us have to work tonight."

"Drew, quit whining. Everyone knows all you do is sit around old houses and wait for ghosts to show up." Kayla pointed to the door again.

Drew groaned as he walked out. "It's important work. I have to keep alert all night."

Zack followed him. "Aw, poor baby." He pushed his friend

forward, and they both stumbled out of the apartment laughing.

Kayla tossed her hands into the air with mock exasperation as she trailed after them.

Tristan shook his head as he watched them go. How had he survived those two years in Wilmington without them? More importantly, he was grateful they were there the whole past year when he thought he was losing his mind. He had known Drew since they were kids and Zack and Kayla since college. No matter how crazy he sounded, they always had his back.

He pulled off his light blue University of North Carolina baseball cap and pushed back the curls that fell into his eyes. He took in the small dining room/living room combination. Light brown hardwood floors and white walls waited for him to put his mark on them. A sliding glass door that led to a balcony stood across from him. He turned into the kitchen on his right and ran a hand over the smooth off-white counter tops. It was a good place. Despite the visions, it had a good energy. He could learn control here.

Originally, Tristan hadn't wanted to leave his parents' house. After everything that happened in Wilmington, he wasn't sure the real world was for him. Then Zack and Drew suggested he move to Asheville, a city nestled in the Blue Ridge Mountains, and finish his master's degree. He was hesitant, but he trusted them. Zack and Kayla lived down the hall. Drew was a quick phone call away.

It was a place where he could forgive himself. Even though he missed the crash of the ocean and the salty, humid air, he was glad to move back to the crisp and cool mountains. His family and friends didn't blame him for what happened, but he blamed himself. His cousin Karie's screams still haunted him. Details of the vision that almost destroyed them both played over and over in his mind. Flashes of anger and intense rage. He still felt the solid wood in his hand.

He pushed it away. It wasn't going to happen again. He refused to let it. Control. He had to learn control.

As Tristan ambled back to the door, a cold breeze brushed his cheek. He shivered. A quick glance around the room told him no windows were open. He started to walk again.

A woman's laugh rang in his ears, and he froze. He took a deep breath. He didn't acknowledge the breeze or the laugh. It was probably some remnant of the past, begging to be let in.

The air cooled. The temperature on the air conditioner control panel dropped from seventy degrees to forty and kept going. Tristan's breath made white circles with every puff. Chill bumps formed on his sweat-soaked arms as he folded them. His shoulders hunched as his body shook. He lifted an eyebrow. It was the end of the summer in the mountains. Temperatures were cool, but they didn't drop that fast. And definitely not on their own.

The front door slammed, loud enough to cut through the eerie silence.

Tristan's heart jumped into his throat. Just the wind. That was all. He glanced at the sliding glass door that led to the balcony and noticed it was closed. No wind, then.

He grabbed the doorknob, his breath sucking in as he touched the cold metal. Fighting the stinging iciness, he wrapped his hand around it and pulled. The door wouldn't budge. He yanked and turned, but it stayed closed. Tristan's calm melted away as his heartbeat picked up. Panic rose, swift and all-encompassing. His mouth dried. Rattling the door, his stomach rolled and threatened to sour.

The cold kissed his skin as he continued to work the knob. No movement. Not a creak. He was stuck in his apartment. His ever-increasingly cold apartment. Was it possible to freeze to death in an apartment in the summer? Why didn't the stupid door open? He banged on it with his fist.

"Zack! Drew! This isn't funny! Open the damn door!"

The woman laughed again next to his left ear. Something cold and soft trailed down his neck. He held his breath, but his heart continued to pound. What was that?

He stood still while every cell in his body told him to run. But where to? He was stuck inside his apartment, and he wasn't alone.

What the hell was going on?

A light glow appeared in the corner of his eye. He pivoted to face it, and his jaw dropped. The ghostly shape of a woman wearing a simple white sundress stood in the middle of his living room. A nonexistent wind lifted her long, white hair off her shoulders. Her piercing green eyes were the only spot of color on her. She studied him for a moment before gliding toward him, a hand outstretched. Her feet never touched the floor.

It took him a long moment to find his voice. "Who the hell are you?" It came out as a whisper, as if a louder volume might cause her to attack.

She cocked her head to the side, studying him as if he were a specimen. Her eyes held no life.

Tristan's muscles refused to move. He barely even breathed. *It's another vision,* he told himself. But deep inside, he knew this woman was not in his head. She was too transparent. Tales of Drew's ghost hunting ran through his memory. Ghosts pulled energy from the room, making the air colder than it actually was. But didn't they show up at night? The day was bright and warm outside the windows.

He shut his eyes and counted to five before opening them again. He dug his fingers into his arms as he jerked away. She had moved closer; an inch or two was all that stood between them.

Fascinated and terrified, he watched as she lifted her hand. She touched his cheek with icy, hesitant fingers. Wanting to back away, he told his feet to move. They were planted to the floor. Her fingers traced a freezing line down his jaw. She seemed to glow brighter the moment she touched his skin. A few seconds later, his body relaxed, and he sank into the nearest chair.

The fear and panic eased away, leaving a floating sensation. The cold no longer bothered him. Instead, peace spread through his limbs.

Someone jiggled the doorknob. "Tristan, you going to let us in?" Zack knocked on the door.

Tristan opened his mouth to answer, but no sound came out. His eyes were glued to the ghostly girl caressing his cheek. If he could stay there forever, he'd be content.

And then she was gone, disappearing as quickly as she appeared.

The door sprang open, banging against the wall. Zack walked in, his eyebrows turned down in confusion. "Tristan?"

Tristan blinked a couple of times and shook his head. Everything was fuzzy. His brain was sluggish, thoughts forming slowly. He wiped his face with his hands, jumping when Zack's warm hand shook his shoulder.

"Tristan? Did you turn up the air in here?"

More boxes thudded on the floor. "Oh, my God! Is he okay?" Kayla knelt in front of him. "You're pale. Zack, he's pale. Get him some water."

Everything swam into focus. "I'm okay. I promise. I just… I don't…" He glanced from Kayla to Zack. "There's a ghost in my apartment."

The couple exchanged a knowing look.

"What?" Tristan kept his gaze on Zack. "What is it?" His skin warmed as the room itself did. "Did you know about this?"

Zack set a bottle of water on the table. "Don't tell Drew, okay? We'll explain everything tonight."

"Were you planning on telling me?" Tristan gulped down the bottle as if he hadn't had water in a month. "I feel like I ran a marathon."

Everyone went quiet when Drew ambled through the door. He peered around the box he carried and the humor left his face. "What's wrong?"

Zack gave Tristan a slight shake of his head.

Tristan forced himself to smile. "Another vision, man. This one was a doozy." His voice was too high, his breath too shallow. He hated lying to Drew.

Drew's greenish-hazel eyes lit up. "Murder?"

"No, only a hot chick coming on to me." Not far from the truth.

Drew relaxed and set his boxes on the edge of the table. "Well, at least this one wasn't throwing a suitcase at you."

Tristan met Zack's eyes. "Yeah. Thank God for that." His friend had a hell of a lot of explaining to do.

"Anybody want to tell me what's going on?" Tristan sank into his chair with a cold beer. He studied the two friends sitting on his couch. "And maybe why they didn't tell me before I signed a contract?" The bitter taste of beer was welcome.

Zack shrugged. "I didn't think it was a big deal." He studied his bottle, avoiding Tristan's eyes.

Drew had left for his job an hour ago, and Tristan was

ready for answers about the mysterious haunting in his apartment.

"You didn't think it was a big deal?" Tristan leaned forward. "You talk your psychic best friend into moving into an apartment with a ghost, and you didn't think it was a big deal?" His bottle clinked on the dark cherry wood coffee table.

"Look, The White Lady is a part of this place. A feature. I think she's harmless." Zack flashed him a grin. "I've seen her in the hall and my place, too."

Tristan fought to remain calm. "A feature? How long has she been here?"

Zack sighed. "I don't know. Since before we moved in. She doesn't do anything but float around and laugh. She's harmless."

"According to the legend, she's not harmless." Kayla sipped her beer, her voice flat.

"Kayla, not this again." Zack sighed. "It's a legend, a story. It's not real."

Kayla narrowed her dark eyes. "She sure as hell is."

"The legend?" Tristan's stomach dropped. How could this possibly get any worse?

"Ten years ago, three guys committed suicide in this building. Some people say The White Lady made them do it." Zack set his drink on the coffee table. "'If you see The White Lady, you die.'" He made air quotes. "It's bullshit."

Kayla shot him a look. "It's not bullshit. Three different men all decide to kill themselves at the same time?" She turned to Tristan. "I've been trying to get him to tell Drew, maybe get an investigation going around here, but he won't do it."

Zack shook his head. "She's a ghost. She can't hurt anybody," he insisted. "There's no point in having cameras all over the place. I don't want Drew watching me sleep."

Kayla groaned. "We don't have to stay here while they investigate, stupid."

"Still. Having people walking around our apartment and filming is creepy."

"Not as creepy has having a ghost haunting us."

"Can we get back to the point?" Tristan's voice rose. His hands shook. His lunch pitched and tossed in his stomach. He leaned forward, his grip tightening on his bottle. "Why did you keep this from me?" He waved his bottle in a circle, encompassing the room.

Zack raked a hand through his hair. "You'd have used it as an excuse, man. You were looking for anything to keep you in your parents' basement, locked away like some crazy person. I wasn't going to give you one." He sat back, his face beaming. "Besides, history bothers you, not ghosts. It'll be fine." He took a swig of beer. "She won't bother you at all."

"But she touched me." Tristan fidgeted in his chair as his eyes darted around the room. The memory of her icy touch lingered in his mind. Part of him wanted to see her again, but the other part wanted her to never come back.

"She touched me the first day we moved in, too. I think it's her way of saying hello."

Kayla snuggled closer to Zack. "I still think there's more to her. I've never seen her, though. She only seems to let men see her." She trembled. "It's weird."

Tristan gulped down the rest of his beer, hoping to dull the nerves. "Yeah, weird."

*I f I ignore it, it will go away.* Tristan wasn't sure how true that mantra was, but he was going to apply it to the ghost situation. She didn't reappear for the rest of the weekend, and for that, he was grateful. She had studied him like he was a curious insect. Why had she touched him? Why had he been so tired after she had? He had seen other ghosts a couple of times before, thanks to Drew's love for hunting them. None had ever touched him, though, or left him feeling like his arms weighed a ton.

Who was she? And why did she haunt an apartment building? If any ghost would haunt that place, he thought for sure it would be one of the three men who had apparently died there. He shivered at the thought. Death visions were the worst, especially when he felt the person dying along with seeing it.

Tristan stepped out of the building late Monday morning, determined to forget all about Saturday night. His days of dealing with the supernatural were over. All he wanted to do was go to class, do his job, and live his life. He was too busy keeping visions out of his head. He didn't have time to deal with a ghost.

He pulled his jacket tighter around him. Even in late August, the mornings were chilly in the mountains. Adjusting the shoulder strap on his messenger bag, he headed for the college.

His building, Hidden Forest Apartments, sat on the edge of the small Blackwood College campus. The college was half the size of the larger UNC-Asheville and focused on the liberal arts. Most of the students who went there continued on to get master's degrees and PhD's. Tinier was better in Tristan's opinion, and being able to walk to school and work was a bonus.

Minutes later, he was following Dr. Isaac Smith out of a medium-sized office.

"I've got a good feeling about you, son. You seem to have a good head on your shoulders." Smith talked a mile a minute as he walked. For a portly, older gentleman, he moved fast. Tristan jogged to keep up with him. "It isn't easy to be a graduate assistant, what with all the freshmen, papers to grade, and your own school work. But I bet you're going to like it." They zipped around a corner.

Tristan broke in when Smith took a breath. "Yes, sir. I'm glad to be here." He was surprised he got a word in edgewise. Smith had been talking since the moment Tristan entered his office two hours earlier. If he had been allowed to head to his own office in the first place, Tristan would have made it there much faster. He was the newest graduate assistant, though, and Smith said that he liked to give tours to the new recruits.

The morning had already been long. He had spent it signing papers and meeting everyone from the history department, probably the whole college. There were so many people he couldn't keep their names straight.

He had said hello to Dr. Ian Cameron, the head of the history department. He was a jovial, slender white man with brownish-green eyes and gray hair who asked Tristan way too many questions. He wanted to know where Tristan saw himself in five years and what he planned to take away from his studies at Blackwood. Tristan couldn't remember the other questions he had been asked after he left Cameron's office.

Smith took a sharp turn and stopped short in front of a wooden door at the beginning of a corner. Tristan caught himself before he bumped into the older man's back. Smith grinned and gestured to the doorknob. "Welcome to your home away from home, son." He stroked his graying beard, pleased with himself.

A smile spread across Tristan's face. He was going to have a normal life, as long as he kept his head down and stayed out of his own way. He placed the key in the lock and twisted the knob.

The office for the history graduate assistants had been a

large classroom at one time. Two wooden desks faced each other from opposite sides of the room. One was to the right, beside the door. Nothing but a computer sat on the desktop. The other one rested between two large windows and had a huge purple bag lying on it. Picture frames, their black backs visible to Tristan, sat around the desktop computer. Wooden bookshelves lined the back wall, filled with musty books. It was everything he had dreamed.

"You'll be sharing this space with one other graduate assistant, Jaime Liu. It looks like she's stepped out right now, but I'm sure you'll get a chance to meet her," Smith said. He indicated the empty desk. "This'll be yours."

A slender woman with long, wavy, brown hair bounced through the door, a bottle of Mountain Dew in her hand. She smiled when she saw Tristan. "Hi." She held out her tan hand. "I'm Jaime."

Tristan shook her hand and introduced himself.

"Welcome. It'll be nice to have someone new around here." She bustled over to the desk near the windows and set down her drink.

"Thanks."

Jaime grinned as she settled in her chair. "First day, huh?"

"Yeah."

She leaned forward. "It's not so bad here, but that one," She pointed to Smith, "will talk your ear off."

Smith chuckled. "Ms. Liu, you flatter me."

Tristan smiled as he touched his desk. It was worn and well used, but it was his. His skin tingled, and his vision shifted. Jaime and Smith vanished. The room changed right before his eyes.

*"Tell me you love me."*

*Empty desks sat in straight rows. A stack of papers and a briefcase lay on the teacher's desk. He had so many papers to grade, but he didn't want to leave the room. Not yet. A beautiful young woman with long, dark hair sat in the corner front desk. Her legs were crossed at the ankle and her red dress stopped at the knees. She smiled, and her whole face brightened. Bangs fringed her eyes, a red hair band with a rose on the side held the rest of her hair back. A hint of lavender wafted past him.*

*She leaned forward. "Tell me you love me." She stood. "Tell me like you mean it."*

*Heat ran through his entire body as his breath caught. He opened his mouth to answer her.*

Tristan closed his eyes as he remembered who and where he was. *She's not real. She can't be real.* He sank into the empty chair, frustration seeping into his chest. His heart pounded. Sweat beaded his brow. He was torn between taking the woman into his arms and pretending she wasn't there. Neither of these feelings belonged to him. They belonged to whoever's past he was witnessing. He had to remember that.

"Mr. Johnson?" Smith's smooth cadence broke through the vision still playing out against the back of Tristan's eyelids. It was enough to anchor him in the present. He opened his eyes to see both Smith and Jaime hovering over him.

He took a deep breath. "I'm good." He forced a smile back onto his face, but it felt more like a grimace. The small bit of pain he felt earlier bloomed into a full-blown headache. He met Smith's worried blue eyes and Jaime's concerned light brown ones. He had to remain calm and seem normal. He didn't want anyone to think he was unhinged on his first day.

Tristan scanned the room once more. Everything looked like it had when he walked in. There was nothing left of the strange vision. Even though he had seen the office when he interviewed for the position, this was the first time he'd set foot in it. He'd expected the usual shadows and whispers, but he hadn't expected an image that strong. He took a moment to adjust the strength of his shields.

Smith cleared his throat. "Well, if you're all right, I'll leave you to the rest of the paperwork. If you have any questions, I'm right down the hall."

"Thank you, sir."

Smith left, his whistle echoing down the passageway.

"You sure you're okay?" Jaime continued to hover near his desk.

He waved her away. "Yeah, I'll be fine." He patted his stomach. "Not enough breakfast."

Jaime cast one last worried look at Tristan before walking back to her desk.

Tristan sank into his seat and prayed he wouldn't see anything else.

## 2

"**O**h, man! How can you handle sauce that hot?" Zack winced as he gulped down his beer. He shook his head, his eyes watering. "I'm going to need some water."

Tristan bit into one of his chicken wings, moaning. Spicy goodness danced on his tongue. It didn't compare to his mother's cooking, but it was still good. "It's in my genes. Besides, I didn't ask you to eat one."

"You know I can't resist a challenge." Zack took a bite out of his bacon cheeseburger.

"How you can eat anything with mayonnaise in it, I'll never understand." Tristan rested his back against the brick wall and put his feet on the empty end of the wooden seat. He finished off the wing, savoring the burn. Ah, the spicier, the better. Even if it wasn't as spicy as he liked.

"You're jealous because mayonnaise gets all the hot girls." Zack nudged Kayla's side.

She rolled her eyes at him. "You're both idiots, you know that?"

"You love me anyway." Zack planted a noisy kiss on her cheek.

Tristan relaxed, half-listening to his friends banter back and forth. This Friday night celebration was needed after making it a full week at the new job. He had spent it planning and preparing for the two classes he was teaching, but the best part was all the visions of the past had left him alone. Well, except for the strange girl he kept seeing in his office. Trying to convince his office mate he was fine was getting harder. Jaime was too perceptive for her own good.

The restaurant celebration had been Zack's idea. They hadn't seen much of each other since Tristan moved in. Zack was busy doing lawyerly grunt work for his boss while Kayla eased her second graders into the school year. And, of course, there was the wedding planning. Tristan had invited Drew to join them, but he said he had a ghost in a church to destroy. Drew had a tendency to exaggerate.

"Okay, I'm glad I've got you here." Kayla grinned, and Tristan knew something about the wedding was coming. "We need to get you sized for your tux."

"Honey, the wedding isn't until April." Zack popped a fry into his mouth.

Kayla pinned him with a glare. "Do you realize how much work goes into planning a wedding? Do you? Everything has to be perfect, Zack. Everything."

Zack held up his hands. "I surrender." Lowering them, he wiggled his eyebrows. "I'm your willing servant."

Tristan chuckled. "Just tell me where to go, and I'll be there."

"Good. I'll get you all of the information. Now." Kayla relaxed as she sipped her drink through her straw. "How is the life of a college professor?"

"I'm not a college professor yet." Tristan popped a fry into his mouth, his head bopping to the rock song playing over the speakers. "Got several more years before I get there."

"Still. What's your office like?"

Tristan thought about the vision of the strange girl and almost shared it with them. No. He wanted the night to be normal. No vision talk. "It's big. Used to be a classroom once. I share it with one other person, Jaime. She's almost finished with her history PhD and knows way more than I do."

"Oh?" Kayla perked up.

"No." Tristan pointed at her with a wing. "No matchmaking."

She nudged his foot. "Come on. You haven't been on a date in forever."

"I'm not dating my office mate, Kayla."

"Any? You know?" Zack twirled a finger around his ear.

"Crazy people?" Tristan asked, welcoming the change in subject.

"No. You know, the vision stuff."

Tristan laughed. "That was not the universal symbol for visions, dude." He shook his head and bit into another wing. Instead of answering, he slid into another line of conversation. "What about your ghost? Seen her lately?"

Zack shrugged and sat back. "Off and on. She looked a little brighter the other day."

"Brighter?"

"More solid, maybe."

Kayla shifted in her seat. "Can we talk about something else?"

And that line of conversation was dropped.

That night, Tristan tossed and turned, but sleep wouldn't come. He opened his eyes and stared at the dark ceiling. Wide awake with energy to spare. Something was off, but he had no idea what. The fine hairs on his arm stood on end.

A white glow appeared at the foot of his bed. He bolted upright and slid back into his headboard. Huddling in the corner, he yanked his blankets to his chin. Cold crept into his bones as the back of his neck prickled. It was like he was five again and terrified of a thunderstorm. A wind only The White Lady felt tossed her long hair around her face.

He'd almost talked himself into believing she wasn't real. But there she was, floating at the end of his bed. And Zack was right. She did look brighter and a little more solid.

"Who are you?" Tristan tried to climb out of the bed, but his legs wouldn't move. Nor did his hands release the blankets. "What do you want?"

She didn't answer. Instead, she floated to the left side of his bed, her unblinking eyes staring at him. A finger rested on her lips signaling for him to be quiet.

Everything inside of him told him to run, but his muscles disobeyed. He stayed still as she reached for him. She placed her hand on his forehead, an unmoving block of ice. Something pulled on his brain as if it were tied to the end of a rope. A small ache pulsed between his eyes, growing more painful with each tug. He opened his mouth to yell, but nothing came out. The longer the ghost touched him, the heavier his arms and legs became. The White Lady glowed brighter until she was solid. The edge of Tristan's vision dimmed. He sank into his pillows. It took so much effort to lift his arm.

"What did you do to me?" he mumbled.

The White Lady removed her hand with a whispered, "Thank you."

When she vanished, the room grew warmer.

He lay there, staring at the empty space where she had been. He winced as a headache erupted behind his eyes. It was as if a truck had slammed into him. Pain killers. He needed a pain killer. He moved the comforter, and his feet hit the cool hardwood. It took effort to wipe his eyes. It had to be a dream. A weird, strange nightmare. For some reason, the ghost was in his subconscious. That was all.

But he was so tired. He shook his heavy head and glanced at the digital alarm clock on his nightstand. Two a.m. He tried to stand and stumbled under his own weight. He pressed his palms against his nightstand, taking a deep breath. Then another. When he was no longer wobbling, he inched away from the support until he had his balance back.

Whatever had happened might not have been a dream after all. He looked back at the place where The White Lady had been. What had she done to him?

Pulling on a white T-shirt, he dragged his feet down the hall. He padded into the kitchen and poured a glass of milk. Grabbing some medicine, he stepped onto the balcony. The cool air hit his skin. He breathed deeply, letting the air rejuvenate him. The night was clear, and he picked out several constellations. The moon peeked out over a line of trees in the distance. He tossed back the pills and chased them with milk before leaning against the railing. He let his head droop forward.

Tristan loved this time of year in the mountains, summer fading into fall. The nights and days grew cooler, and the leaves exploded into different colors. The mountain ranges burst with reds, golds, and oranges. It was much better than the humidity that hung around the coast until January.

A loud crash shattered his thoughts. Tristan's head jerked

up in time to see someone pitch backwards out of a window at the other end of the building. The man's body tumbled down, his scream ringing in the quiet night. He smacked the pavement below, a sick wet thump. Dark liquid pooled around his body. The glass of milk slipped from Tristan's slack fingers.

He shut his eyes. Was it another vision? He checked his shields. Nothing slipped. He ran his hands over his face. He was tired. Maybe he was sleeping standing up. Opening his eyes, he saw the body still there and lights coming on in the windows around the one he fell from.

Tristan raced inside and grabbed his cell phone.

"911. What's your emergency?"

"I just saw someone fall out of a window." He threw on a jacket. "No. No, it looked like someone pushed him."

He flung open his door, racing for Zack's apartment. The man fell from that end of the building. Maybe Kayla and Zack had seen something.

"Sir, what's your address?"

Tristan rattled it off as he raised his hand to knock on his friends' door. It swung open before he had a chance. Kayla stood there, her eyes wild.

"Zack's dead! He's dead! She pushed him!" She ran past him, leaving him stunned in her wake.

Tristan stood in the open doorway. Zack was dead? But he couldn't be dead. He had seen him earlier. Zack was fine.

"Sir?" The dispatcher's voice was distant.

A woman laughed, the sound like musical notes in the hallway. Then, the door slammed in Tristan's face.

## 3

The rattle of nerves came from one direction. The steel of determination floated in from the other. McKenna Ellison pushed them away as she walked down the aisle, passing the empty wooden pews. She searched for one emotion out of the many filling her heart and head. One emotion that identified the spirit she hunted for. He was there. He had been there at the last investigation. He would be there again.

During the last investigation, the ghost's anger and rage had filled McKenna's heart. Her jaw hurt from clenching her teeth the whole night. It had taken all of her effort not to let it consume her.

She was prepared this time. She took a deep breath and focused, her eyes searching the pulpit. "Come out, come out, wherever you are."

"Getting anything?" Tabitha Lawson met McKenna in the middle of the aisle. The streetlights outside the windows reflected off her short, blond and pink hair. She held up her electromagnetic field detector, a black box with a series of colorful lights at the top. Only the first two were lit. "No fluctuations yet. The energy is stable around here."

"I don't feel anything either." McKenna sat in one of the hard pews. "I don't get it. He was here last week. We have the proof." She pushed up her sleeve. Purple and blue marks marred the white skin. "I have the bruises."

The pew creaked as Tabitha sat next to her. "Maybe he decided to move on by himself. I mean, who wants to haunt the First Baptist Church for the rest of your life?"

McKenna cocked her head to the side. "True."

The lights on the detector lit all the way across at the same time McKenna developed an urge to hit someone. Sucking in a breath, she doubled over and clutched her stomach. Pain bloomed in her middle. It was like having her gut punched.

She let out a long, slow breath, fighting the war raging inside her. Her muscles tightened and ached.

"He's here," she said through clenched teeth.

Tabitha switched on her walkie-talkie. "Aaron, Drew, bring in Mrs. Corr."

McKenna watched the pulpit, zeroing in on the anger. The air around her grew colder. She wrapped her arms around herself, standing on shaky legs. Strong emotions knocked the wind out of her every time. But the pain and the fighting urge subsided.

She slid into the aisle and straightened. "Pastor Jones? Someone wanted to come talk to you."

The pulpit shook.

"Her name is Elizabeth. You loved her once, right?"

A small, leather-bound Bible sailed past her head.

McKenna swallowed and kept moving forward. Her fingers clutched the box of salt she carried. She hoped it would be enough to disembody the ghost long enough for everyone to get out of harm's way. "We're here to help, Pastor

24

Jones."

A heavy wooden object slammed into McKenna's shoulder. She gasped at the pain but remained still. The object clattered on the seat of one of the pews. A cross? Pastor Jones tried to hit her with a cross? She shivered. The anger grew stronger. Her muscles tensed, ached.

The ghost of Pastor Jones had terrorized the First Baptist Church for eight years. His outbursts during services drove the congregation away until the church was abandoned. It sat empty for three years. Two months ago, a new preacher had wanted to renovate it and make it usable again. But the ghost had other plans, and several workers were hurt on the job. Out of options, the current pastor asked Restless Spirits, Inc., to help send the ghost packing.

After extensive research, the Restless Spirits team – McKenna, Drew, Tabitha, and her husband Aaron - realized that Pastor Jones had died in a car accident after seeing his fiancé Elizabeth with another man. Hoping that was the reason he was so upset, they found Elizabeth, and the woman explained what happened.

"Stanley was always a little jealous," she had said. "So, when he saw me with my friend Tom, he went crazy. Punched him right there." Elizabeth had sighed. "We were only talking. I hadn't seen him since college and I was asking about his family, but Stanley didn't believe me." Tears had pricked the corners of her eyes. "He died in the car crash later that day. We never got to work things out."

McKenna thought they should do exactly that as long as they could keep Elizabeth safe.

The door in the back squeaked open. A small circle of light bounced down the aisle. As it came closer, McKenna made out the shapes of Elizabeth Corr and Aaron Lawson.

"Where's Drew?"

"He's keeping an eye on things at the command center. I

wanted him to be able to get help if we needed it." Aaron held one of Mrs. Corr's hands while keeping a protective arm around her.

"It's so dark in here." Mrs. Corr's light voice filled the empty space. "Why can't we turn on the lights?"

McKenna took Mrs. Corr's other hand. It was cold to the touch. "This way we can see where he is if he chooses to appear. His energy will give off light."

"Plus, I don't want to give him any more energy he can pull from." Aaron's voice was gruff.

"You know that's only a theory," Tabitha said.

"We'll argue about this later." Aaron's clothes rustled as he shifted. "Mrs. Corr, would you like to start?" His voice was gentle with her.

"I'm not sure what I'm supposed to do." The older woman shook in the cold.

"Get out!" The loud deep voice boomed through the church.

Mrs. Corr stiffened. "Is that any way to treat me after eight years, Stanley?" McKenna jumped at the command in Mrs. Corr's voice. She stopped herself from answering with a "no, ma'am." Aaron, however, mumbled the answer under his breath.

A light formed on the edge of the stairs leading to the pulpit. As it brightened, the air chilled. McKenna huddled against Mrs. Corr. Long sleeves and a jacket were going to be her outfit for the next hunt, whether it was summer or not. Pastor Jones's rage ebbed, giving McKenna some much needed relief. Warm love came from Mrs. Corr, and McKenna held on to it.

"Go away!" Pastor Jones's loud words held less malice.

Aaron encouraged Mrs. Corr to take a step forward. She did, and the ghost glowed brighter, taking the shape of a man. Mrs. Corr's eyes widened in the light, but she showed no signs of fear.

The shape growled. He grabbed a chair and threw it at them. All four of them ducked. The chair crashed into the pews behind them.

McKenna swallowed. So much anger and hate. Over a wife who he thought was unfaithful? Ghosts did tend to let things fester, and they could harbor more emotions than they died with.

Mrs. Corr cleared her throat. "Stanley, it's me. It's Elizabeth."

McKenna prayed the spirit was intelligent enough to recognize the older woman.

The ghost cocked his head at her, his eyes flashing red.

Mrs. Corr let go of McKenna's hold and took another step forward. Aaron made a move with her, but McKenna waved him off. He let go of Mrs. Corr's other hand. Pastor Jones's anger vanished, an edge of curiosity replacing it.

"I think he recognizes her," McKenna whispered.

Aaron shifted from foot to foot. "I don't trust him."

Tabitha took his hand. "Give her a chance."

"Stanley, I know you think I was seeing someone else, and we never got a chance to work it out." Mrs. Corr placed her hands over her heart. "I cried for a solid year after you died. Nearly died of a broken heart myself. If someone told me you were here the whole time, I would've spent every day here." She sighed. "You can't stay here, Stanley. You have to let me go. You have to let us go." Her breath hitched.

McKenna's heart broke for the couple, for the love and life they never got to share. She brushed away the wet tears on her cheeks.

Mrs. Corr straightened. "I love you, Stanley. I always will. And someday, I'll join you. But I can't do that as long as you stay here and try to hurt people."

Pastor Jones dimmed as he took a step towards Mrs. Corr. The older woman stood where she was and let him come to her. She reached out a hand, shivered a little when Pastor Jones touched it.

"Go on, Stanley. Let other people learn about love and light in this building again. Let it be a good place again."

Pastor Jones leaned forward, his eyes a deep brown instead of bright red. He planted a kiss on Mrs. Corr's cheek. She rested her hand on the spot where his lips had touched.

He inclined his head to McKenna, Aaron, and Tabitha. McKenna let out a breath as all the anger dissipated. The warmth of love filled her heart.

Pastor Jones glanced behind him, seeing something no one else could see. He gave one last look to Mrs. Corr before walking up the stairs. His glow brightened into a blinding white light. McKenna held up a hand, blinking in the brightness. The light disappeared, taking Pastor Jones with it and leaving the quiet and the dark in his wake.

McKenna touched Mrs. Corr's shoulders. "Ma'am, are you okay?"

"I will be, my dear. Do you think he passed on?"

McKenna mentally reached out, searched for any emotional sign of Pastor Jones. She picked up Aaron, Tabitha, Mrs. Corr, and Drew, but no sign of the ghost. "I think so."

~

McKenna patted Mrs. Corr's hand. "Are you sure you'll be okay?"

Mrs. Corr slid into the passenger seat of her husband's Honda. "I'll be fine, dear. It breaks my heart that Stanley was stuck there for all these years." She smiled. "I'm glad he's at peace." She beamed.

"We won't know for sure until we check in with Pastor Marion."

"He's gone on." Mrs. Corr tapped her chest. "I feel it in here."

McKenna let go of her hand. "Then I believe it, too." She stepped back as Mrs. Corr closed her door.

"Thank you, all of you, for letting me be a part of this." The older woman paused, her dark eyes thoughtful. "I didn't believe you when you first told me, but I knew I had to be here. Thank you for letting me help."

"Thank you for helping."

The engine rumbled. Mrs. Corr waved goodbye, and the car drove off into the night.

Taking a deep breath, McKenna headed back to the church, her heart lifted. She had been working for Restless Spirits for a year, and it still amazed her how much good they could do. How much good she could do. Years before, she'd struggled with her empathy. Everyone else's emotions crowded hers out, and keeping her sanity wasn't easy. It was still a struggle, but Tabitha and Aaron had helped her learn the control she needed. Control she had lost when her older brother died ten years earlier.

He, along with their grandma, was the only other person in the world who knew what it felt like to feel everything at once.

She shook off the dark thoughts. No thinking of Jason's mysterious death tonight. He would be proud of her work with the paranormal investigation agency. She had helped a soul move on. It called for a celebration.

The church's heavy front door swung open. Drew walked through, a camera bag in one hand and a tripod in the other. "There you are. Aaron was grumbling about where you went to."

AMY RAVENEL

"Had to see Mrs. Corr off. She handled this whole thing better than I would have."

"That was so cool how she stood up to him."

"You weren't even in the room."

Drew lifted the camera bag. "Saw the whole thing on this."

"Did you catch anything that proves Pastor Jones moved on?" McKenna rested her hip on the railing.

"Nothing as far as I can tell. One minute he was there, and the next he was gone." Drew shrugged. "I'll review the tapes tomorrow to see if I missed anything."

"No bright light? Weird." McKenna smiled. "I'll be happy to help you out with that."

"It's a date." Drew continued to the van parked out front.

McKenna climbed the stairs to find most of the equipment packed away. Tabitha clicked a case closed while Aaron packed the last of the small items. His brown eyes caught hers.

"Mrs. Corr make it out okay?" he asked.

"She did. Said she'll be fine."

He raised an eyebrow. "You believe her?"

"I do. Her emotions matched her words. She's a lot stronger than we thought she'd be."

Tabitha laughed, her blue eyes twinkling. "After meeting her, I had no doubt. I hope I'm like her when I'm in my fifties." She bumped Aaron's hip. "I'm already married to someone as grouchy as Pastor Jones."

"Yeah, yeah." Aaron wiped the sweat off his brow. "I need a cigarette." He pulled a pack from his shirt pocket and tapped the bottom of it on his palm. Tucking a cigarette between his lips, he headed for the door.

Tabitha wrinkled her nose. "One of these days, I'll get him to quit."

"But today is not that day," Aaron called back to her.

McKenna laughed as she picked up the box of small equipment. She stepped back out into the cool night air. Drew took the box from her before she started down the stairs.

"I can carry that," she said.

"Yeah, but I'm closer to the car." Drew marched down the stairs and slid the box into the back of the van. He shut the door, wiping his hands on his jeans. "Not a bad night if I do say so myself." He crossed his arms and leaned against the side of the van.

McKenna joined him. "It was a good night." She tuned into each member of the team. Tired, a little grumpy on Aaron's part, but proud over all.

Black Sabbath's "Iron Man" broke the quiet night. Drew pulled his phone out of his back pocket, his eyebrows lifting. "What's Tristan doing calling me at two in the morning?" He pressed the button. "What's up?"

Drew's good mood plummeted. The change was like someone shoved a fist into her stomach. She pushed away from the van and rested a hand on Drew's shoulder.

"Slow down, man. Are you sure?" He adjusted the brim of his ball cap. "She said what?" Drew paced away from McKenna. His confusion and sadness were so strong they shoved through her mental shields.

She took a step forward. "Drew?"

Aaron and Tabitha moved closer to the van.

"What's wrong?" Aaron asked.

"I don't know."

Drew hung up, jammed his phone back into his pocket, and paced back to the van. "I've got to go. Zack...my friend... he's dead." His gaze flickered to the van. "My car's at the office."

"I'll drive you," McKenna offered. "What happened?"

Drew blinked. "Somebody pushed him out of his bedroom window."

Dread filled McKenna's stomach. "Where does he live?"

"Hidden Forest Apartments."

"Oh, God." McKenna closed her eyes. "Not again."

4

———————

Tristan took a step back as Kayla's words echoed in his head. *She pushed him!* Who pushed him? Was the legend true? Had the ghost done this? His heart pounded against his chest. The White Lady's visit came back to him: her hand on his head, his body tiring the longer she held on. Why didn't she kill him? Why was he alive and not Zack?

The noise in the hallway pulled him out of his thoughts. People ran past him and down the stairs. Giving one last look at the door, he followed the flow of traffic. He needed to find out what exactly happened.

He shoved people out of his way as he raced down the stairs. Ignoring their angry comments, he made his way outside. It didn't seem real. Was he still dreaming? He had talked to Zack earlier that night. His friend had been alive and vibrant and safe.

Tristan slowed down as he approached the crowd gathered in the parking lot. Did he really want to see this? Did he want to know? Kayla's voice cut through the chaos.

"Let me through! Zack! Oh, God! Zack!"

He had to get out of his own head. This wasn't about him. Sucking in a breath, he pushed his way into the mass of people. Sirens blared in the distance. Help was on the way.

Out of the corner of his eye, Tristan saw Kayla disappear into the crowd. He picked up his pace, weaving in and out. Nasty comments followed in his wake, but he didn't care what they said. He reached Kayla and dropped to his knees. She was kneeling beside the body.

"Shit!" he said.

Zack lay still, his blue eyes open to the sky. His face was frozen in fear, and his mouth formed a silent scream. The iron smell of the dark red blood permeated the night air. Kayla crouched beside him, her shoulders shaking with sobs. She reached for him, but Tristan held her back.

"Kayla, what happened?" He rubbed her shoulders.

"I don't know." Her voice shook. "I don't understand any of it."

"What do you mean?"

"The White Lady. She was there, out of nowhere. She grabbed Zack and pulled him out of the bed. And then she pushed him through the window." Her sad brown eyes met Tristan's. "I couldn't move. It was like I was pinned to the bed." She paused for a moment. "She said I was free." Her face crumpled, fresh tears falling from her eyes. "I...I don't..." She pressed her lips together and gave into her grief.

Tristan swallowed as he wrapped his arms around her.

Kayla grabbed his shirtsleeve. "It was the legend. It's true. It has to be true." Her breath hitched. "What if she comes after you next?" She let go, fire in her eyes. "I told him we should leave. I told him." Her fists pummeled Tristan's chest. "He said she was harmless. Harmless!" She hit him over and over until she sagged in his arms.

Tristan didn't fight back. He took the punches as they came. His eyes were glued to Zack's body. It was like seeing it on a movie screen or through the eyes of someone in one of his visions. He didn't want to believe it was real, that he could reach out and touch it.

Someone shook Tristan's shoulder. "Sir, I need you to step back, please." A young female police officer stood behind him.

Tristan nodded. He stood, his body reacting automatically, and helped Kayla to her feet. She stayed close and let him pull her away from the body. The crowd parted to let them through as the officer followed them.

"My name is Officer Lopez," the woman said, a pen and pad in her hands. "Did any of you have a relationship with the victim?"

Kayla nodded, but no words came out of her mouth.

Tristan stepped forward. Someone had to answer the question. "She's his fiancée, and I'm his friend."

Lopez studied him with compassion in her light brown eyes. "Can I ask you a few questions?"

Tristan agreed.

"Can you tell me what happened?"

He took a deep breath, his hands fidgeting with the end of his shirt. "I was on my balcony when I saw him crash through the window."

Lopez raised an eyebrow. "You were awake at this hour?"

"I couldn't sleep." Tristan shrugged.

"Ma'am, what happened in that room?" Lopez asked Kayla.

Kayla looked at the officer with empty eyes. "The White Lady pushed him."

Lopez's pen stopped writing, and the officer lifted her head. "The White Lady, ma'am?"

Kayla nodded. "The ghost that haunts our building."

"Are you sure you didn't touch him?" Lopez kept her voice gentle.

Kayla's eyes flashed with anger. "No, I didn't. How the hell could I push him out a window? He's bigger than me!"

Lopez jotted down her answer, not bothering to react. "I'm sorry, ma'am, but I had to ask."

"I didn't kill him."

Lopez never indicated she heard Kayla. Instead, her face remained impassive. "Stay here. The detectives will want to talk to you." With that, she walked back to the crowd.

Kayla gripped Tristan's shirt. "I'm telling the truth. You believe me, right?" She met his eyes. "You can see it. You can see what happened. You can see the truth." She loosened her fingers and slid down the brick wall into the cool, damp grass.

Tristan crouched beside her. "I believe you." However, he didn't know what to believe. He had seen and felt the ghost. The legend echoed in his brain. *If you see the ghost, you die.* Zack was dead, but Tristan wasn't. Why? They had both seen her. He remembered the pain when she touched him, like she was yanking everything out of him. But he was still alive, and Zack wasn't.

Another car pulled into the parking lot, a red light blazing on top. Two men in suits climbed out of the unmarked vehicle and made their way to the scene. They spoke with Officer Lopez before walking in their direction. Tristan roused Kayla from her spot on the ground.

The detective on the right smiled as he approached them, "Hello. I'm sorry for your loss." He stuck out his hand. "I'm Detective Bill Needham, and this is my partner, James Morgan."

Detective Needham was taller than Tristan and didn't seem that much older, maybe five or six years. His dark hair fell across his forehead and his hazel eyes appeared to take in everything. Detective Morgan was a little shorter, but not by much. He had black, curly hair and his dark brown eyes regarded Kayla.

Tristan shook Needham's hand.

"Mind if we ask you a few questions?" Needham positioned his pen over his notepad.

Kayla nodded as she wrapped her arms around herself.

"Okay, walk me through this. What exactly happened?"

Kayla took a deep breath and repeated the whole story. Tristan worried when she mentioned the ghost again, but he had no way of stopping her from talking about it. She was calmer this time, as if this whole incident had happened to someone else. Needham took it all in as if she were sharing a homemade recipe with him.

"Are you sure it was a ghost?" Needham raised an eyebrow.

Kayla's eyes widened. "I know it sounds crazy, but that's what happened. I swear."

Needham exchanged a glance with Morgan. Tristan placed a protective hand on Kayla's shoulder, a muscle in his jaw twitching.

"Ma'am, did anybody want to hurt your fiancée? An ex-girlfriend, maybe?"

Kayla shook her head. "No."

"Did anyone break in? Did your fiancée catch them?"

"No. I told you what I saw. I told you everything."

Needham focused on Tristan. "Officer Lopez said you saw the victim fall from the window?"

"Yes, sir." Tristan took him through everything he saw.

"Did you see a ghost?" Morgan asked.

"No, but I saw it at a different angle. I didn't see anybody at all."

"Kayla! Tristan!" Drew ran towards them, a woman with long, dark hair on his heels. He hugged Kayla. "Are you okay?"

"Yeah, but Zack." Kayla's voice cracked.

Drew let go of her and the dark-haired woman embraced Kayla.

"I'm so sorry," she said. "Is there anything I can do?"

"Oh, McKenna. I'm so glad you're here."

Needham cleared his throat as he and Morgan closed their notebooks. Needham handed Tristan a card. "Call me if you remember anything else." He focused on Kayla. "Ma'am, can you please go with Officer Lopez down to the station? We'd like to ask you a few more questions and contact your family."

Kayla nodded. "Anything I can do to help."

McKenna kept her arm around Kayla. "Can she get dressed first?"

The detectives nodded. McKenna led Kayla back to the building with Lopez walking behind them.

Needham nodded to Tristan and Drew. "Stay in touch." He and his partner followed the women.

Tristan fell back against the wall, all of his energy gone. The ghost had been there. She wasn't a dream. She had been in his room. She had touched him. He crumpled the business card in his hand. She had taken something from him. He was sure of it. What was it? And did it connect to Zack's death?

Zack's death. Zack was dead. His best friend was dead. He took a shuddering breath. What was he supposed to do now? He looked at Drew, who leaned against the wall next to him.

Drew's gaze was level. "You going to tell me what happened?"

"Kayla said The White Lady killed him." Tristan didn't want to go through the story again.

"The White Lady?" Drew pushed away from the wall.

"The ghost that haunts the building."

"A ghost haunts this building? And no one told me?" Drew's voice grew louder with each word.

"Zack said she wouldn't hurt anybody. He didn't want you poking around." Tristan slumped against the prickly brick wall. "Fuck!"

The police blocked off the scene and pushed people away. The detectives hovered over the body while people in white coats scoured the ground.

"I think this might be my fault." Tristan's voice sounded hollow to his own ears.

"Dude, what are you talking about?"

"She was in my apartment tonight. I think she took something from me, something that helped her kill Zack."

"What did she take?"

Tristan wiped his face. "I don't know. I was tired afterwards. I thought it was a dream."

Drew narrowed his eyes. "Come on. We're going to do something about this." He stalked off to the building before Tristan could answer him.

He followed Drew inside and climbed the stairs. This time they moved with the traffic instead of pushing their way through. They stopped in front of Zack and Kayla's apartment. Yellow tape blocked the open door and more people in white coats milled about inside. Kayla and McKenna had probably already come and gone.

Drew turned to him. "See what happened."

"What?" Tristan blinked, unsure he had heard right.

"See what happened." Drew tapped his temple. "Use your power and look into the past. Find Zack's energy or whatever and tell me how he died."

The panic bloomed in Tristan's chest. "I can't."

"You can. I've seen you do it before."

Tristan's breathing picked up as he stared at the open apartment. "There are too many people inside. They won't let us in."

"You can do it here, can't you?" A camera flashed against the back wall, lighting up the living room for a second.

"No. I have to be in the room to get a vision." He kept one eye on the apartment. "What if I tried and the vision took over?" Tristan stepped back. "What if I connect with the ghost and tried to shove you out the window?"

"How do you know you'll see it from The White Lady's point of view? Maybe you'll tap into Kayla or Zack." Drew talked faster as the idea took hold.

"It's not worth the risk. Zack is already dead. We can't help him." He winced at his own cold words, but the panic was already deeply rooted. "Besides, you're forgetting one thing." He indicated the door. "We can't get inside." And then he noticed it. The entire night, he hadn't seen or heard one shade of the past. Nothing pushed against his shields. He wasn't even struggling to keep them in place like he usually did.

Reaching out, he searched for something, anything. All he saw was a few people going back their apartments and the officers searching his friend's apartment. He pushed a little harder, his brow wrinkling in effort. He didn't hear or see anything. Confused, he looked up and down the hallway. Even with his shields down, he didn't see or hear any echoes.

"Something's wrong," he said.

"Tristan?"

He faced Drew, gripping his upper arms. He mentally dropped his shields and braced for the onslaught of Drew's past to bombard his brain. Nothing happened. "I can't...I can't read you."

Drew's eyes widened. "What?"

Tristan let him go and backed away from the apartment. "It's gone. Just like that."

Drew approached him in a slow and gradual way. "You

messing with me? Is this your way of getting out of using your powers?"

"No. I wouldn't lie about this." He leaned against the wall and rubbed his face. This was what he wanted. His curse was gone.

"Maybe you need to get some sleep. We'll try again in the morning." Drew's voice softened.

No! No, no, no! Tristan rubbed the back of his neck, his hand shaking. He stumbled away from Drew and into the nearest wall. He pressed his hand against it, keeping himself upright. His mind felt empty, a part of him gone. Sweat prickled his hot skin.

He always wondered what it would be like without his psychic ability. He used to imagine how nice normal would be. But he wasn't prepared for it to ever happen.

Too shocked to argue, he let Drew take him back to his apartment. Sleep. Yeah, maybe he only needed sleep.

5

Pain filled Tristan's head when he woke up Saturday morning. Opening his eyes, he saw visions of the past occupants of his bedroom lapping over one another. Some were more solid than others. All of them were doing and saying different things. It was like having a marching band play in his head.

He cried out, closing his eyes to block out everything. It didn't work. He smelled thick vanilla perfume. Shouting matches echoed against the walls. He swore his head split apart in that moment.

His power was back in full force. Either that, or he was losing his mind.

Fighting for concentration, he rebuilt his imaginary brick wall. Everything vanished layer by layer. When he felt steadier, he opened one eye to test the room. No shades or shadows remained.

He lay in his bed, letting the headache recede. Apparently, whatever had happened to him the night before wasn't permanent. Sighing, he sat up. The memory of the night before hit him hard: the ghost, the sirens, Zack lying dead on the ground. Zack was gone, and he wasn't coming back. A ball of dread sat like lead in the center of his chest. He fought back tears. It still didn't feel real yet.

Tristan stumbled out of bed. Coffee. Coffee was the answer.

Something that sounded like a buzz saw rattled his living room. He walked in to find Drew stretched out on the couch, snoring away. Tristan shook his head; he remembered that, too. Drew had left his car at work and needed to crash at the apartment because his ride had gone to the police station with Kayla. Tristan shoved him on the arm.

Drew rolled over. "It's not time to go to school yet."

Tristan shoved him again. "Making coffee, man. You want some?"

Drew mumbled and went back to snoring.

Tristan made a pot of coffee and drank his cup before Drew stirred. The warm, rich smell of the fresh black brew filled the room. The caffeine swam through his brain, helping him think clearly. What was he going to do? He relied on Zack and Kayla being there for him, but now, neither one of them would be. Could he do this without one of his best friends?

He got dressed and headed out of the apartment, leaving the rest of the pot for Drew. He had to get out, to do something, had to clear his head. A drive in the mountains would help. He turned away from his door and started when he almost ran into the woman Drew was with the night before. The woman who had gone to the police station with Kayla.

She jumped. "I'm sorry." Her big blue eyes looked up at him, and some of his sadness eased. Dark brown hair fell past her shoulders to the midpoint of her back. She smoothed it down, a smile on her elfin face. Her pale skin glowed in the hallway light. "I didn't expect anyone to come out at this hour." She blushed. "I'm McKenna Ellison."

Tristan dipped his head. "Tristan Johnson."

Her face brightened. "Drew's other friend. He's mentioned you."

"All good things, I hope." He stuffed his hand into his pockets. "How's Kayla?"

"Better now that her sister's with her." Her face darkened. "I think the police suspect she did it."

Tristan shook his head. "No way. I've known the both of them since college. Kayla wouldn't do something like this."

"I don't think she would either." She touched his arm. "How are you doing?"

He tried to ignore how his skin tingled from her touch. "I'll be okay. It's still a shock."

"It usually is." She walked around him. "Is Drew up yet?"

"He was moving around when I left."

"Good." Another smile. "I guess I'll see you around."

"Yeah, maybe." Tristan walked to the top of the stairs and glanced back. She was pretty, this McKenna, but the timing was way off. Regretting it, he jogged down the stairs.

The door of his truck creaked as he opened it and climbed inside. He avoided looking at the spot in the parking lot where Zack's body had been. He wiped his face and turned on the engine.

Rock music roared through his speakers as he drove away from Asheville. Turning north onto the Blue Ridge Parkway, he felt the tension ease from his shoulders. The truck rumbled along the narrow, tree-lined road as Tristan relaxed against the back of the seat. Few buildings dotted the parkway. Mostly, overlooks and nature itself greeted him. Outside was the best place for Tristan to be. The past didn't push as hard against him when he was out in the open, and it gave his mind a much-needed rest. He could even handle a battlefield easier than an old house. Neither he nor his family knew why; he simply accepted it.

He pulled to the side of the road and climbed out. The sun warmed his face as the view of Mt. Pisgah rose in the distance, a tall, blue point. He slid onto the warm hood of his truck, not caring how uncomfortable it was. The last time he had been there was when his dad took him camping as a teenager. No one else was around, and he welcomed the quiet. He let the tears come.

Could he have saved Zack? Maybe he should have told Drew? He remembered The White Lady's cold, impersonal touch. She touched him, but she hadn't killed him. Why? Why Zack? Was Kayla right? Had The White Lady done it? Was that even possible? Was there truth to the legend? The questions piled one on top of the other. He stared out at the mountains, trying to find answers.

*If you see The White Lady, you die.* That was the legend. Had anyone else in the complex seen The White Lady? If she had been around all this time, Zack wasn't the first. So, other than the three suicides ten years before, why wasn't anyone else dead?

Tristan's phone buzzed, reminding him he hadn't turned the ringer on. He dug it out of his back pocket and answered it.

"Tristan, honey, what happened?" His mother's worried voice comforted him.

"Did Drew call you?" His throat was dry.

"No. Your father saw something happen to Zack last night. Woke him out of a sound sleep. I've been trying to call you all morning. Is he okay?"

He told her all of it, including Kayla's suspicion about the ghost. His mother listened and didn't interrupt once.

"Do you need me to come down?" she asked once he finished.

"No, I'll be okay. I just need some time."

"Oh, mijo."

Tristan chuckled. It didn't matter how old he was, his mother loved to use the term of endearment. He never had the heart to ask her to stop.

"Tristan, your father wants to talk to you." Rustling came from the other end of the line and then a deeper, booming voice replaced his mother's.

"How are you doing, son?"

Tristan straightened his back at the tone. "I'm okay."

"Your mother said Zack is dead?"

"Yes, sir."

"How are the police handling it?" Matthew Johnson had retired two years earlier from the Boone Police Department, but he would always be an officer.

"I think they're exploring every avenue. I told them everything I knew last night."

"Did anybody want to hurt him?"

"Not that I know of." Tristan lay down on his hood, the cell cradled in his hand. He knew the beginning of an interrogation when he heard one. He let out a breath, grateful for the distraction his father provided. Think things through, remember the details, and understand the events. That was his father's motto, his way of controlling his ability. Unlike Tristan, Matthew saw what was happening somewhere else in the present.

"Tell me everything again, from the beginning. I want to know all about this ghost."

Tristan took a deep breath and spent the rest of the morning taking his father through the events of the night.

T he sunlight sparkled through the branches of the trees, casting shadows on the curvy mountain road. McKenna knew the road like the back of her hand and made the turns automatically. The quiet was welcome since her head still hurt from the night before.

She had never seen the scene of her brother Jason's death, but she imagined it looked much like the one she and Drew drove into. Police lights flashing, and a crowd gathered at one end of the parking lot.

Jason had died there ten years earlier, the same building and the same way. Over the years, people insisted he had committed suicide. Even McKenna's own parents came to believe the theory, convinced he couldn't handle his empathic gift. For years, McKenna believed it, too. She was terrified the empathy would drive her to the same fate. Then, three years ago, she had found a journal her brother kept buried in the back of a closet her parents never bothered to clean out. Through that, she saw how much he actually *liked* his power, how it helped him understand how other people saw the world. She had smiled. She could see Jason trying to help other people.

When she had turned into the apartment's lot, Drew jumped out of the car before it stopped. Worried, she ran after him, pushing through the crowd. The swirl of emotions slammed into her – peaked curiosity, utter shock, naked disgust. Kayla's raw grief was the strongest, and McKenna stumbled beneath it. She gasped, a black ball of sadness in her heart.

It reminded her of Jason's funeral. All the feelings of her family and friends caved in on her until she had to hide in her bedroom. She was a grieving fourteen-year old who had no idea how to control it all. Thank God for her grand-mother, a woman who understood and stayed with her the whole time. To this day, McKenna didn't know how her grandma blocked all of the emotions in that house and still stood.

Kayla's story had her wondering if there were more to Jason's death. In her line of work, she had never seen anyone more convinced they had seen a ghost, or that the ghost had actually killed someone. She wasn't sure about the last part. She had never seen a ghost kill someone, but then, she had only been with Restless Spirits for a year.

At the police station, McKenna had to stay in the waiting room while Kayla was taken into the back for questioning. She could've told them Kayla didn't do this. Her friend's grief and pain were all too real. The emotions bled through her shields. They were raw and fresh and powerful. So much, in fact, that she couldn't ease them.

Kayla's sister Angela arrived in record time. McKenna told her everything before heading to her own apartment to get some sleep.

After dropping Drew off at his car the next day, McKenna wasn't sure where to go. She didn't want to go back to her apartment, even though her cat Oscar would greet her. No. She needed the mountains and the fresh air. So, she found herself driving north on the Blue Ridge Parkway.

She didn't expect to see a green truck parked in her favorite overlook spot near Mt. Pisgah. Pulling in beside it, she saw the man sprawled out on the hood, his eyes closed. His long legs hung off the end and dangled above the ground. For a second, she thought about driving away. She really wasn't in the mood for conversation. When he turned his head and opened his eyes, though, she recognized him. Tristan. She had only met him for a short time that morning, but she remembered unruly black curls, the golden-brown skin, and those light green eyes.

When she stepped out of the car, he sat up. She held up a hand. "I didn't mean to disturb you."

Tristan shook out his curls. "It's okay. Didn't expect to see you."

McKenna slid onto the hood of her car, welcoming the heat. "It's my favorite spot, especially when there aren't that many tourists out and about." The sun warmed her face. "Less people to deal with."

A corner of Tristan's mouth lifted. "I know what you mean." He rested his forearms on his knees. "Drew get home all right?"

"He went straight into the office before I left."

"Sounds like him. Tinkering with things. That's how he deals."

McKenna studied the beautiful man beside her. So much sadness lingered around him, and she didn't think it was all from Zack's death. Something about him made her want to shelter him from the world.

Tristan cocked his head, those green eyes trained on her. "So, are you and Drew together?"

A laugh escaped her. "Oh, no. Drew is a little too wide open for my taste." She leaned back and took in the view. A cool breeze blew her hair into her eyes. "We work together."

"Ah, you hunt ghosts, too."

"I do." She tucked her hair behind her ears, choosing to ignore the disdain in Tristan's voice. "Never thought I would, but it seems like it's a good fit. You?"

"Teaching history to college freshmen."

"Really? They certainly didn't make history professors that look like you when I was in college." McKenna raised an eyebrow. "I'll tell you this much. If you were my history professor, I wouldn't hear a word you say."

Tristan threw back his head and laughed. His grief lifted for a moment, and that made McKenna's heart swell. Exactly the reaction she wanted. His laugh was long and loud, and it brightened his whole face. He didn't look as serious. She chuckled along with him.

"We'll see how it goes," he said. A moment passed and the sadness crept back in. "I can't believe he's gone."

McKenna didn't say anything. She didn't offer condolences, remembering how sick she got of hearing the phrase after Jason died.

Tristan met her eyes. "You work with ghosts. Do you think it's possible a ghost killed him?"

"I don't know. I don't know enough about them." She shifted on the hood. "I've seen them throw things and push people, but I've never seen them kill. But that doesn't mean it's not possible."

Tristan nodded. "I'd like to know what happened."

"I think Drew wants to know, too." She waited a beat. "Maybe the same thing happened to my brother."

"He died the same way?"

"In the same building. Ten years ago."

"Your brother was one of the three suicides?" Tristan asked.

McKenna's mood darkened. "It wasn't suicide."

Tristan nodded again. "I'm sorry. I didn't mean to sound like an asshole."

McKenna lay down on the hood, letting the silence stretch between them. It wasn't awkward, but companionable. It had been a while since she felt this comfortable with a stranger. After a weird night, it was what she needed.

After a while, she cleared her throat. "Have you eaten yet?"

"No. I think I forgot to grab breakfast."

McKenna hopped off her hood. "Come on, I'll buy you some lunch."

"You don't have to do that."

"I don't have to do anything." She tossed her hair over her shoulders. She wasn't ready to let this man go, not yet anyway.

"Where did you have in mind?"

She smiled. "Follow me."

Tristan settled in his seat across from McKenna at the Pisgah Inn restaurant. They sat next to a wall of windows, the bluish mountain range stretched out before them. He sipped his drink as he focused on the story McKenna was telling. It was a welcome distraction.

McKenna's smile seemed to make the place, hell, the whole world, better. Her nose wrinkled when she laughed, and she couldn't seem to eat without dropping food into her lap. It was the most adorable thing Tristan had ever seen.

Leaning over her half-finished plate, McKenna waved her hands as she spoke. "So, there we are at the breakfast table. The empty milk carton hanging from my fingers, and the front of Jason's shirt dripping." She fell back into her chair, her laughter ringing in the half-empty place.

"For a six-year old, you were pretty determined." Tristan finished off his glass of Pepsi.

"Yes, I was. He had it coming." She sighed. "What about you? Any brothers or sisters?"

"No. Only child. Although, Drew, Zack, and I got into some pretty sticky situations." It hurt to think about Zack. All he could see was his best friend lying on the ground, dead eyes staring at the sky.

Her eyes lit up. "Oh, you have to tell me embarrassing stories about Drew. It'll make my day." He let her distract him from the pain.

"Let's see." Tristan looked out the large wall of windows,

trying to think of a good one. "Okay, Drew had this thing for a girl in high school named Samantha. She was gorgeous, tall, and wouldn't give him the time of day. So, he decided he was going to go all out with a big romantic gesture."

"Uh oh, I'm afraid of where this might be going."

Tristan flashed her a grin. "Oh, you're going to love it." He moved closer to her and almost forgot what he was saying when he caught her scent. She smelled like an ocean breeze on a summer's day. He struggled to find his train of thought. "You know how he loves his gadgets, right?"

"I do."

"Well, he made a robot to bring her flowers and declare his love for her."

"Did you help him make it?"

"I was up to my elbows in grease and old motor parts."

McKenna laughed. "I can't picture it. You, the book nerd, with his hands covered in grease."

"Oh, it happened. It happened. Anyway, Drew sends the robot into her algebra class, and it does its thing. There's applause, Samantha's blushing, all good things. Drew walks in, his chest puffed out, ready to take the credit. But somewhere between the door and her desk, he hit a button on the remote. The robot rolls over to him and pulls his shorts down."

McKenna's eyes widened. "Oh, no."

"Oh, yeah. Drew is standing in the middle of class in nothing but green boxer shorts."

"At least he wore boxer shorts."

"Thank God for small miracles."

McKenna met his eyes. "Was Zack there?"

Tristan swallowed. "No. We didn't meet him until college." The memory of Zack as a straight-laced skinny college student brought a smile to Tristan's face. "He was our voice of reason. Drew usually came up with a crazy idea, I'd shrug and go along with it, and Zack would tell us why it was a bad idea."

McKenna rested her chin on her hand. "Did you ever listen?"

"God, no." Tristan chuckled. "College was about the time Drew got into the whole ghost hunting thing." He shifted in his seat as he launched into the story. "You know the Devil's Tramping Ground, right?"

McKenna sipped her iced tea. "Absolutely. A circle in the middle of a field where nothing grows, and if you put something in it, it'll be outside the circle by morning. Aaron's been trying to get permission to investigate it for a while now."

"Well, Drew had the terrible idea to spend the night there. He wanted us to tie him down in the middle of the circle to see if he'd move."

"Oh, that does sound like a terrible idea."

His mood lifted as he continued. "I backed him up on the idea, but Zack kept listing all the reasons we shouldn't do it."

"Was he right?"

"Of course he was right. We were eighteen and stupid."

"What happened?" McKenna leaned closer.

"For some reason, we put Drew in charge of finding the place. He got us lost in the backwoods of Chatham County. We didn't realize it until we walked right into the business end of a rifle."

McKenna's eyes widened. "Y'all weren't shot, were you?"

"No, Zack was the one who saved us. He talked our way out of it, and the farmer helped us find our way back to the car. Never did find the tramping ground." The memory eased some of the pain. He could still see Zack holding his hands up, smooth talking the farmer whose land they had trespassed on.

"What is it?" McKenna asked.

"What?"

"You've got a line between your brows. What are you thinking about?"

"Oh." Tristan pulled himself back to the present. "I was just thinking how easily Zack could always talk his way out of things."

"Yeah?"

"Yeah. If someone had broken in last night, and Zack was awake, he would've found a way to talk them down. There'd be no reason for throwing him through a window. Out of the three of us, Drew is the most likely to go through a window, not Zack." He eased back into the chair. "The whole situation doesn't make sense."

McKenna's soft hand laid across his. She didn't say anything; she didn't have to. He placed his other hand on top of hers, the contact reassuring.

"Thank you."

"You're welcome."

She smiled. "Give me your phone." She moved her hand out from between his and reached out. He handed his phone to her, and she punched her number into it. She then took a silly picture of herself to go with it. "In case you need someone to talk to."

She paid the bill, and the two of them walked out into the parking lot.

"You'll get through this, Tristan, and the police will find out what happened." McKenna took his hand.

Tristan found he didn't want to let her go. "What if Kayla's right, and the killer is already dead?"

"Then you know who to call."

He raised an eyebrow. "Is that a Ghostbusters joke?"

"Maybe. But you know some actual Ghostbusters now, don't you?"

"I guess I do."

They said good-bye, and he watched her drive away. She

was a bright spot in all of this darkness, a bright spot he wanted to see again. But later. He had to take care of his friends. He owed Kayla and Drew so much after the way they took care of him after Wilmington.

He walked to his truck and stopped halfway there, a realization hitting him. He had sat all the way through lunch, in a building he hadn't been inside in years, and not one shade of the past bothered him. He glanced in the direction McKenna went. She was more of a distraction than he thought.

---

## 6

Sunday had been rough. He and Drew had spent the day with Kayla, making sure she was handling everything. She was still sad, but she had moved on to anger.

Kayla threw her arms around Tristan and Drew the minute they had walked in the door. "I'm so happy to see you."

"How are you doing?" Tristan asked when she let go.

She nodded as she stepped into the kitchen. "Two days in, and I'm holding it together." She picked up a knife and continued to chop the tomatoes she was halfway through. It was a steady rhythm of pop, pop, pop with each cut. "I'm not thinking about it. I won't let myself think about it." The rhythm slowed. "If I let myself think about it..." Her shoulders shook, and she couldn't finish the sentence.

"Hey, we're going to figure this out." Drew rubbed her shoulder.

Tristan leaned on the counter. "Any news from the police?"

"Other than me being suspect number one, nothing." The

chopping went faster. Pop, pop, pop became bang, bang, bang. "They haven't found any evidence that I did it, but they don't want me to leave town."

Tristan's heart broke for her. "I'm sorry. Is there anything we can do?"

The knife stilled. Kayla lifted her head, her dark eyes meeting his. "There is something you can do."

"Anything."

"You won't like it." She held his gaze.

Dread filled his whole body. "You want me to look for her, don't you?"

Kayla dropped the knife and grabbed his hand like a lifeline. "You can see who she was, what she wants."

"Kayla, I don't know the first place to start. Hidden Forest is twenty years old. A lot of people have passed through that building since then. Finding one person's past isn't easy, and you know my control sucks. Remember what happened in Wilmington?" He recalled the anger that raged inside of him. Karie's screams still rang in his ears. The visions had been full of violence and terror, taking him over completely. Even his shields cracked underneath the emotions from long ago. He couldn't trust himself, and he refused to put anyone else in harm's way.

She let go of his hand, turned, and chopped faster. "I can't believe you won't try to help me." She plopped another tomato on the cutting board. "Nobody wants to help me. Not you, not the police. My own sister doesn't even believe me."

Kayla's eyes filled with tears, and Tristan crumbled beneath the sight. When Zack had introduced her to him and Drew, he wasn't sure how well she might fit in with their small group. But over the years, she had become like a sister to him. She was in so much pain. Dashing her hopes wasn't an option. He sighed. "I'll try. I don't know if I can do it, but I'll try when the police clear out."

Kayla wiped her eyes. "Thank you."

Drew moved between them. "In the meantime, my team and I can look for proof."

Hope sprang into Kayla's face. She stopped cutting the tomato and laid the knife down. "Drew, I didn't even think. Of course."

"You've both seen her so there's bound to be a trail Restless Spirits can follow."

Kayla's brow creased. "I don't know how much I can pay you."

"We'll worry about that later. I'll talk to Aaron, work something out."

Kayla blinked back tears and her features hardened. "I just want to find that ghost and send her back to whatever hell dimension she came from." She picked up the knife and stabbed the tomato.

~

Monday morning came early. Tristan covered his head, blocking out the rays of the advancing sunlight. Despite what he was feeling, he had to face the real world again. This time, though, he welcomed his work and his classes.

He had made promises to himself. Promises he desperately wanted to keep. But in the face of tragedy, it was hard to hold onto them.

He sighed as he pushed back the covers and stared at the ceiling. Ice-cold air kissed his skin, his breath making small white clouds. Was the air conditioner on too high? He swung his feet to the floor and froze.

The White Lady stood at the end of his bed. Her hair fell in rings down her back, unmoving. Her green eyes watched him, studied him. Her entire body and her dress glowed white while her features were hard to distinguish. The cold kissed Tristan's skin as he narrowed his eyes.

"What do you want?" His voice came out steady, but he shook all over.

She said nothing.

"What did you do to me? Why didn't you kill me?" He slid back against his headboard. "Why did you kill Zack instead?"

Her face was stone. "You feel the same." Her voice was light, emotionless.

"The same as who?"

Her eyes flashed red. "You all have to pay." Her mouth curved into a smile, but it didn't reach her empty eyes. Her hair lifted off her shoulders as she floated higher. Throwing her head back, she let out an ear-piercing scream.

Tristan covered his ears, his heartbeat spiking. His ears throbbed as the scream continued. Then it stopped, leaving deafening silence in its wake.

He kicked at the covers wrapped around his legs. *Get out! Get out now!* Every part of him was on high alert.

The bed lifted off the ground and shook. Tristan gripped the sides, hanging on for dear life. His bones rattled. Breath rushed out of him. This was it. The legend was true. He didn't want to die. He wasn't ready. He braced, preparing for her to throw him out the window.

The White Lady lowered her head and the bed crashed to the ground.

Tristan's jaw ached from grinding his teeth together. Every part of him was rattled. He opened his mouth to answer her, but she was gone before he could.

The room warmed, but he sat there, shivering. What the hell was that? He let go of the bed and dropped his bare feet to the freezing floor.

❧

Tristan strolled into his office, trying to forget the morning's encounter. He thought about calling Drew several times, but how did he explain that the ghost who may or may not have killed his best friend was stalking him. He chose to ignore it and focus on his lesson plans. Lessons pushed all other thoughts of The White Lady and Zack's death out of his mind.

"Tristan!" Jaime jumped from her window desk. She met him in the doorway. "Thank God you're okay. I was worried sick when I heard about the guy who was killed over at the Hidden Forest apartments this weekend. Didn't you say you live over there?" She hugged him before he could stop her.

"I'm okay. It wasn't me." He wiggled out of her embrace and took in a breath of fresh air. Dropping his bag on his desk, he sank into his chair. He wasn't ready for this conversation. He swallowed. "It was my best friend Zack."

She sat down across from him. "I'm so sorry. Does anyone know how it happened?"

"No. The police haven't found anything yet."

Jaime rubbed her arms. "That's terrifying. I've heard that building's cursed. How are you doing?"

"I'm doing okay."

She patted his hand. "Are you sure?"

He forced a smile. "Yeah." Her expression told him she didn't think he was serious. He pulled his hand out from under hers. "I promise."

"I'm here if you need to talk." Her tone was sincere.

"Thank you."

She stood. "I'm going to grab a Mountain Dew from the machine. Need anything?"

"Some coffee?"

"You got it." She sauntered out of the room.

*"Tell me you love me."*

Tristan turned his head, searching for the source of the voice. His heart picked up as he gripped the arms of the chair. Pressure built against his psychic walls. She was back, the girl he kept seeing. But this time, urgency came with her. *See. See. You have to see.* Against his better judgment, he lowered his shield.

The room shifted.

*He looked out across the classroom. Evening had settled in outside the window, and the room was empty, except for one remaining student. She walked to the desk and perched on the corner. His whole body yearned for her as her lips kissed his. Something in the back of his mind screamed about how wrong this was, but he didn't want to let go of her.*

*She slid back, her heavy lids shadowing her eyes. She beamed, the smile on her face lighting up the whole room.*

*"Come on, tell me you love me." She ran a hand through his hair. He moaned. "You never say it out loud."*

*He wrapped his fingers around her hand, removing it from his hair. He moved his chair back. "You know I can't. We can't. There are too many eyes here." She had to stay a secret. His secret.*

*She pouted. "Then where?"*

*"I might know a place."*

Someone squeezed Tristan's shoulder. He started, torn between what was real and what was the vision. The girl and the feelings that weren't his own disappeared into mist, leaving the office the way he remembered it. He blinked a few times, struggling to put his mental walls into place. The hand on his shoulder steadied him.

Dr. Ian Cameron looked down at him with concern. "Mr. Johnson, are you all right? I didn't mean to scare you. I knocked, but I guess you didn't hear me."

Tristan ran a hand through his hair. He breathed in and out, steadying his pumping heart. He stood. "I'm okay, sir. What can I do for you?"

"I wanted to come by and see how you were doing. I ran into Ms. Liu in the hall. She told me you lost a friend this weekend. I'm sorry for it." Cameron settled on the edge of the desk. He was a tall, lanky man with salt and pepper hair and wrinkles in the corners of his hazel eyes.

Tristan blinked. "Thank you, sir."

Cameron's eyes grew serious. "Seems like that building's never had any luck. Almost like it was cursed from the beginning."

"Jaime said the same thing. What are you talking about?"

Cameron faced the rest of the room. "Have you heard of the three young men who died there ten years ago?"

"Yes, sir. I heard they all committed suicide, but that's all I know." Tristan settled into his seat, wondering where this was going. His knees still shook from the vision.

"It was strange and tragic, really. All three happened within weeks of each other. The police never found out why they took their own lives." Cameron shook his head. "If I remember correctly, each one jumped out the window."

Tristan swallowed. "Like Zack."

"The troubles didn't start there. My friend Paul Martin owns Hidden Forest, and his company had the devil of a time building that place. They'd put up a wall one day and find it knocked down the next. Took him forever to finish it." The older man pulled his eyes away from the far wall. "People tried to talk him out of finishing it, but he was like a man obsessed."

"What was there before Hidden Forest?" Tristan leaned forward.

"Woods, mostly. I think kids used to go out there and throw parties." Cameron chuckled. "I was too old to attend them."

Tristan raised an eyebrow. "How old were you?"

"Thirty. A young and naive professor, making his way

through his first year." The older man stood. "But enough about me. If you need anything, maybe some time off, you let me know."

"Thank you, sir. I will."

After Cameron left, Tristan sat back in the chair. Nothing had been in the space Hidden Forest currently occupied. Had she lived there, the woman who became The White Lady? But apparently only three men had died there before Zack. No women. Where had The White Lady come from? He opened an empty document on his computer and jotted down questions. Who was The White Lady? Who had to pay? Why did they have to pay? And why did she keep stalking him? All questions he planned to send to Drew.

The memory of her eerie green eyes came back to him. He stopped typing. Her green eyes. He remembered the girl in his office visions. She had green eyes, too. But hers were a darker color and much warmer. She couldn't be the same woman, could she?

He ran a hand over his face. Lack of sleep and grief were getting to him. He was leaping to conclusions and trying to connect a random vision that didn't have anything to do with his apartment building. A headache pounded against his temples as he dropped his head onto his desk.

The strong, warm smell of coffee permeated his senses. He lifted his head to see Jaime smile at him.

"This should help. Coffee makes everything better."

He accepted it. "More than you know."

## 7

McKenna regarded the wealthy older lady sitting across the desk from her. Dressed in a navy-blue pantsuit with white hair framing her features, Mrs. Williams appeared regal and elegant. Despite her stoic looks, she was an emotional mess. Sadness and grief came off the woman in waves.

McKenna fought to mentally block out the emotions. "Let me get this straight, ma'am. You say your dog is haunting you?"

"Do I look like I am making this up, young lady? Yes, Fluffy is haunting me. He won't let go." Mrs. Williams's voice broke on the last word.

McKenna handed her a box of tissues. Mrs. Williams took one and dabbed at her eyes. "How long has this been going on?" McKenna kept her features as neutral as possible. The client must never see judgement in your face. They were searching for a sympathetic ear and for someone to believe their claims.

"It started two weeks ago." Mrs. Williams clutched the tissue. "I thought I was imagining things at first. I felt him crawl into my lap and, every once in a while, I heard him whimper. But last night, I saw him. I saw my Fluffy lying in his little bed." Her brown eyes widened. "You think I'm crazy, don't you?"

Mrs. Williams's melancholy pushed against McKenna's mental shields. She shoved back, trying to keep it from overwhelming her. It wouldn't do any good to cry in front of the client. Too much sympathy was a little weird. "No, ma'am. Sometimes the bond between an owner and a pet is so strong, the pet might keep an eye on the owner long after it's gone." McKenna walked around the desk and sat down in the chair next to the potential client. She patted the older lady on the hand. "Maybe if you open your home to another dog, Fluffy will know you're okay and can move on?"

"I don't know if I'm ready to do that." Mrs. Williams took McKenna's hand. "My dear, do you think you can lay him to rest?"

"I can't make any guarantees, ma'am. It depends on why he's holding on. But I can bring the case to my boss and see what he thinks." McKenna hurt so much for this woman that she considered sending calming emotions to her. However, she knew her grandmother would cluck her tongue in disapproval. No, she had to take care of this the normal way. Mrs. Williams had to find her own calm.

"Oh, my dear, thank you so much. How much do I owe you?" Mrs. Williams pulled McKenna into a hug.

"You don't owe us anything today, ma'am. Consultations are free." She patted the older lady's back. "As soon as I know whether we're taking the case or not, I'll call and work out a schedule and a price."

The door to the right of the front desk clicked open. McKenna looked up to see Aaron peek his head out. She didn't have to read him to know what he was feeling. His light brown eyes expressed concern.

"Everything all right?" he asked.

McKenna nodded as she untangled herself from the hug. "We're finishing up." She turned back to Mrs. Williams. "Do you need to take some time? Maybe visit the restroom?"

Mrs. Williams stood, her back ramrod straight. "No, I'll be fine. You've given me hope." She held McKenna's hand and reached for Aaron's with the other. "Thank you. Both of you." She let go of Aaron, and McKenna led her to the front glass door.

"Have a nice day, ma'am," McKenna said as Mrs. Williams left the office. After the older lady left, McKenna closed the door and faced her boss.

"Fluffy?" he asked, amusement in his eyes.

"Another pet case."

Aaron nodded. "It pays the bills."

The bell over the door rang again. McKenna's heart skipped a beat when she saw Tristan walk in behind Kayla. Drew had told her that Kayla would be coming by that afternoon, but she didn't think Tristan would join her. What a pleasant surprise.

She soaked him in. "We keep meeting like this."

The corner of Tristan's mouth turned upward. Was that a hint of happiness she felt, or was she hoping he felt the same way? "We do."

Pushing her own feelings aside, McKenna hugged Kayla. "How are you? We didn't get a chance to talk before."

"I'm hanging in there." Kayla pulled away. "I know we're a little early."

"You're fine." Aaron led Kayla past the desk. "We're going to meet back here."

McKenna walked beside Tristan. "I didn't expect you to come along."

"Kayla asked me to. It's the least I can do."

She picked up a twinge of guilt. What did he have to be

guilty for? "I'm sure she appreciates it." She reminded herself not to pry. If it was none of her business, she needed to stay out of it.

He didn't answer. Instead, he pressed his lips together and indicated that she enter the room ahead of him.

According to Drew, Kayla wanted to hire Restless Spirits to investigate The White Lady and her legend. Aaron mentioned he thought it was too soon. The police were only three days into the investigation, and he never liked getting involved with them. No matter how legitimate he tried to make his business, law enforcement never seemed to understand. However, Drew pushed, and Aaron agreed to hear Kayla out.

The conference room seemed smaller with six people crammed into it. Drew and Tabitha were already seated at the oval-shaped light brown table. McKenna slid into one of the soft black leather chairs across from Drew and Tabitha. Aaron sat next to her while Tristan and Kayla slid into the empty ones at the front.

Kayla cleared her throat. "Drew told me this isn't how you normally take on cases."

"They usually go through me," McKenna answered. "But Drew brought this one in. You're practically family."

"Well, thank you." Kayla shifted in her seat. Her mouth turned down, and she kept her shoulders back. She appeared confident, but a mix of worry, grief, and nervousness surrounded her. McKenna was light-headed from all the emotions.

Kayla took a deep breath. "The police are still poking around our apartment, and they haven't released Zack's body yet." She swallowed. "But I know they're not going to find anything."

"How do you know?" Tabitha asked.

"Because I saw the whole thing. I saw that ghost, demon,

whatever the fuck she is, pick Zack up and throw him through the window." Kayla's temper flared.

McKenna jerked back at the force of it. She rubbed her head, knowing she was going to need some serious alone time later.

"What exactly happened?" Aaron's voice softened.

"The cold pulled me out of a sound sleep that night. I'm used to the weird temperatures in our building, but this was different. More intense." Kayla studied the tabletop, her fingers tapping steadily. She lifted her head. "I never saw her before. Only felt the cold air and saw things move. But there she was at the end of our bed." Her eyes widened. "She was solid. As solid as all of you right here. And Zack stared at her like she was the most amazing thing ever." She stopped, and her breath shook.

"Take all the time you need," McKenna said. Fear mixed in with all of Kayla's other emotions.

"It all happened so fast. Her eyes turned red. She grabbed Zack and threw him through the window like he didn't weigh anything." Kayla shuddered. "I'll never forget the sound of that window breaking, nor will I forget how cold her touch was."

She swallowed. "I thought I was next. When she turned those red eyes on me, I thought it was all over. But she didn't do anything. Instead, her eyes changed to green." She paused, and everything in the room held steady. "She said I was free, and she vanished."

All of Kayla's emotions pounded against McKenna's wall, one boulder after another. Her muscles tensed as she fought to hold everything together. She didn't blame her friend; she remembered her anger after Jason's death, and how no one knew how it happened.

Kayla continued. "I don't know much about the building,

but I do know the legend of The White Lady. 'If you see her, you die.' Other people must have seen her, too."

"I saw her." Tristan looked around the room, his eyes stopping on McKenna.

"When?" McKenna asked.

"The day I moved in, right before Zack died, and this morning." He ran a hand through his black curls. "She touched me."

Drew pushed away from the table. "Why didn't you tell me?"

"I didn't think it was important."

Drew's hazel eyes narrowed. "Everything about this ghost is important. You can't keep stuff like that from me."

McKenna breathed in, projected serenity throughout the room, and breathed out. The anger cooled around her. Drew sat back down. Tristan sank into his chair. When everyone relaxed, she spoke. "Let's all take a minute and focus on the problem at hand." She crossed her arms. "It doesn't matter who told who what. What matters now is Kayla is coming to us, and I think we should do everything we can to help her."

"I second that," Drew said.

McKenna stretched her legs under the table. "Tristan, how did she touch you?"

He scratched at the dark stubble on his chin. "She touched my face the first day. Then she touched my head the night Zack died."

"She didn't hurt you?" Aaron's leg shook under the table. His brows dipped as he took notes. A spark of surprise came from his direction.

"No. She came and she went."

"And the third time?" Drew asked.

"She didn't touch me at all. She shook the bed, though, and said, 'You feel the same,' and 'You all have to pay.'"

Drew rubbed his face. "Tristan, you can't keep shit like that to yourself. It's important."

Tristan leaned forward. "I thought it was in my head."

Drew opened his mouth to argue, but then quickly closed it. An unspoken conversation passed between the two friends, and the discussion ended there. McKenna glanced from one to the other. They knew something, but they weren't willing to share.

"What does 'You feel the same' mean?" McKenna asked.

"I don't know." Tristan shrugged. "None of it makes sense."

"What about Zack? Did the ghost ever touch him?" Aaron leaned forward as he launched into another line of questioning.

Kayla nodded. "He said she did on the first day we moved in, but that was it. After that he only ever saw her."

Aaron rocked back in his chair and swiveled it from side to side. "I'm interested. I definitely want to know what the hell is going on."

Tabitha held up a hand. "But we need to consider that we can't get into the apartment right now." Her chair swiveled back and forth as well. "The cases we take on are usually of the long-dead variety."

"Have you ever dealt with a ghost that kills?" Drew asked.

Aaron and Tabitha exchanged a look.

"It was a while ago, before we started Restless Spirits." Aaron studied the table, a black mood settling over him. Neither Aaron nor Tabitha liked to talk about working at The Greene Institute for Paranormal Research before they opened Restless Spirits, but that didn't stop McKenna from wondering. She didn't know much about the organization, only that their home base was Charlotte. "I'll spare you the details, but it was the hardest damn thing I ever did."

"*We* ever did," Tabitha added. A wave of sadness passed between them.

Aaron shook off the past and faced Kayla. "Here's what we can do. We can research, find out more about the building and if anyone else has seen the ghost."

"According to one of the professors at my college, two other guys died the same year McKenna's brother did," Tristan said.

"The other two suicides." McKenna nodded. "They may be connected." She bit her bottom lip, her brain already working through the possibilities. "I'll look into it."

"Your brother was one of the suicides?" Kayla asked. "Mac, why didn't you tell me?"

"It was ten years ago, Kay."

Aaron continued. "Once the police are finished with your apartment, we'll make plans to set up our own investigation."

"Thank you. How much will it cost?"

"We'll work that out later." Aaron waved her concerns away. "Now, the police could find something. If that happens, we won't have a leg to stand on. We'll have to drop the case. Understand?"

Kayla nodded. "I do. But either way, I can find out what happened to Zack." She looked around the table. "I have to know."

McKenna agreed. "I understand." It wouldn't hurt to find out what happened to Jason, either.

Tristan reached for McKenna's arm as everyone else filed out of the room. Her light blue sundress swished when she faced him, the color bringing out her eyes. For a moment, Tristan stared at her, not saying a word.

"You wanted something?" she asked.

71

"Yeah." He shoved his fingers into his back pockets. "I want to help."

"That's not necessary. We've got it under control."

"I know you do, but I need to do something. I'm pretty good at research. I can give you a hand." He waited as a beat of silence passed between them. He felt helpless the past couple of days. Drew was working with the team. Kayla dealt with the practical things, like the apartment and the funeral. Tristan had the promise he'd made to Kayla, but he wasn't sure if he could pull it off. The thought of it terrified him. But the research, the facts, the history were all familiar to him. He could do that.

McKenna chewed her bottom lip again. He noticed she did it when she was thinking. "I'd have to ask Aaron."

"Please. I feel like I owe it to Zack, you know? He's done so much for me; this is the least I can do for him."

McKenna touched his arm. "I'll see what I can do."

He relaxed. It was a small thing but being able to help meant the world to him. "Thank you."

She smiled, and his whole world tilted again. "Don't thank me yet. Aaron can be a stickler for rules."

## 8

A quiet and empty office was the best way to start the morning, at least McKenna thought so. Cars rumbled past her as she sauntered up busy Haywood Street. People opened their own shops and businesses and some waved as she passed them.

Emotions swirled around her, activity buzzing in the back of her brain. Anticipation, happiness, sadness, and others bumped against her mental shields, but none of them were strong enough to knock her off her stride.

She breathed in, feeling much better than she had in days. It was amazing what some alone time and sleep could do.

She reached Restless Spirit's big glass window, the logo covering most of it. "Restless Spirits" was in large block, white letters. The R was larger than all the other letters. A line ran underneath "estless Spirits." Written below the line in smaller letters were "Paranormal Investigators."

"Clean and simple. Nothing fancy," Aaron had declared.

McKenna opened the door, the bell tinkling above her. She locked it behind her, settling into her desk. A quick glance at the clock told her it was eight a.m. Her nerves kicked in, butterflies fighting in her stomach. Tristan would be there in thirty minutes.

She pushed the anxiety away, but it shoved back. Why did seeing the history teacher again make her feel like she was back in high school? At twenty-four years old, she was a grown woman. She wasn't trying to catch the eye of the mysterious loner dude in the corner anymore.

It had taken a little work, but Aaron agreed to let Tristan help with the research end of things. It freed Tabitha to go with him to talk to Paul Martin, whose company had built and owned Hidden Forest.

Secretly, McKenna was excited to spend more time with Tristan. She thought about the lunch and the conversation they had shared. It was so easy, so open. She wanted more like it. She planned to pursue it once the current investigation was over. That would be a good time to tell him about her empathy. Lay it all out there in the open at the beginning. Things probably would have gone differently with her ex-boyfriend if she had told him ahead of time.

She remembered Logan's reaction when she laid all her secrets bare. He had accused her of messing with his emotions, of making him love her. She flinched at his words and tried to explain. Empathy was a part of her, like her brown hair and blue eyes, but she had never messed with his feelings. The thought had never crossed her mind. But he wouldn't hear of it. He broke up with her then and there, calling her a freak.

She hoped Tristan would never call her a freak. The hateful way Logan had spit out that word drove into her like a sharpened spear.

Pushing the aching memories aside, she dove into the public library's online research databases. Logging into the Citizen-Times archive, she searched for any articles mentioning the Hidden Forest deaths ten years earlier. It didn't take her long to see a picture of Jason beaming at her.

An old wound broke open, filling her heart with pain.

Black and white eyes stared at her from the past, but she remembered how they were reflections of her own. He smiled in the picture, the wind tossing his hair. Tears threatened at the edge of her eyes as she recalled him. His loud laugh. His way of always teasing her. How he taught her to shut out all of the emotions around her. McKenna didn't realize how much she missed him.

Even though she had started out as a reporter, she never searched for the articles about his death. She wasn't ready to face it. Ten years on, she still wasn't sure she was strong enough.

A series of sharp knocks on the glass door caught her attention. Tristan grinned and waved at her, and she found herself returning it. Taking a deep breath, she rose and let him inside.

He nodded to the computer. "Starting without me?"

"I couldn't wait." She wiped the corner of her left eye.

A line appeared between Tristan's brows. "Hey, are you crying?"

McKenna shook her head. "It's stupid." She sat back down at the desk. "Found the article about my brother."

Tristan pulled up a chair. "You don't have to look at that, you know. I can do it."

"And what else am I going to do?"

He pulled three folders out of his satchel, set it on the desk beside the computer. "Look at the reports on the other two victims." He pulled the bottom folder out. "I'll research your brother."

"Where did you get these?" McKenna tapped the folders.

Tristan leaned back in the chair, a confident expression on his face. "Told you I was good."

"No, seriously."

He chuckled. "My dad. He was the chief of police up in Boone, but he still has friends in other departments. I called in a favor and picked these up on the way over. Don't worry, these aren't the originals, only copies."

"They'll be a huge help." Her earlier melancholy melted away. "We may have to keep you around."

"I don't know about that." Tristan shook his head. "Now, let me look over your brother's stuff."

"No." She turned back to the screen. "I need to face it. Like you said, you owe it to Zack to find out the truth. Well, I owe it to Jason." She let out a humorless laugh. "Besides, it's been ten years. You'd think I'd be over it by now."

Tristan ducked his head. "He was family. I don't expect you to be over it."

McKenna stared at the screen, determination set. She scrolled past the picture. "No, I've got this."

"What was he like? Your brother?"

"An annoyance." Another laugh escaped. "Okay, not all the time. He looked out for me, even though I was the baby sister who followed him around."

"The milk incident. I remember you telling me."

"Yeah." She sat back, a tight coil unrolling inside of her. "He was protective," she said after a quiet moment. "I followed him around, but he stood up for me, especially against our parents."

"Your parents?"

McKenna slid her eyes to Tristan. *Tell him,* she thought to herself. *Tell him everything.* She ignored the instinct and returned to the computer. "There were some things our parents didn't understand about us."

Tristan nodded, but didn't press her to explain herself. Instead, he rolled away from the computer and set up shop at another desk in the back. "I'll be over here if you need me."

"Same here." A weight lifted. She would tell him, but not now.

McKenna went back to the article, concentrating on the research at hand. She took notes on all the details she could find, but there wasn't much she didn't already know. Over the course of a week, three young men had lost their lives when they fell from their windows. At the time the article was written, the deaths were still unexplained. She jotted down the notes.

After a couple of minutes, Tristan broke the silence. "You know, this report is so similar to Zack's death, I could've given it."

McKenna blinked, pulling herself out of research mode. "What do you mean?"

"Jason's window was closed, and to some of the bystanders, it looks like he was pushed." Tristan's mouth made a thin line. "How could any officer worth his salt declare that a suicide?"

"I don't know." The revelation that Jason went through a closed window was new. No one had ever revealed that detail to McKenna. Did her parents know? Curious, she picked up the folder on top of the small pile. "Cory Monroe also crashed through a closed window." She flipped open the last file. "Keith Craft, too."

Tristan dragged his chair closer to her. "The police knew something weird was going on, but they couldn't find any evidence to convict anyone. No fingerprints or DNA."

McKenna went cold. "A ghost wouldn't leave that behind. But they ruled them suicides anyway."

She tapped the monitor. "Obviously, they didn't release the window detail to the press."

Tristan shoved his curls out of his eyes. "Why would they? The whole city would probably panic about a serial killer that doesn't leave fingerprints."

"But that still doesn't explain a cover-up or why they would stop searching for a killer." McKenna looked at him. "It's like someone wanted this case closed and quietly."

"And when no one else died that year, they had their opportunity." Tristan's knee bounced up and down while his eyes remained thoughtful.

McKenna rubbed her eyes, the new information rolling around in her head. Three dead young men, all pushed through windows. How strong did a man have to be to have the power to do that? How could a ghost, leftover energy, have the strength to do that?

"This isn't going to be enough." She waved a hand at the papers strewn across her desk. "We need some first-hand accounts and to start at the beginning."

"You want to determine if the ghost actually did this," Tristan said, seemingly following her train of thought.

"Exactly. I want as much information as possible before we set up anything in your building."

McKenna skimmed the high points. "According to this, Cory was the first victim. His roommate didn't see anything, but he heard the crash."

"Or maybe he did and didn't want to tell the police." Tristan peered over her shoulder.

"Good point. He might not have been as confident as Kayla was. The police didn't get suspicious until Keith died the same way a week later." McKenna drummed out a rhythm on her desk with the end of a pen. "Jason died a week after that. Same way."

"And that was it?"

McKenna went back to the main archives. No other articles about Hidden Forest existed. Her drumming got faster. The erratic pattern matched her frustration.

"Yeah. Nothing until Zack last weekend."

Tristan folded his arms. "So, ten years." He nodded to the computer. "Go ten years back."

McKenna knew what he was searching for – a pattern. Her fingers flew over her keyboard. Articles from ten years earlier appeared. "There's nothing about Hidden Forest here, nor strange murders that match."

"Not even the death of a woman who matches The White Lady legend?" Tristan asked.

"Nothing."

She jumped away from the computer and paced the length of the room. "Four men dead, three were killed ten years ago, but no one died before them." She stopped. "When did they build Hidden Forest?"

Tristan dropped into McKenna's vacated seat. He entered his realty company's website and clicked on Hidden Forest. "1999. Twenty years ago."

McKenna switched directions and ambled back to the desk, lifting her hair off her shoulders. "What were the dates?"

"The building was built? I don't know."

"No, I mean the deaths." She shuffled through the papers. "I know Jason died on September twelfth." She pulled out the reports on the other two."

Tristan studied them. "August twenty-ninth and September fourth." He straightened, his face losing all color. "Friday was the twenty-ninth."

McKenna turned on her heel, moving towards the back wall. "A timetable. If Zack's death is connected to these three, then someone else could be in danger this Friday." Her head snapped up, dread pooling in her gut. She raced back to her desk. "We have to get out there. We can't let anyone else die like that, and we have less than a week." She walked away from her desk again, her pace still brisk. Why hadn't she looked at all of this sooner? Why hadn't she researched Jason's death before now?

"Whoa. Whoa." Tristan stepped into her path and rubbed her upper arms. "One step at a time. The police were clearing out of the apartment this morning when I left. You've got three days. You'll get in there."

She shook her head. "You're right." She glanced at the reports again. "In the meantime, we've got to share this with my team, and I have some people to talk to."

$\approx$

McKenna started with Keith's family and friends. All of his family members hung up on her before she could explain why she wanted to talk to them. She couldn't even find recent information on his former roommate. But then, she found Selah Harris, Keith's girlfriend at the time.

Mrs. Harris lived on the outskirts of Asheville, along the parkway. Her two-story log house had a picture window in the living room with an amazing bird's eye view of the city. McKenna sank into one of the cushy chairs in front of that window as she studied Mrs. Harris.

The woman was in her early thirties with bright hazel eyes and short dark hair. Her face darkened when McKenna asked about Keith.

Keith had been a chemistry major in his senior year. He wanted to start grad school at Duke in the fall. Science was his passion. He loved learning how things worked, why they worked, what their base components were. According to Mrs. Harris, he was happy, excited about the future. Not like a man who wanted to kill himself.

"You have to understand, Ms. Ellison, I loved that man. Loved him with all of my heart and soul. We had plans." She set her glass of sweet tea on the coffee table. "My family means the world to me, but he should've been the father of my two boys."

"Did he leave a note behind?" McKenna kept her voice as gentle as possible.

"No, because it wasn't suicide."

"How do you know?"

"Like I said, we had plans. Why would you make plans if you were going to end it all? He had asked me to marry him the night before." Tears formed at the corners of Mrs. Harris's eyes. "I still have the ring. My friends, my family all told me to get rid of it or pawn it. I just couldn't, you know?" She was telling the truth. Her sadness seeped in, pressing against McKenna's heart.

"This is going to be a crazy question, ma'am, but did he ever mention seeing a ghost?" McKenna compartmentalized the emotion so it wouldn't affect her. She glanced down at her own untouched glass of sweet tea resting on the coffee table.

Mrs. Harris's confidence wavered, letting a little anger in. "He told me about seeing her, how he started seeing her after the other boy died." She rubbed her hands on the arms of her chair. "I didn't believe him, but he insisted it was true." Her breath hitched. "Hearing about the man who died last weekend brought it all back for me. God, what his family is going through."

"I know." McKenna folded her hands in her lap. "My brother Jason died after Keith did. It isn't easy losing someone and not knowing why."

"Exactly." Mrs. Harris stared out the window. "Maybe there is some truth to that legend that started after they died. I don't know." She pulled her gaze back.

"Did you ever see the ghost yourself?"

"No. Never." Then her eyes widened. "Wait." Mrs. Harris paused, holding up a hand. "I do remember stuff being moved. Like I'd leave my pocket book on the floor and find it on the counter the next day. And that apartment was always so cold, even in the summer when we'd leave the air-conditioner off and open the windows. But that's it. I wish I had more to tell you."

"No, this is good. Thank you for talking to me."

Mrs. Harris smiled. "People would think I was crazy talking to a paranormal investigator. But a ghost is about the only theory other than suicide I've heard lately." She leaned forward. "Promise me something."

"Yes, ma'am?"

"If you find out what happened to Keith, to all of them, tell me. I don't care how weird it is. Tell me. I have to know why he died."

McKenna touched the other woman's hand. "I promise."

"We heard about the ghost the day we moved in." Will Benton, Cory's former boyfriend, held the top of his coffee cup, making circles on the table with it. "The story didn't have the whole 'If you see her, you die' part to it then. It was more along the lines of a creepy ghost girl was haunting the place." He looked up, his brown eyes distant, lost in the memory. He chuckled. "I haven't thought about Cory in so long." Love and heartbreak swirled around him.

"I know this is difficult and a little strange. Thank you for talking to me, Mr. Benton."

His eyes crinkled at the corners. "Call me Will, please."

"What was Cory like?"

Will shook his head, his eyes bright with the memory. "He always had his head in the clouds. A total dreamer." He laughed long and loud. It was infectious. "He was a writer, you know. Was going to be the next Stephen King."

McKenna chuckled along with him. "So, the whole ghost thing was right up his alley?"

"Absolutely."

She sipped her mocha, the sweet taste of chocolate on her tongue. "What were some of the ghost stories you heard?"

"Let me think." Will slid back in his chair, his gaze fixed on the shelf behind her. He was quiet for a moment. Then he continued. "One version of the story was that she was a jilted bride who hung herself in her apartment. Another version was that she was a leftover spirit from a torn-down mansion that used to be on the site. My favorite was the girl who died in a car accident and was searching for the driver of the other car." He sipped from his cup. "Of course, at the time, they were all just stories." Melancholy crept in.

"Did he ever tell you he saw the ghost?" McKenna asked, her voice near a whisper.

"Once. He said he saw her floating by his bed one night."

She leaned in. "What did she look like?"

"He said she was white from head to toe. She wore a short, white dress, and her eyes were so sad. He said her eyes were bright green, unlike the rest of her." He rested his arms on the table. "He started working on a story about her that night."

"Did you ever see her?" McKenna moved closer to him, torn between remaining professional and wanting to comfort him.

"No." Will lowered his shoulders. "Never saw her once."

"Do you still have the story?"

Will sighed. "I'm a sad fool, but yeah, I do. I'll be happy to bring it to your office if you think it'll help."

McKenna sipped her coffee. "Every detail helps. Was anything ever moved? Was the apartment cold?"

Will blinked. "Yeah, now that you mention it. I used to see things moved all the time. I'd leave the remote on the couch, go do something, and come back to find it in the kitchen. And Cory hadn't been in that room at all. And the place would get so cold at night. I had someone check the air conditioner once, and they couldn't find a thing wrong with it."

McKenna shifted. She dreaded asking the next question. "Did Cory kill himself?"

Will's head shot up. "No." He didn't even hesitate. "Like I said, he was going to be the next Stephen King. We were happy. I never saw any signs." His jaw tightened. "Besides, he crashed through a window and landed on the ground on his back. Wouldn't you jump face first out of an open window if you were committing suicide?"

"I honestly don't know."

Will took her hand. "I don't know if I believe all this ghost stuff, but if you find out, you'll tell me, won't you?"

"Yes, sir, I will."

## 9

A wooden bench in Pritchard Park wasn't the most private place in the city, but that was where Justin Sanders, Jason's old college roommate, wanted to meet. McKenna settled on the hard bench, her back against the brick wall, and glanced up and down the sidewalk. Cars and people hurried past her on their way to their destinations.

It had been a long time since she had seen Justin, and she hoped she recognized him after all that time. In her memory he was still the big, strong guy she had had a crush on. But he wasn't twenty anymore.

She reviewed her notes on Cory and Keith. The descriptions of the ghost matched up to Kayla's, but no one had definitive proof if The White Lady had killed them. And sadly, no one even agreed on who The White Lady was. McKenna chewed the end of her pen. The only connection the three young men shared was the apartment building.

Jason was going to be a high school math teacher. Helping people, especially kids, learn was his way of dealing with his empathy. He had dated a few girls, but he hadn't been seeing anyone at the time of his death. As far as McKenna knew, he hadn't known Cory and Keith, and Cory and Keith hadn't known each other.

Where was the connection? What was she missing?

She called her parents, but they didn't want to talk about Jason. She wasn't surprised. They never wanted to talk about Jason. It was like they locked his memory away in a room, and that was it. The whole phone conversation had been tense. Her father refused to answer her questions, while her mother argued with her.

"Why are you bringing this up now?"

McKenna held the phone away from her ear. Her mother's voice grew louder with every word. "Because someone died in the same place in the same way." She pinched the bridge of her nose.

"My heart goes out to his parents, but I won't talk about Jason. I can't." Her mother's voice gained another octave.

"Mom, I think something supernatural killed him. Please, do you ever remember him ever mentioning a ghost?"

"McKenna Rose Ellison, I don't want to hear this talk again. I knew I shouldn't have let you spend those summers with your grandmother. Ghosts and psychics, and now you're bringing your brother into it, God rest his soul."

"Mom, you know there's a possibility that it's true." Tara Ellison had perfected the art of denying her empathy a long time ago. McKenna didn't know how her mother was able to ignore all of the emotions that surrounded her on a daily basis. She sometimes wondered if her mother had closed off all of her feelings. It explained a lot.

"This conversation is over." After that, her mother hung up on her.

She tried her grandmother in Charlotte but got her

answering machine. She'd left a message, but she hadn't heard anything since.

McKenna smacked her desk in frustration, then spent the next few minutes trying to shake the pain out. Cory and Keith each had a connection to the ghost. Kayla swore up and down she saw the ghost kill her fiancé. All they needed was a connection between Jason and the ghost. McKenna reached out to Justin in a last-ditch effort. His reaction was different from her parents.

When she had mentioned the ghost over the phone, his end was quiet for a long moment. Then he mumbled under his breath. "She's not supposed to be real."

"Justin?" She hadn't expected that response.

"I spent years convincing myself I was crazy, that I had too much to drink that night. The police, everybody, thought I was crazy." Justin wanted to meet her in person to talk about it, so they set it up for the following day.

McKenna fidgeted on the hard bench and stretched out her legs. Justin was five minutes late. Maybe he didn't know where the park was? Maybe he changed his mind? She bit her bottom lip. She was so close to possible answers. The hustle and bustle of the city continued around her, but she tuned out the noise. She retrieved her cell, pulling up a note-taking app.

"McKenna?"

She looked up to see a tall man with dark skin standing over her. His hair was short and dark, and he no longer sported a tiny goatee, but she recognized his chocolate brown eyes and his smile. This was the guy who used to tease her when he stayed with them during school breaks. The guy her fourteen-year-old self had developed a crush on. He hadn't changed a bit.

She smiled back. "Justin?"

"In the flesh." He sat and hugged her. "Ten years did you justice. No more braces, huh?"

"No. It's been a few years since I wore them." She sighed. "I wish we were meeting under better circumstances."

Justin's face sobered. "I do, too. I can't believe it's happening again."

"What do you remember about that time? Did you know Keith and Cory?"

Justin leaned back against the bench. He extended his arms along the short brick wall behind them. "We didn't run in the same circles, but Jason and I said hi to them in the hall. I had a couple of classes with Keith, but that was it." His eyes teared up, and he took a shuddering breath. "I'm sorry. I haven't thought about this in years."

McKenna touched his arm. His sadness crept in, and she swallowed the grief. She mentally sent him calm feelings, and his body relaxed. "When did you and Jason first see the ghost?"

Justin pulled off his jacket, tossing it on the bench beside him. "She showed up the first night we moved into Hidden Forest. It was pretty weird. She just floated there, all white and glowing."

McKenna noted the description matched the one Tristan and Kayla had given her. "Did she do anything?"

"No." He shook his head. "Wait. Yes, she did. She looked at both of us for a long time, and then she touched your brother." He shrugged. "The next minute she was gone."

"Did Jason ever figure out why?"

"If he did, he never told me."

McKenna tapped the end of her pen against her chin. "The newspaper clippings I found said the deaths happened within a week of each other, starting at the end of August. Do you know how they happened?"

Justin sat forward and rested his elbows on his knees. He

stared at the restaurant across the street. "I didn't see what happened to Cory and Keith." He met McKenna's eyes. "But I remember what happened to your brother."

Her breath caught in her throat. She had never heard the story of how Jason died, not in detail. Part of her wasn't sure she wanted to know, but the other part had to know. She let out the breath. "What happened that night?"

Justin tensed. He closed his eyes for a second. He opened them and answered, "One of the guys who lived below us, Jacob, had a party that night. The whole building was on edge after Cory and Keith died, and Jacob thought it was a good idea to blow off some steam. I had a few beers."

"You were a little drunk."

Justin nodded. "More than a little." He moved closer to her. "McKenna, if I had been there that night instead of that stupid party, maybe you'd still have your brother."

Her stomach twisted with his guilt. She rested her hand on his. "It's not your fault. You were, what? Twenty years old?"

"For the past ten years, I've been asking myself, 'What if?'"

"Don't be ridiculous. My family's never blamed you for it, ever. You know that."

Justin glanced at the sidewalk. "Still."

"Tell me what happened that night."

He took a deep breath and told her.

The loud music filled the room, the bass thumping against the walls. Justin danced in the middle of it, people crammed in the tiny space. Laughter and conversation echoed around him. He brought the beer in his hand to his mouth and gulped it down. He raised his bottle.

"To Cory and Keith!" he roared.

*The crowd roared back. He took another swig.*

*"It's too bad Jason didn't want to come!" The tall blonde's voice purred in his ear. He pulled her closer to him. What was her name again? Rachel? Susan? Lanette? Catherine? He couldn't remember. He didn't really care.*

*He grinned. "I know! The douchebag wanted to stay in our room!" Ever since Keith's death, Jason did nothing but brood around the apartment. Justin had to admit his roommate looked exhausted and seemed to have a hard time functioning.*

*"Maybe we should go get him!" Busty Blonde suggested.*

*Why was she so interested? It didn't matter. Justin thought Jason needed to get out of the apartment anyway. He shrugged. "Okay!"*

*He danced to the door with Busty Blonde in tow. He promised Jacob they would be back with Jason and headed out the door. Once Jason was out of their room, Justin might get lucky. The hallway was eerily quiet compared to the party noise. No wonder. Most of the building was stuffed into Jacob's apartment. Justin stumbled as they climbed the flight of stairs to his floor. It was a good thing Busty Blonde was there to steady him, even though he wasn't drunk. He was feeling good, that was all.*

*When they reached his door, he banged on it. "Yo, Jace! You gonna come out of there?"*

*No answer.*

*Groaning, he pulled his key out of his back pocket and stuffed it into the lock. It didn't budge, absolutely would not turn. He jiggled it, but still, it refused to move. He yanked his key out and jammed it back into his pocket.*

*He knocked on the door again. "Jace, my key's not working. Can you let me in?"*

*Again, no one answered him. He flattened his hand against the door. The wood was ice cold. He jerked his hand back.*

*"This door feel cold to you?" he asked Busty Blonde.*

She giggled. "Stop playing around." She put her hand on the door and yanked it back. "Weird."

What was going on? The last time anything felt that cold he had seen a ghost appear in the middle of the living room. His partying mood melted away.

He banged on the door. "Jason? You okay, man?" He exchanged worried looks with Busty Blonde before handing her his bottle. He took three steps back and charged the door. His shoulder rammed into it with an audible crack. The door remained closed. His shoulder throbbed, and his mouth went dry. "Jason, open the door!" He stepped back to run at the door again when it swung open on its own.

Busty Blonde took off running.

"Get away from me! You can't have it! No more!" Jason's voice came from his bedroom.

Justin didn't think twice. He ran through the apartment, knocking into furniture. When he reached the room, he swore the alcohol had gone to his head. The pure white ghost he had seen several weeks earlier stood next to the window, her hair blowing in a non-existent wind. Her eyes were bright red, like a demon. She gripped Jason's throat, holding him off the ground.

"You're the last one. You have to pay," she hissed.

She hurled Jason through the window. The crash reverberated around the room mixing with Jason's scream.

Justin's feet froze to the floor. Not a muscle could move. His heartbeat moved in double time when the ghost whipped her head in his direction. Sweat trickled down his face.

She lowered her arms, and her eyes changed from red to green. Her wind-blown hair settled against her shoulders. She cocked her head to the side, looking young and innocent. "It's over," she said before she vanished.

Justin took a step back. "Holy shit."

McKenna doubled over. She clutched her sides, struggling for breath. She opened herself and felt everything: all the fear, the guilt, and the shock as Justin told the story. Fumbling with her bag, she grabbed a half-empty bottle of water and brought it to her lips. The cool liquid calmed her down. Bit by bit, she regained control.

Justin brushed her elbow. "Are you okay?" His voice was concerned. "I'm sorry. I didn't mean to upset you."

McKenna closed her eyes and took a deep breath. And then another. "I'll be okay. Just give me a minute."

She identified the emotions that weren't her own. Picturing a box, she gathered the black ball of guilt, the quaking of fear, and the icy blast of shock. One by one, she placed them inside. In her head, she pushed the box away. Her lingering sadness remained.

As her breathing returned to normal, she opened her eyes. She didn't expect Justin to still feel that strongly about what happened.

"Are you sure that's what you saw?" she asked after a moment.

"I swear to you, that's how it happened. Now you know why people thought I was drunk or crazy."

McKenna sipped her water. "You said Jason told the ghost she couldn't have something. What was she trying to take from my brother?"

Justin shook his head. "I don't know. It never made sense to me."

She wrote down her questions and notes. The ghost had touched her brother the first time. Tristan had said she touched him, too. Kayla had mentioned the ghost touching Zack on that first day, but McKenna didn't know if The White Lady had touched Cory and Keith. Wait! Tristan had said the ghost took something from him, like she apparently took something from Jason. What did Tristan and Jason have in common?

Justin indicated her phone. "Is that enough to help?"

She came back to the present, frustrated she had another question. She flashed Justin a half-hearted grin. "I think it is. Thank you for telling me."

"Thank you for believing me." He stood. "I hope you can stop it from happening again. Nobody deserves to die like that."

McKenna placed her phone back into her bag. "No, no one does."

Tristan studied the notes he had taken. Cory, Keith, and Jason had all died the same way as Zack. There was a connection, but damned if he knew what it was. All morning, he and McKenna pored over the reports, the article, and anything else they could find.

After McKenna started scheduling interviews, Tristan pulled out the pictures of each guy. Why these three? What was the ghost searching for? He compared the pictures to one another. Zack and Jason resembled each other. They were both tall, lean blonds. But did that mean anything? He studied the other two victims. Keith was stout with short dark brown hair while Cory sported a softer body type and long ash blond curls. They didn't seem to fit any kind of type and certainly didn't match Zack and Jason.

*You could open to the past,* a small voice in the back of Tristan's mind said. *It could be so easy.* He pushed away the uncomfortable feeling. Not now. Besides, he only saw the past of the building he was in. And he was planning to try it that night in Zack and Kayla's apartment.

Coming out of his apartment that morning, he had seen

the police clearing out of his friends' place. They ripped the yellow tape off and packed it away. His grip tightened on his door. He had a promise to keep, and he intended to go through with it. No matter how much it scared him. Maybe if he kept everyone out of the room, nothing would go wrong.

He hoped he would find something about the ghost during the research session so he wouldn't have to try. If he could give Kayla a solid piece of evidence, his own sanity would be saved. But the reports and the article didn't offer much. McKenna said that she wasn't sure where to start digging for The White Lady, either. Dead end after dead end. Maybe McKenna would have more information after her interviews.

He shoved his phone into his back pocket. As much as he wanted to know the truth, he had to focus on his actual job. He heard voices coming from his office as he turned the corner. Was Jaime meeting with a student? He stopped right outside, giving them some privacy.

"He teaches a class at two so I'm sure he'll be here soon." Jaime had on her "professional" voice. He? Were they talking about him? Tristan inched closer to the open door.

"Is it okay if we wait for him here?" A familiar deep male voice asked.

"I guess, but I have a lot of work to do." Jaime's tone was clipped. Barely working together for two weeks and already she was protecting him. He smiled to himself. He'd have to thank her later.

Chairs scraped against the hard floor. "We'll stay right over here." A different voice spoke this time. At least two men were in the room.

Tristan braced himself for whoever was waiting for him and stepped inside. Detectives Needham and Morgan stood and adjusted their suit jackets.

"Mr. Johnson, do you have time for a few questions?" Needham asked.

"I don't know what more I can tell you." Tristan dropped his satchel on his desk. "I told you everything I remember." He ran a hand through his hair.

Jaime moved between the two detectives. Tristan didn't miss her glare at each of them. "I'm going to get some coffee. Do you want anything?" she asked him.

"I'm good. Thanks."

Jaime narrowed her eyes at the detectives one more time. She tossed her hair over her shoulder and headed out of the door like a woman on a mission.

Morgan smiled, holding out his hand. "We're sorry to barge in on you like this."

Tristan shook it. "That's okay. I'd love to help, but I don't know how." Judging by the scowl on Needham's face, he figured Morgan was playing good cop. Why did they need to act out the roles? He kept his guard up, ready for anything.

"We want to clarify a few things about Mr. Beckett's death."

"Okay."

Needham cleared his throat. "Let's review, Mr. Johnson.

You said you saw Mr. Beckett fall from his window while you were on your balcony, right?"

"Right." Tristan crossed his arms over his chest.

"Can someone confirm you were on your balcony?"

Tristan didn't miss a beat. "No, I was alone. What are you getting at?"

Needham gestured to the chair across from him. "Why don't you sit down, Mr. Johnson?"

"I think I'll stay where I am."

Needham stood as well. He seemed to be a man who didn't like people towering over him. Tristan was still taller by several inches. "Johnson, we did some research on you. You left Wilmington rather quickly, following your cousin's hospital visit. And you stayed with your parents for a year after that?"

Tristan opened his bag and pulled out his lesson planner and other materials. He refused to let Needham intimidate him. "What does that have to do with anything?" His voice was nonchalant. "I had some personal issues to work out." He didn't like where this conversation was going.

"How did your cousin wind up in the hospital? You were the one that brought her in, weren't you?" Morgan's tone was more casual than Needham's, as if they were having a conversation while watching a ball game.

*Lost in a violent vision. Karie screaming.* Tristan shoved the memory away. "I was, but I don't see how any of this has to do with Zack." He faced the two men. His jaw tightened.

"You wouldn't know what happened to her, would you?" Needham hedged.

Morgan put a hand on Needham's shoulder. "Bill, this isn't how we're going to approach this." He gave Tristan another reassuring smile. Tristan was anything but reassured. "Let's all sit down."

"Am I a suspect?" Tristan gripped the edge of his desk.

Morgan answered before Needham could open his mouth. "No." He sat down. Needham grunted, but followed his lead.

Tristan relaxed and lowered himself into his chair. Needham and Morgan wanted the answers as much as he did. Arguing wasn't going to get them anywhere. He took a deep breath. "Karie, my cousin, and I were in her house. She'd just bought an old Victorian, and she wanted me to see it. I did. She hadn't moved in yet, but renovations were going on. She tripped over a stack of wood, fell, and hit her head. I took her to the hospital. That's it." Short, simple, and leaving out any psychic details.

"How did you feel about Zack?" Needham's voice was softer but kept a steel edge.

"He was one of my best friends, Detective. If you think I killed him, you're wrong. I had no reason to hurt him."

Needham and Morgan exchanged a look.

Morgan rested against the back of the chair. "What about Kayla Collins? How close are you two?"

Tristan hunched over his desk. "I've known her since college. She and Zack hit it off the first time they met, and she's always fit right in. I count her as one of the best people I know."

"No romantic feelings?"

Tristan laughed. He and Kayla would never work as a couple. They would wind up killing each other. "No."

"Your fingerprints were in that apartment," Needham said.

"Because I visited them. I bet our other friend Drew's fingerprints are there, too. I promise you, I didn't kill him." Tristan's gaze was level with Needham's.

"All right. Thank you for talking to us again." Morgan straightened his suit. He replaced his smile. "You still got my card?"

"Yes, sir."

"Don't hesitate to call if you have any new information." Morgan nodded and walked to the door.

Needham lingered, continuing to glare at Tristan. "Wait. One more question. Why did your father request copies of the suicide cases ten years ago?"

Tristan tried to hide his surprise at the question. "Kayla still believes The White Lady killed Zack. She hired a paranormal investigation team, and I'm helping them with research."

Needham's laugh reverberated off the walls. "We'll be in touch, Mr. Johnson." He joined his partner. Without another word, they left.

Tristan blew out a breath he didn't realize he'd been holding. He sagged in his chair.

Jaime and her rich coffee with a hint of vanilla strolled into the room. "What was that about?"

"They wanted to ask me more questions about last Friday." Tristan rested his forehead on the desk. "I think they think I did it."

"Do they have any proof?"

"I don't think so." He looked up. "I don't see how since I wasn't in the apartment."

Jaime set another cup of coffee in front of him. "Have some. It'll make you feel better."

"Thank you." He sipped the hot liquid gratefully.

*WE'RE AT KAYLA'S PLACE. COME ON IN WHEN YOU GET HERE.*

Tristan stared at the text until the letters didn't make sense anymore. With the research and the detectives, he had forgotten about his promise to Kayla. He had seen the police tear off the yellow tape that morning. He had jogged past a couple of policemen on his way out of the building. But things didn't connect until he saw Drew's text.

Anxiety rolled in his chest. He stopped dead outside of Hidden Forest, his heart racing. *What if it all goes wrong? What if I hurt someone? What if I lose my sanity altogether?* He wiped his sweaty palms on his jeans. The memory of Karie's wide eyes flashed into his mind.

Everyone said it wasn't his fault she was hurt. He didn't remember everything that happened, but his cousin's terrified face was etched in his brain. She never told him what she had seen when she looked at him, but he knew it had been bad.

His phone dinged. Another text from Drew.

*WHY ARE YOU STANDING OUT IN THE PARKING LOT? GET IN HERE.*

Screwing up his courage, he put one foot in front of the other. He would be fine this time. He would keep his shields in place and not let too much in. Control. Focus. He'd worked on it with his father for a year. He could do this.

His courage faltered when he heard her voice as he sauntered into the apartment.

"This place is so pretty." McKenna was there, in the same building, in the same apartment. He hoped Drew had a plan to get her out of there. He didn't want her to see any of this. Oh, God. What if he wound up hurting her? The thought chilled him to the bone.

"Thank you," Kayla said. "They opened up the apartments to all residents, not only students, nine years ago. I heard they were having trouble renting to only students. Now I know why."

Drew was the first to see him. "There you are, man."

Tristan waved, moving all the way into the living room. "Hi, everyone."

The room was full. Kayla and Drew claimed opposite ends of the couch while Tabitha lounged in the recliner. McKenna perched on the arm of the couch. He wasn't prepared to explain his powers or share them outside of his immediate circle. A spark of hope flared. Did this mean Kayla had changed her mind?

"What are y'all doing here?" he asked.

Tabitha struggled to her feet, the chair threatening to hang on to her. "Preliminary interviews with the residents. McKenna and I ran into Drew and Kayla so we're taking a break before hitting the bottom levels."

"I thought the big ghost hunt was this Friday." Drew had told him Mr. Martin had given Aaron the go ahead to prepare a hunt. Tristan planned to be far away from his apartment on that night.

"It is," McKenna said. "But we wanted to lay the ground work before we started setting up equipment."

Tabitha glanced at her watch. "We need to finish, Mac. Aaron promised to have dinner ready for me when I got back."

Tristan set his bag on the kitchen table. "You're welcome to stay. I didn't mean to interrupt." The longer they stayed, the longer he could put off using his powers.

McKenna waved away his concern. "You aren't chasing us off. How about I meet you for dinner?" She stood. "We'll probably be done by seven."

"Yeah."

Drew cleared his throat. "Are we all invited?" Kayla kicked his leg. "Never mind. I'm sure Kayla and I can find our own dinner."

Tabitha rolled her eyes. "Let's go, Mac."

"Right behind you."

Tristan moved closer. "Oh, did you find out anything else at the other interviews?"

"I did. Justin, Will, and Selah all described The White Lady the same way you and Kayla did. That's not definite proof she killed them, but all of the victims saw her. We'll see what the residents have to say tonight, and then on Friday, we'll see what Drew's equipment has to say."

Tristan relaxed his shoulders. It felt like they were closer than the police were. "Where do we go from there?"

"If she's real…" Tabitha began.

"She's real," Tristan interrupted.

"Then we try to find out who she was, what she wants, and how to banish her." She continued without acknowledging the interruption.

"How do you do that?"

"It's different with every case. We'll have to see how this one plays out."

"Good." Kayla stood. "The sooner you get rid of her, the better."

"We've got you covered." Drew touched her lightly on the shoulder.

McKenna and Tabitha agreed, then made their way out of the door. As soon as they were gone, Kayla beamed at Tristan.

"Are you ready?"

The hope in her voice caused Tristan's nerves to rattle. He wiped his hand on his jeans again. "I don't know."

Before Kayla could respond, someone knocked. She opened it to find Paul Martin, the building's owner, on the other side.

"May I come in?" He was a short, robust man with close-cropped dark hair. His dark brown eyes glanced from one person to another.

"Yes." Kayla took a step back. "What brings you here?"

"Two paranormal investigators dropped by my office today. Said they think a ghost killed Mr. Beckett." He nodded to Kayla. "I'm sorry for your loss."

"Thank you. You could've sent a card." The confusion was evident on Kayla's face.

Paul chuckled. "I know." His eyes darted around the room as he shuffled from foot to foot. "I thought something like this wouldn't happen again." He rubbed his hands together. "It's been ten years." He sighed. "It's like my building's cursed."

Tristan exchanged a look with Drew. "Can we do something for you, Mr. Martin?" He asked as he crossed to the older man.

"No. No." He shook his head. "But I do want to know why you hired paranormal investigators without talking to me. Some of the other residents are a little spooked."

Tristan and Drew closed in on Kayla like two bodyguards. Tristan leaned on the edge of the door. "Are you saying she can't do that?"

Paul straightened to his full height, which only reached Tristan's chest. "I'm saying she should've spoken to me first."

"*She* is standing right here." Kayla's voice held an edge to it. "I can't explain what I saw when my fiancé died, Mr. Martin, but I do know it wasn't normal. Something is in this building, and I want to know what it is. I don't want anyone else to get hurt."

"Ms. Collins, maybe we can work something out."

Goosebumps traveled the length of Tristan's arms. All of the fine dark hairs stood on end. Something rattled behind him. A vase on the left end table rose on its own. It sailed through the air as if thrown and crashed into the opposite wall.

Paul's cheeks paled. "Just talk to me in the future." He scurried out of the apartment as fast as a rabbit.

Kayla slammed the door shut. "That was my grandmother's vase, bitch!"

The air warmed around them.

She rounded on Tristan. "What do you need to do your thing?" Tristan stumbled back at the fury in her eyes.

"I need you to stay out here." He glanced at Drew. "Both of you."

Kayla softened. "Are you sure?"

"I'd feel a lot better." He swallowed. "I don't know what's going to happen, or if I'll even see anything we can use, but I promise I'll try my best. I may lose it, though. If that happens, I want you as far away from me as possible."

"But you only see the past," Kayla pointed out.

"If he's in too deep, he starts channeling it," Drew said. "And there's no telling who lived in this apartment before you."

Tristan walked into the bedroom. Since this was the last place The White Lady had killed, he hoped he could connect with her there. One sliver of her past might help them learn who she was. Granted, he had only read buildings and living people up until that moment. Trying to pick up the past from an actual ghost could be a completely different experience. Or it might not happen at all. Sitting on the bed, he pushed his worry aside.

"You ready?" Drew asked.

"As I'll ever be." Tristan held up a hand, palm out, when Drew stepped into the room. "Stay out there, man. Please."

Drew backed up. "I'll be here if you need me."

Tristan took a deep breath and closed his eyes. He pictured his shield, the thick red brick wall that only a few glimpses could get through. He imagined the wall sliding down halfway. He opened his eyes. Incorporeal images of the past overlapped each other. None of them had defining characteristics. It was like watching several different movies play at once with the sound off.

He concentrated on Zack first. The room around him transformed from day to night. The goosebumps were back as the temperature in the room grew colder. He was no longer on the bed, but in it. He was no longer Tristan.

*Zack sat up in bed and peered down at his girlfriend. No, fiancée. Kayla was going to be his in a few more months. God, how could one man get so lucky? She rolled over, snuggling under the covers.*

*The room was too cold. Icy. He knew he had set the thermostat at seventy. Why was it freezing? He crawled out of bed and planted his bare feet on the cold floor. It wasn't busted, was it? That didn't make any sense. If it weren't working, then it would feel like an oven in here. He groaned.*

*A loud shriek echoed in his ears. Zack's head whipped up. The White Lady floated in front of him. Her ethereal beauty filled the room. Her eyes were different this time. Red. Angry. His eyes darted to Kayla. Protect her. Whatever happens, no matter how terrified he was, he had to make sure she was safe. He opened his mouth, but no sound came out. He stumbled backwards. The ghost grabbed his T-shirt, lifting him off the ground.*

Tristan fought against the fear. He wasn't Zack. He wasn't going to die. The White Lady. He had to concentrate on her. Who was she? He dropped his mental shield another inch.

*Anger. Pain. Confusion. They have to pay. They all have to pay. She held the terrified man in the air, strength and energy coursing through her. He did this. He and the others. Why won't they die? She had killed this one before. She had killed them all before. They always came back to torment her. Why didn't they stay dead?*

The scene changed.

*She ran through the woods, laughing. Twirling in a circle, her heart burst with joy. He was coming, tonight. They were going to run away together and get married. No one would know. She clutched the note in her hand. It wouldn't be long. He would be there. He never broke his promises.*

Tristan dropped his shield a little more. He was so close. If he could hear a name, see a detail, anything. He pushed harder. The vision shifted again. The woods and the girl were gone.

*Asshole! His friend was going to wish he had never touched her. He burst into the apartment and took a swing. His fist connected with his friends' face.*

Another change.

*She slid under the covers, her skin warm. She was ready for this. Pressing her body against his, her heart fluttered. He tucked her hair behind her ear.*

Tristan's fingers dug into the sheets. The images moved faster, changing from one person to the other. He was losing it. He had to focus, return to The White Lady. Who was who? Which one was she? Tristan slid off the bed and fell to his knees. He grabbed his head. Other images came through. A student worried he wouldn't pass his final. A woman locked in a passionate embrace. A man punched another one in the face. Someone yelled, and it took Tristan a minute to realize it came from him.

"I can't! Too much!" His voice was lost in the din of voices, all clambering to be heard. His careful shield crumbled, and everything rushed in at once. A tornado of images and sounds and emotions swirled around him.

"Tristan?" Drew's voice was faint.

"You!" He gritted his teeth, struggling against the urge to shove Drew against the wall. He fought to hold onto himself. Who was he again? He shut his eyes, willing it all to stop. The voices grew louder as the panic overtook him.

McKenna rested her elbows on the table. Luke Connors, the young man sitting across from her, grinned, his white teeth glistening. He believed he was telling the truth with all of his heart. She didn't detect any deception from him.

"I'm telling you, The White Lady is a woman who killed her husband and then herself and now wants to kill fresh meat." Luke adjusted his black-framed glasses. His blue-green eyes were as round as saucers. "She uses the apartment as her hunting ground."

McKenna exchanged a look with Tabitha.

Tabitha smiled reassuringly at Luke. She lifted her camera and snapped a picture of his living room. "If that's true, Mr. Connors, then why did she wait ten years? And only kill three guys before this?"

"And why hasn't she killed every man in this building?" McKenna added.

Luke swept his dark brown hair off his forehead. "No one knows. That's the mystery."

McKenna sighed. They were getting nowhere. She and

Tabitha had spent the rest of the afternoon interviewing the other residents of Hidden Forest. Between the numerous people who closed the door in her face and the different versions of the legend, McKenna was tired of getting no answers.

Luke was the third resident she and Tabitha had spoken to that afternoon, and none of them had shed any new light on the ghost or her origins. The first resident they spoke to, a harried young woman, had said the ghost would sometimes watch her when she brought a date home. The second resident, an older man, said that he had seen the ghost a couple of times, but she never bothered him.

Luke had been more than happy to share his theories the minute McKenna and Tabitha had introduced themselves.

And all of the stories shared two characteristics. She killed, and she didn't like men. McKenna sighed. That was the problem with urban legends. Everyone told a different version.

"So, you really don't know who The White Lady is or why she's here?" Tabitha asked, her spiky hair, streaked red that day, bounced with each movement. She walked around the table, taking a picture from another angle.

"I swear every word I'm telling you is the truth." Luke held up three fingers in the boy scouts' honor sign.

"We appreciate you telling us the story." McKenna smiled. "How did you hear it?"

"From my cousin. She lived here ten years ago, when the other three guys bought it."

McKenna nodded. "Did she tell you anything about what happened then?"

"Just the story I told you."

McKenna pressed her lips together. "And where did she hear the story?"

Luke slumped in his chair. "I don't know. I think her boyfriend at the time told her."

"Did she have any proof? Pictures or anything?"

"No. Just what she heard."

McKenna wrote down what he said, adding the legend to others she had heard. People always seemed to latch onto a good ghost story, but none of them knew who The White Lady was or where she came from. She had already gone through all the newspapers she could. No women had died in the building or the woods. A few young women had died or went missing before the building was constructed, but they weren't connected to the building or the area. Dead ends popped up no matter which way she turned.

"Do you mind if we set up a camera or two in here?" Tabitha asked, bringing McKenna back to the present. "Since you've said you've seen her."

Luke shrugged. "Go ahead. I'll be visiting a friend out of town. I'll leave a key for you."

"We appreciate it." Tabitha shook Luke's hand. "Thank you for your time, Mr. Connors." She handed him a card. "If you see or hear anything, just give us a call."

Luke took the card. "I'll keep an eye out."

McKenna followed Tabitha out the door. She rested her back against the wall when Luke's door closed. "We're not getting any closer. All we have surrounding this ghost are legends and sightings. We don't know any more than we did."

Tabitha tapped her on the shoulder. "I know it's frustrating. Hopefully, we can get some footage of her. That will give us more details to go on."

McKenna gestured to Tabitha's camera. "Anything in the pictures?"

Tabitha flipped through her last few shots. "I need to look at them closer, but so far, nothing." Lowering the camera, she tapped her temple. "You?"

McKenna shook her head. "Nothing. I can pick up everyone in this building, and with so many people, I can't tell which one might be a ghost."

"So, off to meet Tristan now?" Tabitha moved toward the stairs.

McKenna pushed away from the wall. "Absolutely."

Tabitha nudged her. "What is it about this guy?"

"I don't know." McKenna's cheeks burned. "There's something vulnerable and mysterious about him. Plus, he's pretty hot."

"He is that."

McKenna placed a foot on the first step. A wave of panic knocked her backwards. She registered Tabitha's hands steadying her, but the erratic emotion filled every one of her senses. Her breathing picked up as she clutched her chest.

"McKenna?" Tabitha's voice was far away.

"Someone's in trouble." McKenna bolted up the stairs, zeroing in on where the emotion was located. She turned right when she reached the third-floor landing. Skidding to a halt, the panic emanated from the closed door of Zack and Kayla's apartment. "It's here." She walked inside.

"Man, it's me!" Drew.

"Drew, what's wrong with him?" Kayla.

Both of them were worried, but the panic didn't come from them.

McKenna rounded the corner and gasped. Kayla hovered at the end of the hall. Drew was on the floor, scratches on his cheek and blood trickling from his mouth. Tristan stood over him, one hand clutching Drew's shirt. His other hand was balled into a fist.

"Man, this isn't you." Drew wiped his lip.

"You have to pay!" Tristan growled out the words.

"Tristan?" McKenna took a step forward, but Tabitha held her back.

Tristan's head snapped up, his green eyes wild and unfocused. McKenna swallowed. This wasn't the guy she planned to have dinner with. This wasn't the guy she had flirted with last Sunday. He stepped over Drew, advancing on her, Kayla, and Tabitha. She pushed the other two women behind her, her eyes never leaving Tristan. Whatever he was seeing, it wasn't them. She knew that unfocused look. He was lost in a vision.

Drew grabbed his leg and yanked it out from underneath him. Tristan crashed to the floor. His face contorted in pain as he grabbed his head. When he looked up, his eyes filled with tears.

"She killed him!" he yelled. "She killed him!" He shook his head. "Make it stop!"

McKenna pulled free from Tabitha. She crouched down and touched Tristan's arm. "What happened?"

Tristan grimaced again. The anger was back in his green eyes. He grabbed her wrist and squeezed. She yelled, a sharp sudden pain shooting up her arm. She tried to yank her arm out of his grasp, but his grip was locked on. Drew reached her in no time. He pried Tristan's hand off her. McKenna crab walked out of his reach.

"He wanted to try to see what happened to Zack." Drew held his friend down. "He let too much in. I can't bring him back."

"It's my fault. I asked him to try," Kayla said.

"What do you mean 'he wanted to see'?" McKenna kept her eyes on Tristan. His anger turned to fear, and he thrashed against Drew's hold.

Drew gave an uneven chuckle. "I'm not supposed to tell you."

"Drew, I don't think it matters right now. He's in pain."

Tristan screamed, his back arching. His eyes met McKenna's. Even though they weren't seeing her, they pleaded with her.

Drew swore. "He's psychic. I think the fancy term is retrocognitive."

"He can see the past?" Tabitha asked.

"Yeah, but his control is all over the place. If he lets too much in, he loses himself. He becomes the person he's seeing. And when he opens up like this, he's more than one person."

McKenna caressed Tristan's arm. He flinched. "I think I can help him if you can hold onto him."

"How?" Kayla dropped to the floor.

"No time to explain, but you can trust me."

"Are you sure?" Tabitha grabbed one of Tristan's legs.

"Yes."

Kayla grabbed the other leg while Drew kept his grip on Tristan's arms. Tristan thrashed and kicked. He was strong, but they held onto him.

Kayla grunted with effort. "Whatever you're going to do, do it now."

McKenna placed her hands on either side of his head. She tuned the other three people out as she looked into Tristan's unfocused gaze. She sent every peaceful and calming emotion to him she had. It was like shoving against a wall. "Tristan? Can you hear me?"

The wall gave a little. He stopped thrashing as the tension eased out of his muscles.

McKenna kept her voice steady. "Picture a wall. Put the wall up." She imagined her own shield; how safe it was. She sent that emotion to Tristan. His breathing slowed.

Minute by minute, Tristan's eyes cleared. His gaze moved from seeing through her to seeing *her*. McKenna kept her hold. "Tristan?" She continued to call his name over and over.

Tristan blinked. When he didn't move, Drew, Kayla, and

Tabitha let go. He lay on the wooden floor, his breathing ragged. He nudged McKenna's hands away from his head. "McKenna?" He blinked again.

She let out a breath she didn't realize she was holding. "Yeah. Are you okay?" She sat there, too tired to move. She sagged against the nearest wall.

"Yeah." He sat up. Slumping, his whole body appeared as tired as McKenna felt. He wiped his face with his hands, glaring at Drew. "So much for watching my back, huh?"

"It wasn't his fault," McKenna said. "I felt your panic."

"You felt my panic?" He dropped his head into his hands, not giving her a chance to explain. "You can run away now that you've seen the freak show."

H e was a failure, plain and simple. All the things he had seen and felt churned in his brain. None of it fit together in any kind of sense. Were any of the people he had seen The White Lady? He had no idea. His focus had been all over the place.

Tristan glanced around the room. His stomach sank when he saw Drew's split lip and the bruise on McKenna's wrist. McKenna. She was another puzzle. A psychic like he was, only with better control. How had she pulled him back? When he realized where he was and who he was, her face was the first one he had seen. He wanted the floor to open and swallow him right then and there. Why was she still here? Why were Drew, Kayla, and Tabitha still here? He slouched on the couch in his apartment, dropping his head in his hands.

At least Drew had the common sense to lead Tristan back to his apartment. It was brighter, and no visions plagued him.

"Y'all should just go," he grumbled.

A glass of water and a plate with a slice of pepperoni

pizza appeared on the table in front of him. "You need to eat and drink something," Kayla said. He raised his head to see the determined expression on her face. A look that said she wasn't going anywhere.

He obeyed her, lifting his pizza off the plate and biting into it. The tangy sauce made him realize how hungry he was. He wiped a dribble of it off his chin.

"I'm not going anywhere," McKenna declared. "Besides, I don't think I can move." She sat on the other end of the couch curled into a ball. She took her time chewing.

"All right, we have food, we have drink. We have two psychics who are semi-conscious." Tabitha propped her feet on the coffee table. "Who would like to tell me what's going on?"

"It was my idea." Kayla settled on the floor. "I knew Tristan's control was all over the place, but I pushed anyway. I thought he could see who the ghost was."

"It's not your fault." Tristan tossed back two aspirins. Pain rumbled against his skull. "It was my choice."

"But I pressured you into it."

"It doesn't matter who talked who into what." Tabitha leveled Tristan with her gaze. "How long have you been psychic? How trained are you?"

Tristan hadn't expected anybody to be this abrupt about his ability. The corners of his mouth twitched. "Since I was eleven and not very."

"Hereditary?" McKenna asked as she popped a pepperoni into her mouth.

"It goes from father to son in my family."

"Only men?"

"Only men." Tristan took another bite of his slice. Since no one was making a hasty exit, he chose to learn more about McKenna's power as well. "What about you? How did you do that?" He met her bright blue eyes. She sipped her own glass of water, her face pale. "Pull me out of the vision?"

"Luck, mostly. I'm empathic, I read and send emotions. I sent all the good, relaxed ones I could feel to you." She ate another pepperoni.

Tristan's legs shook, rattling the coffee table. "Is yours hereditary, too?"

"It is, but everyone on my mother's side of the family has a degree of empathy. Couldn't hide anything from my grandmother. My mother, however, denies her gift." She dropped her eyes and studied the gooey cheese dripping onto her plate.

Tristan let her answer sink in. Denial. He had gone through denial in high school and college. Wanted to get rid of the images that plagued him. But it wouldn't shut off. It got worse the more he tried to ignore it. "Just the women?"

"No. My brother was empathic, too."

Tristan let the information hang in the air between them. Had the ghost taken anything from him the way she took Tristan's strength? He wasn't sure how to ask that question. He tossed the rest of his water back. "Well, thank you. For what you did."

"You're welcome." McKenna wiped her mouth. "I'm glad it worked."

He lifted his head. "Me, too." He sighed. He could sleep for a week if everyone would leave and let him. A drumbeat pounded in his head, and his muscles were like rubber.

What was he thinking, trying to will a vision? He knew he didn't have the control. It was stupid of him to try, to risk his friends' wellbeing in the process. He glanced at McKenna again. She had risked her wellbeing to save his sanity. How could he repay that?

"I wish you had told us the plan." Tabitha stretched her

short legs. She polished off her slice. "We could've been there from the beginning." She shot a disappointed look at Drew.

Drew knocked back some of his beer. "I thought we had it under control. I've seen him do the whole psychic thing before."

"Still. You should've told us."

"Wasn't my secret to tell."

"He's right." McKenna swallowed. "When you first meet people, you don't lead off with 'I'm psychic.' You have to trust them first."

"It took him a long time to trust me," Kayla said. Her face was drawn. "Damn it, Tristan. I'm sorry. I didn't believe Zack when he told me how hard it was for you. I thought you just stared off into space and came back with an answer. I didn't know how much of a risk it was." She pushed to her feet. "You should've told me."

"It's okay." He nodded to her. "Like I said, it was my choice."

Kayla scowled as she found a small towel in one of the kitchen drawers. She dug around in the cabinets until she found some cleaning solution. Armed with both, she went to work on the kitchen counters.

"Were you able to get any answers?" McKenna asked.

Tristan looked at all four expectant faces. Rubbing his hands on his jeans, he wanted to be anywhere but there. "I saw a lot of different things, and I still haven't sorted all of it out yet. I saw Zack. Kayla told the truth there, but we knew she was. As for The White Lady, it seemed like she remembered killing all of the victims, but to her, it was the same person or people." He drew his brows together. "I don't know which."

Tabitha's eyes widened as she leaned forward. "You read the past off a spirit's energy?"

"Yeah. Didn't think I could do it, but she is energy, I guess.

That's what I pick up from buildings and people." He ran a hand through his hair. "Why?"

"It's rare. I think I've only heard of one other person who could do that."

"Who?" Drew asked.

"A guy my grandfather worked with, back when he started the Greene Institute. Daniel Johnson, I think." She took a bite out of her slice of pizza. "Any relation?"

Tristan's mouth quirked. "I'm not surprised. Daniel is my grandfather."

Tabitha settled back into her chair. "I heard he was really good."

"Which explains why he was always disappointed in me." Tristan stood and wobbled for a few seconds before finding his balance. He grabbed another slice of pizza.

"Anyway, how can a ghost keep thinking she's killing someone over and over?" Kayla brought the conversation back to the original topic. Her hand flew over the front counter, scrubbing out coffee stains.

"Sounds possible. From what I understand, ghosts have a different perception than we do. If they're the conscious kind, they don't realize time has passed," Tabitha polished off her slice and set the plate on the coffee table. She leaned back, soda propped in her hand.

"More than likely, all four looked like someone she knew. Possibly the man who killed her." McKenna wrapped her blanket closer around her.

"But all four guys don't look alike. Isn't that what you told me, Tristan?" Drew set his beer on the coffee table.

McKenna jerked, wincing when she moved too fast. "No, all four don't look alike, but Zack and Jason both had blond hair and tall, lean frames. I think some of their features were the same, but I'd have to go back and look."

"Didn't Keith have dark hair, and dark eyes?" Tristan rubbed his stubbly chin.

"And Cory had wavy blondish-brown hair." McKenna fell back into the cushions. "I'll study the pictures closer tomorrow."

Drew groaned. "Tristan, did you see anything else?"

Tristan tried to recall more images. Most of them were snippets of memory. "Some guy punching his friend. A woman about to lose her virginity. And a girl running through the woods. She was going to meet somebody there."

Tabitha arched an eyebrow. "A girl running through the woods? That doesn't match the apartment."

"I know. I usually pick up things that happened in the room I'm in, so I don't know where that one came from."

"Maybe it was from before the apartment was built," Drew suggested.

"Still doesn't make any sense." Tristan sank into the couch, his head lolling to the side. "I'm sorry I'm not much help." If they would only let him sleep, his focus would be better.

"Don't apologize. You were brave to try." McKenna nudged his leg with her toe. "Maybe we can try it together when you get your strength back?"

Panic squeezed his chest. "No!" He shook his head. "No. I won't do it again."

"But if I'm there…"

The mere thought terrified him. "No. Something worse than bruises could happen. I can't."

McKenna sighed. "You might not pick up anything violent."

"I don't care. Something violent always comes through. That's the strongest energy. I won't hurt you again."

Tabitha stood and stretched. Picking up her camera, she flipped through some of the pictures. "Maybe I caught something today, and we'll have something more to go on. Drew, you have your laptop. Can you bring these pictures up?"

"Sure." Drew pushed to his feet. "You guys want to see the pictures?"

McKenna chuckled. "I don't think I can move."

"I'm going to stay right here." Tristan finished off his water.

Kayla climbed to her feet. "I'd like to know what you're looking for."

"Okay." Drew searched the area where he sat, and his face fell. "Kayla, I left it in your apartment."

"Come on, let's go get it."

When Drew, Kayla, and Tabitha left, silence filled the room. Tristan studied the ceiling. His arms and legs were heavy, as if he had lifted more than his weight. He rolled his head to the side. McKenna burrowed into her corner, her eyes closed. For a moment, he thought she was asleep.

She opened her eyes. "What happened the first time you realized you were psychic?"

Tristan smiled at the question. At least she wasn't pressuring him to try again. "I was in class. The teacher was droning on about something...I don't remember. I started seeing people fade in and out in the room, and then the room changed completely. I must have freaked out because when the vision ended, I was on the floor and the teacher was standing over me. Drew held everybody back as best he could."

"Did you know it was coming?"

"I did, but I didn't think about it. I knew my grandpa could see the past. He loved to read family members at Christmas time, dredging out all their past secrets. I also knew my dad could see the present. Couldn't lose a thing in our house. And I know they told me it was coming, but I guess I didn't believe them." He sipped his water. "You?"

McKenna chuckled. "I was ten and thought I was having the worst mood swings ever. My mother didn't tell me a thing, and I guess Jason didn't think to mention it. One minute I was happy, the next I was crying. The guidance counselor thought I was crazy.

"Jason was the one who picked me up from school. He was sixteen at the time. He explained everything and tried to teach me as much as he could. We went to Grandma's house that following weekend. You know, she used to work for the Greene Institute back in the sixties, too. Maybe she crossed paths with your grandpa."

Tristan nodded. "Maybe. I'll have to ask."

McKenna cocked her head. "So, why didn't anyone teach you to control your ability?" Curiosity laced her tone.

The question cut through him. "It's my fault. My dad and my grandpa both tried, but I wouldn't listen. I didn't want this thing in my head. I learned how to shield and how to deal with the bits of the past that leaked in, but full on using it? No way. I didn't want to have anything to do with that."

He glanced at McKenna to see what her reaction was. Would she lecture him? Would she tell him how the whole empathy thing came naturally for her?

She let the silence hang there for a moment until she spoke. "I don't blame you. It wasn't easy for me either." She caressed the back of his hand.

He twisted his empty glass in circles. A small bit of condensation formed on the table's wood. "Really?"

McKenna chuckled. "Oh, yeah. It took several lessons with Jason and with Grandma until I was no longer an emotional mess."

"And your mother stayed as far away from it as she could?"

"I think my mom cut herself off from all emotions. She blocks her own, and she blocks the others. I don't know how she does it. I know she loves me, and she fell apart when Jason died, but she doesn't show affection."

He felt for her. "I'm sorry."

"Don't be. I've dealt with it."

"I know, but I felt like I needed to say it." He indicated her empty glass. "Want some more water?"

"Yes, thank you."

Tristan took her cup and tensed with every step to the sink. His muscles still ached from fighting against Drew's hold.

"Was today the first time you tried to see the past in a while?" McKenna asked.

Tristan held the glass under the running water. The rushing sound gave him a couple of seconds to gather his thoughts. He hadn't shared the whole story with anyone in a year. He cut off the water. "No. I tried a year ago for my cousin Karie." He handed the water to McKenna. "She wanted to buy an old house and wanted me to get a feel for it. Tell her if anything bad had happened in it."

"What happened?"

He sighed as he sat down. He pushed his cup around the coffee table, avoiding her eyes. "Last year, I was teaching in Wilmington. My cousin lived out there near me, and she knew about the family secret." He let go of the glass. "Anyway, she invited me along to check out this house she was thinking about buying. Halfway there, she told me she wanted to know its whole history. I told her no, but she talked me into it. After all, she's family." He paused, the memory flashing into his mind. He tightened his jaw.

"Is she okay?" McKenna's quiet voice filtered through.

Tristan nodded. "Yeah, she's okay. I...I went to her place and tried to see. She stayed in the room with me." He looked up and saw soft blue eyes watching him. "It was an old house, and a lot of stuff happened there. I saw it all. Everything. And I felt it, too. Like I did here. And then, it happened."

McKenna sat straighter. "What happened?"

"Somebody from the past with a strong personality shoved through. I saw a man beating a woman, and I could feel his hate for her. It was a massive, twisted, ugly thing. All that rage built up inside of me. All of it was from his point of view. I got lost in it. It was like I wasn't me anymore. I was him."

"How did you snap out of it?"

"I don't know. Karie was screaming my name. Somehow, I heard her. At some point I grabbed a wooden board lying in the middle of the living room, but I didn't touch her, thank God. But she fell and broke her leg while trying to get away from me. She was terrified of me. *I* was terrified of me." His heart broke as he recalled her lying on the floor, fear in her eyes. Fear he had put there. "I moved away and hid out in my parents' house. I couldn't face it." A lump lodged in his throat. "What if I lost it in my classroom? What if I hurt one of my students?"

"Tristan, no wonder you keep a tight lid on it. I channel emotions, and I've never had that happen to me." She scooted closer to him and wrapped her arms around him. He leaned into her. "I'm sorry."

"Like you said, I dealt with it."

Her lean body fit perfectly in his embrace. Tristan buried his face in her soft hair, the clean, salty scent of the ocean surrounding him. He pulled her closer. He should push her away, tell her it wasn't safe to be around him. But McKenna hadn't turned away. She had seen the worst of it, but her eyes never reflected the same fear. She tightened her hold on him, and he didn't want her to let go.

～

It was past nine o'clock when McKenna entered her apartment. She tossed her keys on the table and pressed her back against the door. The memory of Tristan's melancholy, everyone else's concern, and her own fear churned inside of her. Her body shuddered, and the dam broke. Tears streamed down her face. Wiping at them, she collapsed into the nearest chair.

A meow caught her attention. "Hey, Oscar." A large gray and white cat hopped into her lap. She petted him as he curled up. His soft fur helped to chase away the stress. "It's good to see you, too." He meowed again as he rubbed against her palm. "It's been a long day, buddy."

Tristan's wild eyes and erratic behavior haunted her memory. What if she hadn't been able to pull him out of it? What if he was lost in his own mind forever? She swallowed down the fear. He was okay. He was safe for now, but his ability was dangerous. No wonder he didn't want to use it or tell anyone about it.

But he had tried for a friend. He knew what might happen, and yet, he wanted to help. Her heart swelled at the fact Tristan had been willing to take the risk.

She rubbed her arms, remembering his embrace. He trusted her with every fiber of his being. Did she fully trust him? She had seen the worst of him, and she hadn't run. But she had thought about it. She had wanted to grab Drew, Kayla, and Tabitha, shut the door behind them, and run. But his panic had been too strong. No, leaving him was out of the question.

Picking up the heavy, soft cat, she made her way to the bedroom. She changed into her pajamas and crawled under the covers. Oscar's rhythmic purr was the only sound in the quiet room. He lay down beside her, a warm, furry body.

McKenna wasn't sure what to make of Tristan. He

intrigued her. That much was for sure. She wanted to be near him, to know more about him. After all, he was the first guy not related to her who comprehended what it was like to be psychic. As she understood it, she was the same for him.

But she saw what happened to him if he let too much in. He must be exhausted trying to hold it together all the time. He needed training, more training than he had. She didn't blame his father, but she did blame Tristan. A gift that powerful deserved respect, and Tristan had spent most of his life not respecting it. She had to convince him he needed to learn to control it. Maybe she could be the one to help him. She wanted to be.

She smiled as she remembered her own early training sessions with her grandmother. Grandma was like a drill sergeant, making sure McKenna knew exactly what she possessed and how to use it. She didn't want the empathy to drive McKenna or Jason mad. Nor did she want them to sever all their emotions and live in a shell like their mother did.

McKenna was terrified of going crazy. She didn't even want to entertain the idea of getting lost in a sea of emotions. Maybe that was why she didn't understand how Tristan could hide and do nothing. Yes, she had to help him. There was no choice.

She clicked off the lamplight and burrowed under the covers. There was more to Tristan than his powers. He made her heart flutter every time he walked into the room. She always found an excuse to touch him or talk to him. No, her reasons for wanting to help him weren't completely selfless.

With thoughts of Tristan dancing in her head, McKenna drifted off to sleep.

A lone. Finally. Tristan leaned against his front door, taking in the silence. He wasn't sure he had the energy to keep up anymore. He sauntered away from the door, his hand reaching for the light switch. His mental shields shook. They weren't rebuilt yet, and a vision slid in.

*He tossed clothes into an open suitcase. He had to get out of the apartment. He had to get out now before anyone else died.*

*Dead. Two people were dead. His heart thundered in his chest.* My fault. All of this is my fault. *Two guys he didn't know were dead. Their bodies had crashed to the ground. Their eyes left wide open, staring at nothing.*

*She had come on the same night for the past two weeks. She would come that night. He felt it in his bones.*

*He had seen her both times before they died. Felt the icy kiss of her breath. Had all the energy yanked out of him against his will. She needed him to kill. He had figured out that much. How many more would die because of him? Well, no more. He intended to be out of the apartment this time before she showed.*

*He pulled open more drawers and threw more clothes into the suitcase. She couldn't follow him home, could she? His breath stopped when he thought about his baby sister. Would the ghost take her energy, too? She didn't have the control yet; she would be a sitting duck. Out. He had to get out.*

*Cold air swirled around him.* Keep moving. Keep moving. *The lights flickered and went out. Her ghostly glow cast the only light in the room. He raised his head to see her eerie green eyes.*

*Pounding on the door. "Jace, my key's not working. Can you let me in?"*

*Justin! He had to keep his roommate away. What if he was next? He wouldn't let her kill him. Jason picked up a chair and held it between them.*

*"No. I'm done." He took a step back. "You can't have anymore."*

*She knocked the chair out of his hand as if it weighed no more than a feather. "You have to pay," she hissed. She advanced on him.*

*More knocking. "Jason? You okay, man?"*

*His eyes were glued to her face. Fear planted his feet to the floor. The wind moved faster around him, cold and bitter. He closed his eyes. "Justin, please go away."*

*The pounding was harder. "Jason, open the door!"*

*He opened his eyes, kept his gaze steady.*

*The White Lady lifted her hand. The front door swung open. Justin stumbled inside, his dark silhouette blocking out the hallway light.*

*Jason grit his teeth. "Get away from me! You can't have it! No more!"*

*She gripped him by the shirt. His feet left the ground. She cocked her head to the side. "You're the last one. You have to pay." His back crashed through the window.*

Tristan blinked. The room around him returned to normal. Sweat ran down his back. It beaded his brow and stuck his curls to his forehead and neck. He gripped the back of a kitchen chair for balance. Raking his hair back, he took one breath, and then another, trying to return his thumping heart to normal.

The man's words ran through his head. *"No more."*

What had he seen? He concentrated on any information he could remember. Jason. He had seen Jason, McKenna's brother. His brow furrowed as he tried to recapture the details. The White Lady had visited Jason before every death, like she had visited Tristan before Zack's. Each visit had left Jason tired. He had tried to get away before she came back, but she said he was the last one. Worry knotted in his stomach. The last one. Oh, God. Did that mean he was the last one, too?

Dropping into the chair, he noticed how cold the room was. He shivered. A frigid room meant one thing. The White

Lady was coming. He swore. Jason was empathic, like his sister. The White Lady must have used his psychic energy to kill. He swallowed. Had she used his own energy to kill Zack?

The lights blinked, then went out. The kitchen table shook underneath his hands. He jumped to his feet, his eyes adjusting to the darkness. He fumbled with the lock on his door. The knob twisted, but the door stayed closed. Tristan pulled, but it was like it was glued shut. Ice caressed his back. He whirled around.

Her outline appeared first, followed by her whole form. A soft glow accompanied her. The White Lady hovered next to him, an inch or two away. She radiated demur and innocence, but Tristan knew she wasn't. He had seen her past, experienced her rage when she killed. She floated closer, and he sucked in a breath.

"Who are you?" he whispered. "What do you want?"

She remained silent as she reached out and brushed his arm. The glow brightened when she made contact. Tristan pulled his arm away. He pressed his back to the door. Nowhere to run. Nowhere to hide.

"You need me, don't you? To keep killing?"

She blinked. Her cold hand traced the line of his jaw. His body shook, the cold freezing him inside and out.

"You used Jason the same way, didn't you?"

No response.

Tristan forced his voice to stay steady. "You won't get it. I won't be here tomorrow night. I won't help you."

The White Lady smiled. She grabbed his arm, fingernails like chips of ice digging in. Tristan sucked in a breath, gritting his teeth against the pain. Her nails sank into skin, blood pooling up at the marks. Second by second, his muscles doubled in weight while she became more solid. His eyelids fluttered as he breathed heavily. His knees hit the floor. Icy sharp pain stabbed through him. It took all that was left of his strength to look up at her.

"Please don't do this."

She put her finger to her lips, quieting him. "It's not time yet. He will pay." She let go and vanished.

The lights blinked back on as the room warmed. Tristan lay down on the cool floor and rubbed his arm. He had to stop the bleeding. He had to move. But no energy was left. Fighting with every ounce of what little energy he had left, he crawled to the kitchen. Getting to his feet, he ripped a square of paper towels and pressed it to his wound. Then he dragged himself to his bed and dropped into it.

In the end he lost consciousness.

## 13

"Tristan, open the door!" McKenna jiggled the knob, her heart in her throat. Pressing her hand against the door, she reached out for him. His emotions were faint, his energy a flicker. She pushed her panic down, searching for a way to get inside. If only she knew how to pick a lock. Should she call the cops? Find out if someone could let her in? She banged on the door once again. "Tristan, please."

After everything that happened the night before, McKenna had decided to check on him and make sure he was all right. He had been tired and worried when she left him. She had even thought about staying the night, but he told her to go and get some sleep.

She spent most of the morning calling him, but he didn't answer. No texts, no return calls. After leaving a third message on his voice mail, she started to get anxious. At first, she thought he might be busy. She could understand that. After all, he probably had classes and Zack's viewing would be that night, followed by the funeral on Saturday. She was busy, too, with the upcoming hunt.

She headed to the college, telling herself she wasn't pushing. She only wanted to see if he'd like to go to lunch with her. That was all. It took some navigating to find his office, but only one person was there. She glanced up when McKenna walked in.

McKenna smiled. "Hi. I hate to bother you, but have you seen Tristan?"

His officemate returned the smile. "I'm sorry but I haven't seen him all day," she said. "He might be in class."

"Oh." Her shoulders dropped. "Can you tell him I came by? I'm McKenna."

"Sure, but you can check with Dr. Cameron down the hall. He might know where Tristan is."

"Thank you."

Dr. Cameron was genuinely surprised when McKenna asked him.

"I'm sorry. He wasn't in class this morning, and he didn't show up for the class he teaches after that." He rubbed his stubbly chin. "I asked my secretary to call him, but she said there was no answer."

McKenna chewed her bottom lip. "Thank you."

She then found herself at Tristan's front door, pounding away.

Right when she was about to give up, the lock clicked. The door creaked open and a green eye peered at her. "McKenna? What are you doing here?" He croaked out the question.

Surprise and confusion seeped into her mind. She breathed a sigh of relief. "I tried calling you, and then you weren't at work. I barely felt your emotions through the door. Are you okay?"

The door opened wider. He pinched the bridge of his nose. "Yeah. What time is it?" He stepped away and she followed him inside, closing the door behind her.

"It's one o'clock."

He whirled around to face her. "What?" Panic blossomed. "Shit! I missed my morning classes." He fumbled for his phone. "I've got to call Dr. Cameron."

McKenna noticed he wore the same jeans and T-shirt from yesterday. His skin was pale, but color was coming back. When he moved his right arm, she saw five crescent moons above the elbow, dark with dried blood.

"Tristan, what happened to you?" She held his elbow, inspecting the marks.

He studied them, confused. Then it seemed to dawn on him. "She was here." He blinked and grabbed his head. "No wonder my head hurts again."

McKenna led him to the couch. "Who was here?"

"The White Lady. She showed up after you left, after…" he paused, his eyes darting around the room. "After that vision."

"What are you talking about?" She sat next to him, her hand rubbing his back.

He ran a hand over his face. "After you left, I saw your brother. He was scared, packing, trying to leave. She came for him."

McKenna bit her lip. "You saw it? You saw him die?"

He looked at her. "Yeah, but there's more." He touched the hand she rested on his arm. "She took his energy."

"What?"

"She took his energy. Used it to kill the other guys, I think." His curls bounced when he shook his head. "I knew she took something from me the night Zack died. My powers were gone afterwards. Came back full force the next day." He winced. "In fact, they came back full force when I woke up a few minutes ago. Thought you knocking was another vision."

"You think she took your powers?" McKenna tried to sort

all the details out in her head. It didn't make sense. The ghost took psychic energy. She needed a psychic to exact her revenge? Could ghosts even do that? "How does that even work?"

"I don't know. All I know is my head is killing me." He sucked in a breath.

McKenna grabbed a couple of aspirins and a glass of water. She handed both to Tristan. He knocked them back.

"Thanks."

"Why didn't you tell us about this earlier?"

"I didn't think about it. Didn't think it had anything to do with it. I mentioned it to Drew. And I didn't want anyone to know."

"Of course." McKenna sighed. "Drew wouldn't betray you."

"Exactly."

"Come on." She held out her hand, gesturing him to take it. "You've got to tell the rest of the team. You might be able to draw the ghost out tonight."

His head snapped up. "No. I won't be here tonight." His eyes flashed. "I'm going home." He walked past her.

McKenna regarded him. "You're running again?"

"All I've done is hurt people. I can't be here." He headed into the kitchen and grabbed a beer from the fridge.

"Seriously? You can help stop her." McKenna followed him and leaned against the other side of the counter.

Tristan set the bottle on the counter with a clink. "Exactly. I'm doing that by not being here." He popped the top.

"You don't know that. She might still kill without you. For all we know, you're just an added power boost." She straightened, her whole body vibrating. "If you draw her out, we can get a fix on her. Maybe talk to her, see what's holding her here. You're a guarantee."

Tristan took a long drink. "You think she's the chatty type? No, she isn't. She'll use me, and she'll finish her next victim. I won't help her this time."

"But, if you just…."

"No."

"Tristan."

He leveled her with a glare. His voice dropped an octave. "Just leave me alone."

She stumbled back as if he had slapped her. Silence passed between them. He couldn't be serious. She searched his emotions, looked for anything that she recognized. He was going to run, and she couldn't stop him.

"Fine." She turned on her heel and walked to the door. "Run away. It'll make my job so much easier." She slammed the door behind her, turning her back on him.

With equipment scattered throughout, the Restless Spirits team had transformed the lobby of Hidden Forest into a command center that night. Computer monitors, keyboards, and hard drives covered a folding table resting next to the far-left wall. People could still walk in and out of the doors, but many of them tossed dirty looks towards the equipment.

McKenna scowled at them. "Sorry for ruining your perfect Friday night," she mumbled.

Tabitha popped her head up from underneath the table. "Are you going to mope all night?"

"No." McKenna unwrapped another cord. "But I will continue to wallow for the next hour."

"So, Tristan didn't want to come help. It's not a big deal." Tabitha grabbed the end of the cord and ducked under the desk.

McKenna plugged her end into a monitor. "That's not the point. He shouldn't run. He's a part of this, too."

"I can't play the world's smallest violin for you right now so suck it up." The monitor flicked to life. "Let Tristan deal with stuff in his own way."

"Even if he's being a baby about it?"

"Even if."

McKenna thought about Tabitha's words. Her friend was right; she was pushing again. Not every psychic loved their powers. Some of them ran away to deal with it, even if it wasn't dealing with it at all.

Drew jogged in through the front door, peeling off his tie. Determination replaced his normal good humor. "Everything still in one piece?"

Tabitha crawled out from under the desk. "What are you doing here? Aaron told you to take the night off."

Drew dropped his tie on the table. "No way. Not when I can help find Zack's killer. I'm in this, Tabby." He swallowed. "Seeing his family tonight made me realize I owed them this."

She tossed her hands in the air. "You and Aaron can work it out."

"How was the wake?" McKenna asked.

Drew slid into the chair in front of one of the monitors. His fingers flew over the keyboard, and the program he searched for appeared on the screen. "It was okay." His mood dipped. "Still can't believe he's gone."

"Sounds brutal." McKenna sat down next to him.

Drew shook off the melancholy. "Not going to think about it. We've got to find a ghost tonight." He unbuttoned the top button on his shirt. "And I've got to get out of this suit." He jumped out of the chair and grabbed the bag he dropped at his feet. He disappeared up the stairs.

"I've never seen him like this." Tabitha started the same

program on the other computer. "I hope he'll be okay. He's really close to this case."

McKenna nodded. "I think he will be. At least he's not running from it."

Tabitha rolled her eyes and picked up her walkie-talkie. "Ready when you are, Aaron."

The small screen in the top right corner of both monitors went from blank gray to a black and white living room. McKenna recognized it as Kayla and Zack's apartment.

"How does it look?" Aaron's tinny voice asked.

"Looks good."

Tabitha set the walkie-talkie down. "You keep an eye on the monitors, okay. And stop worrying about Tristan." She hoisted a camera under her arm and headed up the stairs to another apartment.

McKenna sighed. Tabitha was right. She had more important things to worry about than Tristan. If he was going to hide in his parents' basement again, then she would let him. The team didn't need him to find and stop this ghost.

Sadly, they weren't any closer to discovering out who The White Lady was. McKenna had spent most of the day searching through a list of missing women from twenty to ten years ago. No one from the apartment had gone missing, but several women had disappeared from the campus between the late nineties and the early two thousands. She had planned to show Tristan the pictures she collected, but the idea had flown out of her head during the argument. She grimaced at the thought. Because of that slip-up, the team was going in blind. Another thing she could blame on Tristan.

Another room appeared on the computer screen.

"How's the angle?" Drew's voice crackled through the walkie-talkie.

"Move it a little to the left." The room inched across. "Perfect!"

McKenna glanced around the empty lobby. The sun had gone down long ago, and several people were settled in for the night. Others had gone out, and she hoped they wouldn't come back drunk and stumble into the equipment. Drew might never recover if that happened.

More rooms appeared on the monitor screens, and McKenna approved each one as they were placed at the correct angle. Once finished, the rest of the team joined her at the command center.

Aaron cleared his throat. "All right, gang, we have more area to cover than usual, but we're sticking to our protocol. Two people here with the equipment, keeping an eye on things. Two people investigating the apartments we've been approved to investigate." He propped his foot in one of the empty chairs. "I want to start in Zack and Kayla's apartment. McKenna, you and Tabitha are heading out first. Tell me if you feel anything that might identify our spook."

McKenna collected one of the walkie-talkies. "You'll be the first to know." She pushed Tristan and their fight to the back of her mind.

"Sounds like a plan," Tabitha agreed.

"Remember, we're not only looking for The White Lady, but also looking for the reason she's still here. I want y'all to be on alert." Aaron sized up his team. He dropped into the chair and crossed his arms. "Okay, people, let's do this!"

McKenna stilled, feeling for something in the dark. The quiet and the solitude surrounded her. Anticipation and determination resided in the apartment to her left. Happiness reached in from the apartment downstairs. Living emotions, all of them.

Picking up emotional energy from a ghost was next to impossible. Most of the ones she had come across were created from residual energy. No soul was there, only the imprint of who had been there. Those kinds had no emotions. But ghosts who were aware had traces of emotion swirling around them. The preacher they had recently laid to rest was full of burning anger. It was hot, like a living person's. It had felt like a fire inside McKenna's heart. She reached for that same feeling.

She situated herself on the couch, keeping the front door in her sights. Her mental shields remained in place, letting in one emotion at a time. She couldn't lower it all the way because the emotions of the other tenants would bombard her. However, she scanned for intense, dark feelings.

A small tape recorder rested in her right hand, the record light glowing in the dark. "Hello," she said into the darkness. "Are you here?"

No answer.

"We're not here to hurt you. We just want to know who you are and why you're here." *That's right, Mac. Keep it nice and even.*

Nothing.

She shifted her position. "What happened to you? Did the man who used to live here do something to you?" *Did my brother?* she thought.

No trace of emotion or a presence.

"Are you mad all of these people live in your building?"

McKenna sighed when there was still no response. She wasn't surprised. Many of the investigations Restless Spirits had conducted turned out to have no results at all. The team spent those nights sitting in the quiet dark with not one glimmer of ghostly activity. Going through the footage later was long and tedious. Investigating the paranormal required patience, and there were times when McKenna had none. She shifted again. It was turning into one of those nights.

The cushions in the chair next to her rustled. "Don't worry. It's only me." Tabitha's reassuring voice floated out of the dark. The bluish glow of the street lamp outside bounced off her outline.

"Nothing in the bedroom?" McKenna asked.

"I didn't expect there to be. She's already finished in this apartment. She probably won't come back to it." She tapped the recorder. "Any luck here?"

"I haven't heard anything, nor have I sensed anything." McKenna stretched her legs out in front of her. "Hopefully, the recorder picked up something."

"Maybe I should give it a try."

McKenna laughed. "Are you going to ask your usual questions?"

"Well, yeah. My questions are interesting." Tabitha cleared her throat. "Why white? Why not add some color to your wardrobe?"

McKenna sighed. "What does that prove?"

"What kind of taste this ghost has. Obviously, the whole white look washes her out." Her laugh echoed off the walls.

McKenna rolled her eyes. "Sure, I'll give it to you." Even though she couldn't hear anything, she knew the tape recorder might pick up an electronic voice phenomenon, or EVP for short. Sometimes, a ghostly voice used a different frequency than the rest of the world. She handed the tape recorder to Tabitha.

"Mac, how are you doing? Really?" Tabitha's concern came through loud and clear. "Still worrying about Tristan?"

"I'm okay." McKenna studied the door. "This isn't about him anymore. He can do what he wants to do. Besides, I need to focus on this ghost. I don't want her to kill another person like she did Jason and those other guys. If she, in fact, did it."

"Did Jason ever talk about seeing a ghost in his apartment?"

"If he did, he didn't tell me." McKenna sank into the pillows. She then closed her eyes when she remembered what Tristan had told her. "Crap."

"What?" The couch squeaked.

She told Tabitha all about Tristan's vision, how Jason had not only seen the ghost, but may have been an unwilling partner. How The White Lady might be using Tristan the same way.

"No wonder you wanted him here. Why didn't you tell us?"

McKenna shook her head. "I forgot. I was so focused on his reaction." She swept her hair off her shoulders, tying it all up into a knot, and letting it fall back down. She drummed her fingers on her knee. "I wish The White Lady would show up. I'd like to see her for myself."

"I wouldn't mind it, either," Tabitha answered. "But the legend says only men see her. Maybe we can't see her."

"Kayla saw her, remember? Told her she was free."

A chill ran across McKenna's arms, raising goosebumps on the skin. A flash of cold anger shoved past her shields. She straightened, grabbing the feeling and holding onto it. Something feather-light brushed her cheek.

"You can't save him," a female voice whispered in her ear. "He will pay."

McKenna jumped. She turned to her left, but no one was there. "Who? Who will pay?"

No one answered. The cold anger disappeared, and the chill was gone. McKenna wrapped her arms around herself. Her whole body shook. She couldn't seem to get warm again.

"Mac? Are you okay?" Tabitha's warm hand touched her shoulder.

"She's here."

"Where?" The couch groaned. Tabitha's silhouette crouched in front of McKenna.

"Beside me." McKenna mentally searched for the icy anger, but it was no longer there. "She's gone. You didn't hear her? Feel her?"

"Mac, I didn't hear or feel anything."

McKenna searched the room, hoping The White Lady left something behind. It was as dark and as quiet as it was before. "It felt like she was looking for something. She said, 'You can't save him. He will pay.'" McKenna took a deep breath, her heart racing in her chest. "It's so cold."

Tabitha draped a large afghan over McKenna's shoulders.

"Let's get you back to the lobby."

## 14

The all-night diner was practically empty with a few people scattered throughout. Pop music played over the speakers, and the salty smell of French fries filled the air. Tristan stretched out in the corner booth, his jacket and tie lying next to him. The sweet taste of home-made strawberry ice cream lingered long after his last bite.

Across the table from him, Kayla pulled her fork out of her mouth, a look of delight on her face. She swallowed her last bite and opened her eyes. "Thank you for this idea, Tristan." She pointed her fork at him. "I needed to get out of that place and away from everybody."

"I thought you might need to." His head fell back, all the tension draining out of his muscles.

Zack's viewing had taken plenty out of him. Seeing pictures of his best friend alive, smiling, and happy had almost done him in. It had been one thing to see Zack die, but the idea he may have helped scared Tristan to death.

Kayla had taken the whole evening worse than he did, though. She stood stoically beside Zack's parents in the line, greeting and thanking people for coming. Zack's mother hardly glanced her way the whole time. He and Drew had taken turns bringing her food and drink, but when Kayla begged him to get her out of there, he had done so without a second thought.

Kayla sighed. "The vanilla ice cream was always Zack's favorite." Her expression clouded over. Tears swam into her eyes. "I miss him so much, Tris." Her breath hitched.

"I know." He rubbed her arm. "I miss him, too."

Kayla wiped her eyes. "Distract me. Talk to me about anything but the ghost or the funeral. How are things going with Drew's coworker? What's her name? McKenna, right?"

Tristan arched an eyebrow. "What do you mean? Nothing's going on."

One corner of Kayla's mouth turned up. "I'm not blind, Tristan. I saw how the two of you looked at each other last night. Now, spill."

"Shouldn't we focus on you?"

"No." Kayla shook her head. "I'm tired of being sad, tired of dealing with condolences, tired of being useless. Tell me something happy."

His forked clinked a steady rhythm on the side of the empty bowl. "There's nothing to tell. I helped her with some research, and she pulled me out of my own head. That's it."

"That's it, huh?" Kayla cocked her head to the side, her mouth an even line.

"Yeah." Tristan studied the artwork above her head. A stack of strawberry pancakes floated in pink-tinted space, stars decorating it.

"Tristan, I've known you for seven years now. You really like her, don't you?"

He met her eyes. He pictured McKenna, her dark hair falling down her back, her big blue eyes watching him. His lips turned upward. "Maybe a little." He groaned. "But it won't work. I'm too unstable, and she wants too much."

Kayla chuckled. "You've known her for a week. What's too much in your book?"

Tristan gave her an edited version of their earlier argument, leaving out the part where the ghost may have used his energy to kill Zack. "She wanted me to help with the investigation tonight, and I told her no."

"Why would you do that?" Kayla's eyebrows shot up.

"You saw me last night."

"Yeah, and I also saw her pull you out of it. You two make a great team."

Tristan slumped. "It won't work."

Kayla threw her hands into the air. "Tristan, you're an idiot, you know that?"

He shrugged. "Maybe. But I'm going to my parents' house tonight. I want to be as far away from this as possible."

"Ah." Kayla sat back, her arms crossed over her chest. "So, it's Wilmington all over again."

"It's not…"

"It is. You lose control, and then you run away. You need to learn to embrace who you are and deal with it." She pointed her spoon at him. "Apologize to her tonight, before you leave. Zack would be really disappointed in you if you didn't."

Tristan's mouth fell open. "What?"

"Do you know how your friends took your running away the last time? Both Zack and Drew worried about you, especially when you wouldn't call or email or even see them. I'd never seen Zack look so lost. You were his best friend, and he couldn't even reach you. Neither one of them gave up on you. You can't give up on yourself." She narrowed her eyes. "What are you going to do? Hide in your parents' basement for the rest of your life? You have friends who care about you, and you've met a woman who understands you. Don't let that slip away." Her breath hitched.

"People you love can be taken away from you at the blink of an eye."

Her words rang in his ears. She was right. McKenna was right. He was running again. He sipped his coffee without giving Kayla an answer.

"Well?" she prompted.

"I'm thinking about it."

Kayla rolled her eyes. "Stop being stupid, Tristan. Go talk to her."

~

B lack and white images held steady in every corner of the monitor McKenna watched. The dust settled on the furniture in the room, but no ghosts appeared. Two hours in, and McKenna only had the one personal experience. Was The White Lady biding her time? McKenna still heard the ghost's warning in her ears. Who couldn't she save? Who was The White Lady's next target?

McKenna nudged Aaron. He looked up from his monitor and pulled one of his headphones away from his ear. "See anything yet?" she asked.

"Nothing. Feel anything yet?"

"Only the annoyance of the people walking by." She climbed to her feet and stretched, pulling off her own headphones. "Want something to drink?"

"Grab me a Pepsi, will you?" Aaron situated the headphones back over his ears.

McKenna started to turn away when an angry older man with salt and pepper short hair wearing a flannel shirt and black pants stalked over to their table. He glared daggers at Aaron.

"You call this subtle?" he demanded.

Aaron pulled off his headphones. "Mr. Martin, I didn't expect you to be here."

"I got a call from one of my tenants, telling me a crazy group of people had equipment all over the lobby." Martin clenched his teeth. The heat and force of his anger rolled over McKenna like a wave. It knocked her breath from her lungs. "We had an agreement, Mr. Lawson."

Aaron stood, his height putting him several inches taller than Martin. His hands were on his hips, making him appear bigger. "With all due respect, sir, you said we were free to set up anywhere in the lobby as long as our equipment didn't block the doors." He kept his voice controlled as he indicated how all the wires were behind the table and the table was well away from the doors. "As you can see, we did that."

A chill swept through the air. The monitors blinked off and then back on. Martin shivered, taking a step back from the table. He and Aaron glanced around the lobby.

McKenna recognized the moment of icy anger that came with the dip in temperature. She studied the extra electro-magnetic field reader resting on the table. The numbers jumped before returning to normal.

"Mac?" Aaron asked.

She tried to hold onto The White Lady's emotion, but it slipped through her fingers. Animosity replaced it, filling her up. "It could've been her, but I can't feel anything except you two right now."

"Wrap up this investigation. Quickly." Martin's voice lacked the conviction it held earlier. A spike of fear joined his anger.

Aaron's fists tightened. "Yes, sir."

Satisfied, Martin sailed past them and climbed the stairs. "Let's see if I can fix the damage you've caused."

"Weird." McKenna set a can of Pepsi in front of Aaron.

"What?"

"The mere possibility of the ghost terrified him." She slid into her seat.

"Think he knows more than he's told us?" Aaron sat next to her, his eyes on the stairs.

"I don't know, but he's definitely hiding something."

❦

A half an hour later, darkness and silence surrounded her once again. McKenna clutched her flashlight as she crept through the second apartment of the night – Tristan's apartment. Her empathy was on high alert, but all she picked up was the calm of the tenants below them. No flashes of anger and no cold patience. All was quiet.

Drew's footsteps echoed behind her. He muttered as he watched the screen on the small infrared camera he held. If there were a fluctuation in temperature or if he saw a shape he didn't recognize, he would let her know. So far, nothing out of the ordinary had appeared.

McKenna clicked on her walkie-talkie. "Aaron, do you or Tabitha see or hear anything?"

"A whole lot of nothing," Aaron's tinny voice responded.

"You'd think she'd have made her move by now," Drew said, his voice hard. "Maybe killing my best friend was enough for her." His hate caught her by surprise.

"You've been hostile during this whole investigation. Maybe you should take another turn at the command center."

Drew sighed, his mood calming. "I'm sorry. The wake and everything messed with me."

McKenna faced him. "You haven't said much to anyone this whole week. How are you doing, really?"

"You want to have this conversation now?"

She pointed the flashlight at him, avoiding his eyes. The

dress shirt was untucked, and his hair was pushed under his baseball cap. Stubble covered his chin. "Maybe talking about it will draw her out."

"He was one of my best friends, Mac. Zack was the steady one, the one that held us all together. He'd hold me back from fights and keep Tristan grounded so he wouldn't lose his mind. I've never seen anyone have that much patience and respect for people." He set the camera down on a nearby table. He directed his speech to the room. "If you had to kill somebody, why Zack? What the hell did he do to you, anyway?"

"You know she didn't do it because it was Zack. She thought he was someone else, remember?"

His jaw twitched. "Yeah, I remember." He raised his voice to the walls again. "You still didn't have to kill him."

A frosty breeze brushed McKenna's arm. She looked at the detector again. One point six. Her fingers dug into the arm of a nearby chair. It was an effort to keep her breathing steady.

"Are you standing next to me?" Closing her eyes, McKenna concentrated on the emotions around her. Curiosity and anger answered her, the same mix she felt earlier in the night. Her eyes flew open. "She's here." Frustration blended with the other emotions. "I think she's trying to get to her target but can't."

"Who is her target?" Drew picked up the camera and aimed it in McKenna's direction. "Mac, a faint signature is standing next to you."

McKenna swallowed. She fought the urge to run. Her body trembled under the effort of keeping still.

"Who are you looking for?" she asked the ghost.

A cold touch rested against McKenna's cheek and she jerked away. She tripped over a chair, slamming onto the hardwood floor. Rubbing her aching backside, she lifted her head and her mouth dropped open. The image of a girl in a short, white dress flickered. The detector beside her flashed. As she reached for it to see the number, a light glow caught her eye. She froze.

The White Lady floated in the center of the room. She fit the description everyone had given – long white hair, white dress, and bright green eyes. Those eyes regarded McKenna, never blinking once.

"Where is he?" the ghost demanded. Her voice echoed around the room and inside McKenna's head all at once.

McKenna gaped at the apparition.

Drew lunged for her, trying to help her to her feet. The ghost flicked her wrist. Drew sailed backwards and slammed into the nearest wall with a loud bang.

"Drew!" McKenna ran for the door, the detector clattering at her feet. The ghost blinked in front of her, blocking her path. Her heart pounded as she tried to read the shimmering woman. Cold anger and determination circled around her, but the curiosity was nowhere to be found. It was as if she had settled on what she wanted. Something wasn't right.

The ghost moved closer. "Where is he?"

"Who? Tristan?" McKenna tried for the door again. The ghost cut her off.

"You feel the same." The White Lady's hair flew off her shoulders like it was caught in a tornado. Her green eyes flashed to red.

McKenna tried to move, but her muscles wouldn't respond. She struggled against the hold, but her feet stayed where they were. The ghost plunged her hand into McKenna's chest. McKenna screamed. Ice spread through her body, sharp, cold, and painful. Breathing was impossible. She swore she'd never be warm again.

"You're not as strong," The White Lady hissed. "I'll take it all."

"Mac!" Something behind her crashed to the floor. "McKenna!"

The ice changed direction. Instead of going in, it pulled out. Emotions slipped through McKenna's consciousness like water. Her thoughts scrambled, making no sense. She couldn't hold onto anything. Her muscles tightened, her head fell back, and her legs crumpled beneath her. Her head bounced off the floor with a loud smack. The ghost was inside her and all around her at the same time. The edges of her vision dimmed.

"Mac?" Drew's voice was far away.

The White Lady yanked her hand out. McKenna expected her to be holding a still-beating heart, but the ghost's hand was empty. She was solid, whole. Energy radiated around her. She waved, and McKenna slid across the floor. Pain erupted throughout her body as she curled into a ball. The ghost glowed as bright as the sun.

"Thank you." The ghost flew through the door.

McKenna barely registered the sound of a door opening and feet running. Drew's scream was the last thing she heard.

15

Tristan walked into the quiet lobby. He didn't want to be there; he wanted to turn around and head out to Boone. The safety of his parents' house called to him. But the need to apologize to McKenna nagged at him more, and that piece of his conscience had a way of sounding like Kayla. True, he could come back and apologize later after the hunt, but getting it out of the way sooner would be better for his sanity.

Apologizing flew right out of his head when he saw the unmanned control center. His brows dipped. Drew told him that two people studied the monitors at all times. Not seeing anyone there meant the investigation wasn't going according to plan.

He raced to the stairs. What if something had happened to McKenna? Details from his vision about Jason came back to him. Jason was terrified the ghost could use his sister. Shit! What if McKenna was her energy supply instead of him?

Tristan put one foot on the first stair.

"No! You can't be real!" His head snapped up at the sound

of a man's voice. Drew? Aaron? No, the voice sounded older, but he couldn't tell who it was.

Tristan climbed the stairs two at a time, rushing towards the voice. He rounded the top, turning to start up the second flight. He paused at the first step.

The White Lady stood on the next landing, terrible and beautiful. Her long hair billowed out behind her. She was solid and beaming, her eyes a bright and dangerous red. A man dangled above the last step. His hands clutched her wrist as he struggled against her hold on his throat. Even in the ghost's light, it was hard to see who the man was. *Please don't let it be Drew,* Tristan thought.

Tristan took the next step. "Don't."

Her gaze whipped in his direction. For a split second, he thought she heard him. She flung out her free hand.

His back slammed into the wall with a loud thump. Sticking to it like a fly in a spider's web, he pushed against the unseen force holding him. He used every ounce of his strength, but it didn't matter. He wasn't going anywhere.

The White Lady turned back to her prey. Her glow brightened. She pulled her arm back and threw the man down the stairs. He was nothing more than a rag doll. He landed at the bottom with a sickening crack, his neck twisted at an unnatural angle.

The ghost's eyes changed back to green as her hair settled onto her shoulders. "They have to pay." She vanished into thin air.

Tristan slid down the wall, his body aching. He crawled to the fallen man. Dead brown eyes stared at him. Tristan's stomach heaved. He knew him, had seen him a day ago. It was Paul Martin.

"McKenna? Can you hear me?" A warm hand touched her forehead. "Mac?"

McKenna's eyelids fluttered open. Everything was fuzzy and a blob of color hovered above her. She blinked, and her eyes focused, little by little. Tabitha looked down at her, the lights giving her pink and blond hair a halo effect. McKenna held up a hand to block out the blaring glow. She groaned with the effort; her arm weighed a ton.

"What happened?" Her voice sounded rough and raw to her own ears. She licked her dry lips. Her body begged for something to drink.

"On camera, it looked like the ghost sucked the life out of you. I've never seen anything like it." Tabitha helped McKenna sit up. "Are you okay?"

McKenna sucked in a breath, her whole body aching. "I feel like a bus hit me." She rubbed her burning chest. To her relief, her heart still beat underneath her hand.

"Here. Drink this." Tabitha pushed a glass of water into McKenna's still trembling hands.

McKenna gulped it down. The water was sweet and cold and answered her every prayer. She set the empty glass on the ground and tried to piece together her memories. The White Lady had come at her, dropping her like a stone. Then the ghost went through the door. What happened next? Drew! She heard the door open, heard him scream. Her eyes widened.

"Drew!" She struggled to get off the floor.

Tabitha held her still. "He's fine."

"I heard him scream."

"He and The White Lady were out in the hall. She had him by the throat when Aaron and I got here. Aaron threw salt at her, and she dropped him. And then she disappeared." Tabitha's expression was grim.

"What? What's wrong?"

"She got someone else. We heard him yell."

Fear gripped McKenna so hard that it was tough to breathe. "Who?" She tried to stand once more. "Oh, God." She grabbed Tabitha's arm. "I have to know." What if Tristan had come back?

McKenna struggled to her feet with Tabitha's help. She gritted her teeth against her aching muscles. She leaned against Tabitha, and they made their way into the hall. Other people had come out of their apartments and crowded the staircase. They pushed through until they could see the bottom of the stairs.

Tristan, Drew, and Aaron surrounded a body. Tristan stood still, his face white. Drew rubbed the back of his neck while Aaron paced and talked into a cell phone. McKenna let out the breath she had been holding. All three men were safe and whole. But her relief was short-lived. The White lady had killed again, and this time, she had used McKenna to do it.

McKenna balanced against the banister, reaching out to feel the emotions around her. Maybe she could keep everyone calm. Her hand lost its grip. Tabitha caught her before she fell.

"What? What is it?" Tabitha asked.

"I can't feel anyone." All she could feel was her own fear.

Tristan pressed his back against the wall, his hands shaking. Another death, and this time he saw it all. The events repeated in his mind. The White Lady's eyes flashed red. Mr. Martin's body flew as if it weighed nothing. His eyes stared at Tristan, open and empty.

"Mr. Johnson? We need to stop meeting like this." Detective Thompson narrowed his eyes. "Can you tell me what happened?"

Tristan's heart sank. How was he going to explain what he saw?

He cleared his throat and took Thompson through an edited version of events. He recalled how the detectives treated Kayla when she mentioned The White Lady. He told him how he saw Mr. Martin fall from the landing, how it happened so fast, how he rushed to the dead man's side. Detective Thompson tapped the end of his pen on his notebook. "You're telling me you saw him fall when you walked up the stairs, but you didn't see anyone push him?" He pinned Tristan with a glare. "It's not even that big a flight of stairs."

"That's what I saw, Detective." Tristan schooled his features to look as neutral as possible. He tried to appear as trustworthy as he could. It was clear Thompson didn't believe a word of it.

McKenna limped through the crowd and leaned into him, squeezing his hand. Her presence reassured him, but she looked like she had been through hell. He opened his mouth to ask her if she was all right. She gave a slight shake of her head.

Thompson shifted his gaze to McKenna. "Which apartment do you live in?"

"I don't live here." She sounded tired and strained. "My colleagues and I were conducting an investigation."

Thompson raised an eyebrow. "What kind of investigation?"

"Paranormal research, sir."

Thompson's mouth quirked at the corners. "Paranormal?"

McKenna winced as she pulled herself up to her full height. "I'm sure you remember Kayla Collins. She asked us to investigate The White Lady legend."

"Oh yeah." Thompson chuckled. "I remember her state-ment." He leaned in closer to her. "Find anything?" Humor laced his tone.

McKenna didn't back down. "Possibly."

Thompson straightened. "Well, Mr. Johnson, I believe you still have my card." He handed one to McKenna. "Let me know if you remember anything else. And stay in town. We may have more questions for you." He moved on to interview the rest of the people in the hallway.

McKenna let go of Tristan's hand and pitched sideways. He caught her before she fell. "What's wrong?" He lowered her to the ground. "What happened?"

Her blue eyes bore into his, grateful for his help. "The White Lady."

Understanding dawned on him. "She used you?" He crouched next her, dreading her answer.

"Yeah." She took a deep breath. "She couldn't find you."

The urge to hit something was strong. "I never thought she'd try to use someone else. I didn't even think."

"Not your fault." She sucked in a breath. "Did you feel like every part of your body was falling apart?"

"I did." He tapped his temple. "Can you sense anything?"

Her eyes widened. "Not a thing. I feel like I'm blind."

"It comes back full force after you sleep for a while."

"We have to stop this." McKenna set her jaw. "We can't let anyone else die."

Aaron, Tabitha, and Drew joined them. Judging by their intense expressions, the police had questioned them as well.

"How are you two doing?" Aaron asked when he reached them.

McKenna waved and smiled.

"We're okay," Tristan answered.

Aaron set his mouth in a hard line. "The cops aren't going

to find a human killer with this one. We need to get our equipment and go. I want to see what we caught."

"We need to sleep first." Tabitha crouched beside McKenna. "Or we're no good to anybody." She nodded to Tristan. "Can you help me get her up?"

"I can walk." McKenna climbed halfway up before sliding back down the wall.

"No, you can't." Tristan hooked one arm under her legs, the other around her back, and lifted her. Her head rested against his chest. He took a deep breath. She was alive. Battered, bruised, and tired, but she was alive.

"You can put her in my car," Aaron said.

"No, you guys get the rest of the equipment. I'll take her home." He waited while Drew programmed McKenna's address into his phone. He then carried her out to his truck.

## 16

A heavy weight rested on McKenna's chest. It took more effort than usual to draw breath. Flashes of white danced across her eyelids. The cold stole her breath as a hand thrust into her chest. The image changed as the ghost reached for her head. Something soft and sharp poked her face. It grew more and more insistent until she realized it wasn't the ghost. She opened her eyes to see Oscar peering at her with his intense green ones. He pawed at her mouth and cheek.

"Oscar?"

Satisfied his human was still alive and could, therefore, fill his empty bowl, the cat jumped off her chest. He landed with a thud and trotted out of the room.

McKenna inhaled, her lungs filling with air, and rubbed her eyes. How had she gotten home? The last thing she remembered was the Hidden Forest stairwell and Mr. Martin's dead body. Sitting up, she shook out her hair. She wore the same long-sleeved shirt and jeans from the night before. No wonder she was uncomfortable.

She sucked in a breath as a ton of emotions hit her at

once. Happiness's flutter, worry's pitch, and excitement's burst of energy rolled together in a nauseating ball. Black anger joined the chaos. She growled at the clock on her nightstand, but she fought the urge to throw it out of the window. It wasn't even going off. She pulled back the covers and her throat closed. Tears threatened at the corner of her eyes. Her stomach twisted in knots.

She wrapped her arms around herself, her whole body shaking. Tristan was right; her empathy had come back at full force. McKenna fought against all the conflicting emotions and focused on her shields. Imaginary iron closed around her, locking all of the feelings out. She concentrated on breathing while visualizing her wall. Bit by bit, the emotions filtered out and lessened.

When her breathing was normal again, she climbed out of the bed, changed into pajama pants and a loose t-shirt, and padded down the stairs. She paused halfway to the kitchen. Tristan lay on her couch, curls in every direction and his mouth hanging open. He had cocooned himself in the red afghan Grandma Ellison had made for her that hung on the back of the couch.

"Well, this keeps getting weirder." She shook his shoulder. "Tristan." He mumbled and rolled over. She shook harder. "Tristan."

He jerked awake. "What?" His bleary green eyes landed on McKenna. "Oh, hi." He smiled and stretched.

She settled next to his legs. "You want some coffee?"

"Yes, please." He wiped his mouth. "As strong as you can make it."

McKenna walked into the kitchen. She watched him through the window in the wall that separated the kitchen and the living room. "Want to tell me why you slept on my couch?"

Tristan shook out his curls. "I drove you home."

"And you had to stay?"

He blinked at her. "I wanted to make sure you were okay."

She bit her bottom lip. Part of her was still mad at him, but her heart swelled at the thought. "You did?" She turned on the coffee maker. "Thank you." The machine bubbled to life as drops of coffee plinked into the empty pot. McKenna returned to the living room. "I thought you didn't want me around."

Tristan lowered his shoulders. "Maybe I jumped the gun a little bit."

She softened. "I did, too. I shouldn't have pushed." McKenna took the other end of the couch and pulled the end of the afghan to her chin.

Tristan shifted closer. "I thought it would be easy, running away again. But when I saw you struggling to stand and then pass out like that, I couldn't." His thumb traced her cheek, light and delicate. "I should've been there. She was supposed to come after me. I didn't mean to put you in danger."

McKenna caressed the hand on her cheek. "She looked for you, but I'm glad she didn't find you." Her face inched closer to his. Butterflies danced in her stomach.

"I could've protected you."

"You don't have..." His mouth touched hers and the sentence flew out of her head. Heat rushed over her body as her lips parted. Her pulse quickened. His hands cradled her face, his kiss hesitant. She wrapped her arms around his neck, pulling him to her. He took her waist and trailed light kisses down her neck. She sighed. On instinct, she reached out for his emotions, and found her own want reflected back to her. The coffeemaker buzzed, breaking the moment.

He pulled away, his eyes meeting hers. "I'm sorry. I didn't mean..."

"No." She smiled. "That was perfect." A little worry crept in. "I didn't…influence you, did I?"

"No. It was all me."

"Good." The rich, warm scent of coffee wafted through the room. "I better get that before it gets cold." She didn't move.

"Yeah. It smells great." He didn't let her go.

With a protesting meow, Oscar jumped between them and stared at Tristan. McKenna took that as her cue to stand.

The moment gone, she poured coffee into two cups. When she looked up, she saw Tristan petting Oscar's head. Content, the cat curled in next to him.

"Cream? Milk? Sugar?" she asked.

"Just black."

She handed Tristan his cup and took a sip of her own. The hot liquid sent a jolt to her already awake system. Glancing at the clock above her television, her happy feeling evaporated. "One o'clock?" She set the cup down and started for her bedroom. "I'm late. Aaron will kill me."

Tristan took her hand. "He said you didn't have to come in today."

"But the footage? Mr. Martin's death?"

He pulled her down to the couch and rubbed her upper arms. "It can wait. Let's have some coffee, and then see how you're doing."

McKenna narrowed her eyes. "I'm fine. My empathy came back this morning. I'm good." She took another sip. "Besides, don't you have a funeral to go to?"

"I do. At three. My apartment isn't far from here. We don't have to rush." Tristan sank into the couch and patted the seat next to him. Sighing, McKenna scooted over to him. "It takes a little while to recover."

She itched to get to the office. "I don't have the time."

"You've got to make the time." Tristan sat forward, resting

his elbows on his knees. "You're no good to your team if you pass out again."

"You've got a point." She fell back against the cushions. "How long did it take you to get back on your feet?"

"About a day, but it might be different for you." He lowered his voice, his tone turning serious. "How are you doing?"

McKenna twisted to face him. "I told you. I'm good."

"I mean about the ghost using you to kill Mr. Martin?"

She let the words sink in as a black feeling formed in the pit of her stomach. "I hadn't thought about it." She nuzzled into his chest. "I know he's dead, and I know the ghost took energy from me, but it feels like it happened to someone else." She gasped as the realization dawned on her. "Is this how Jason felt?" Her hands flew to her face. "He never told me. I never thought. Oh, God."

McKenna's impartiality fell apart the more she dwelled on it. When Zack had died, she had seen it as just another case, a way to find out what had happened to her brother. Even after she spoke to Justin and found out the ghost had been using Jason's psychic energy, it hadn't dawned on her. He thought he had helped kill two people, like Tristan felt he was responsible for Zack's death. Like the responsibility she now felt.

"I know." Tristan's deep voice pushed through her thoughts. His arm curled around her. "I'm sorry."

"Why couldn't we stop her? Why was she so much stronger than all of us?"

"I don't know."

She raised her mug. "After this, I need to get to the office." She paused. "Is my car still at your building?"

"Yeah. We can pick it up on our way."

McKenna lifted a brow. She didn't miss the pronoun. "We?"

"I want to help."

She took a moment before she asked, "Help how?"

"We still need to find out who The White Lady is. We made a pretty good research team before. I think we can do it again. And I want to talk to my dad about this psychic energy draining business. See if he knows anything about it. Maybe how to stop it." Tristan clutched the handle on his mug. "I feel like I have to do something." He drank.

"Do you want to try to see something?" McKenna kept her voice gentle. "I can probably help with the control."

Tristan paused, his eyes flashing. "Not this again."

McKenna sat up and placed her mug on the coffee table. She whirled around to face him. "I can handle you." *Maybe,* she thought. She recalled the wild look in his eyes as he had switched from vision to vision and person to person. She didn't want to see that again, but she recalled The White Lady calling him strong. Tristan's gift was strong, and if controlled enough, he might be able to find answers. "Your fear is the only thing stopping you."

The corners of his mouth quirked upward. "Fear, huh?" He pounded his chest. "I eat fear for breakfast."

McKenna rolled her eyes. "I'm sure you do."

Tristan tugged her to him. She rested in the crook of his arm, her head on his shoulder. "I have a lot to be afraid of, especially when someone precious to me is in the same room."

McKenna's heart skipped a beat. "Precious?"

"You didn't influence that kiss. It was all me, my own feelings." He brushed her hair back from her face. "I won't let you get hurt. Ever."

"What about the next man The White Lady sets her sights on? If she's still following the pattern, she has one more guy to kill. The last guy who hurt her. Jason fed her energy, and he was the last one she killed. You fed her energy this time. She might be planning to kill you next."

"We don't know that."

"We do." McKenna lifted her head. "A woman in white seeks revenge, and in her mind, three men deserve to die." She ticked items off on her fingers. "Each man represents someone, remember? Jason was blond. Zack was blond. Keith had darker blond hair, but Cory had dark brown hair."

"I have dark brown hair," Tristan interrupted. "But I'm not dead."

"No, but Mr. Martin is. He had dark brown hair." McKenna paused. "Wait. He died differently. She threw him down the stairs, not out a window. Why did she change tactics?"

"He wasn't near a window?" Tristan suggested.

McKenna got to her feet and started to pace. "Why go out of your way to kill someone not near a window?" It dawned on her. "Unless you were one of the men she was originally looking for."

Tristan's green eyes widened. "You think he was one of the killers?"

McKenna walked from one end of the room to the other. "He was mad about the whole investigation, even though he gave us permission, and he was nervous and scared the whole time. I knew he was hiding something, but I didn't know what." She stopped. "We have to talk to the people who knew him. We need to know more about him." She started for the stairs.

"Wait. You can't do that."

McKenna stopped. "What?"

Tristan stood. "McKenna, Mr. Martin died last night. The police have probably told his family by now. What are you going to do? Barge into their house and demand to know who he killed ten or twenty years ago?"

She opened her mouth to argue with him. She wanted to tell him she wouldn't barge in. She only wanted answers. Closing her mouth, she let his words sink in. He was right. Talking to a family who already believed in ghosts was one thing, but barging in to talk to a grieving family was something else. She scrunched up her face.

"You're right. We need to find some other way to learn more about him." She sat down on the bottom step.

Tristan sat next to her. "We need to know more about *her*. Last night's hunt didn't give you any clues, did it?"

"Not initially. We might have caught something on video or on a recording."

"And all the newspaper clippings and missing persons reports?"

McKenna wanted to tear her hair out. "We have names of several women who could be her, but that's a lot to narrow down."

"Then let me try something." Tristan grinned. "She might have been a student at Blackwood. I can ask around. See if anybody knows something. Maybe I can help you narrow down your list of suspects."

McKenna studied him, noting the determination in his eyes. His hopefulness made her more at ease with the whole situation. "That is a good idea."

"Then I'll do it on Monday." He gave that smile that made her heart melt. "But, first, the funeral and a visit to Boone."

McKenna returned his smile. "It sounds like a plan. Can I come to Boone with you? I'd like to know more about the psychic energy myself."

Tristan blinked. "Well, ah, you'd meet my parents."

"I look forward to it."

~

The knot in his stomach released as he approached the two-story yellow Victorian house at the end of the street. Tristan exhaled. Home. The perfect place to clear his head. The two-hour drive up Highway 221 was worth it.

It didn't matter how much the past battered his mind or what kind of regular things he dealt with. His parents had a way of grounding him. After the past week, he was anxious to see them.

He glanced over at McKenna, who stared out her window. He was glad to have her with him. He hadn't realized how much he depended on her until she wasn't at the funeral with him. He missed her touch, her voice, her smile. Melancholy settled over him as his best friend's casket was lowered into the ground. Maybe he could've stopped the ghost from taking his energy if he'd only known how, and Zack would still be alive.

The sadness didn't go away until McKenna climbed into his truck an hour later.

He pointed the house out to her.

"That's it?" she asked.

"That's it."

He parked in the driveway and climbed out. After helping McKenna out, they sauntered onto the wrap-around white porch. He smiled at the familiar creek under his weight. The brown wooden swing to his right swayed in the light breeze, creaking with each movement. He reached for the door, but it swung open before he could touch it.

His mother was a welcome sight. "Mijo!" She swept him into a hug. "I saw you pull into the driveway." He closed his eyes. For a moment, he was her little boy again. Everything in his mind quieted when she was there. They stood like that for a long moment, neither one of them saying anything. Tristan broke away and introduced McKenna.

His mother's eyes widened. "Call me Melissa." She pulled McKenna into a tight embrace.

"Oh!" McKenna giggled, clearly surprised. "Nice to meet you, ma'am."

"Melissa, please." She let go and led them into the foyer. The strong, savory smell of arroz con pollo wafted through the house. Tristan's mouth watered. No one made the chicken and rice dish like his mother. No one.

"Mom, you didn't have to make dinner," Tristan protested.

"Nonsense. You've had a bad week, and you brought a friend. Now, come inside and have something to eat." She walked into the kitchen. Tristan grinned at McKenna as they followed her.

Melissa Gomez Johnson was a petite woman with deep golden-brown skin, long, curly hair the same color as her son's, and mischievous light brown eyes. Her height never mattered, though, since she could make Tristan feel guilty with one look. And anytime she yelled at him in Spanish, he knew he was in trouble. He grew up hearing that his mother decided to marry his father after seeing him only once. His aunts all said that Matthew Johnson hadn't stood a chance.

"Mom, you didn't have to." Tristan repeated as he claimed his usual seat at the table, gesturing for McKenna to take the one next to him. Despite his protests, his mouth already watered.

"I never do anything because I have to. You know that." She filled two bowls. She placed one in front of McKenna and the other in front of Tristan. "Eat. Your father will be down in a minute."

Tristan obeyed and dug into his meal. He closed his eyes, savoring the rich flavor. He moaned with pleasure when the touch of spiciness his mother always added kicked in. There wasn't much his mother's arroz con pollo couldn't cure.

"Mrs. Johnson, this is amazing." McKenna's eyes teared as she reached for a glass of water. "A little hotter than I'm used to, though."

"Eat only what you can handle." Melissa slid into the chair next to McKenna. "Now, tell me everything about yourself because my selfish son has told me nothing."

McKenna was the color of a tomato. "Well, there isn't much to tell. I grew up in Asheville and work for a paranormal investigation agency."

"Oh?"

"Mom, McKenna's an empath," Tristan said between bites.

"Is that so? So you know what it's like to have so much going on in your head." She patted McKenna's hand.

"Yes, ma'am."

Tristan's mother pulled the skin off her chicken. "You know, I forever worry about Tristan and those visions he has to deal with. They nearly tore him apart."

"She knows, Mom."

"So, how long have you two been dating?" Melissa's smile was back.

Tristan choked on the chicken. "Mom!"

"I thought that was you." Tristan's father entered the kitchen, a big white man with salt and pepper hair, a full beard and mustache, and green eyes that matched his son's. He held a hand out to McKenna. "You must be McKenna. I'm Tristan's father, Matthew."

McKenna wiped her mouth and shook his hand. "Tristan told you about me?"

"Not a word, but I've seen you."

Tristan's mother swatted him on the arm. "What have I told you about spying on Tristan?"

"I wasn't spying. Just keeping an eye out." He sat down next to his son, reaching for a bowl. He heaped food into it.

Tristan scooted down in his chair, wishing the floor

would open and swallow him. Maybe bringing McKenna along wasn't such a great idea after all.

McKenna looked from Matthew to Tristan. "I'm confused."

"Dad can see the present. He knows what's going on in other places right now."

"Oh. I thought he could see the past, like you."

Matthew waved his fork in the air. "It alternates. Tristan's grandfather can see the past."

McKenna nodded. "Daniel Johnson. I remember." Her eyes gleamed. "So, remote viewing? I've never met anyone who can actually do that." She adopted what Tristan thought of as her interviewing face. Her eyebrows lifted and her lips parted in a small smile. "How does it work?"

Tristan groaned. "Can we talk about that later?"

"I guess," McKenna rolled her eyes as she went back to her meal.

His father took the time to chew. He swallowed before speaking again. "Now, son, how are you?" Matthew studied Tristan with concern.

Tristan wiped his mouth. "I think I'll be okay. A lot of things haven't made sense this past week. Another person was killed and this time I saw the ghost do it."

Matthew sat back in his chair. "Tell me what happened." He was in cop mode.

Tristan told his father about Mr. Martin's death, about the investigation. McKenna chimed in, adding details from her end. Then, he mentioned the theory about the ghost and the psychic energy. "We think the ghost used McKenna's brother ten years ago, used me to kill Zack, and used McKenna to kill Mr. Martin."

"What do you mean, used?" his mother set her fork down, concern in her eyes.

McKenna gulped down some of her drink. "She somehow took psychic energy from us."

"Afterwards, neither one of us could sense anything."

Matthew's chewing slowed. "You couldn't see anything?"

"Nothing. You know how shades sometimes push through my shields. They didn't. It was...quiet." Tristan shuddered. "It was weird."

"Is that possible?" Melissa asked.

"I've never heard of it." McKenna shook her head.

"I'm not sure. It might be." Matthew considered the problem. "I've never personally heard of it happening, but there's a lot about psychic powers I don't know." He stroked his brown and grey beard. "There might be something in your grandfather's journals. He used to do a lot of research on psychic abilities. He wanted to know why he could do what he could do."

Tristan took a thoughtful bite of his food. "I was hoping you'd say that."

Matthew pushed back his chair. "I'll go get them."

"Your grandfather kept journals?" McKenna's eyes lit up with interest.

"Yeah. I've never looked through them, though."

Tristan's mother rested her hand on her son's. "Are you sure you're okay?"

"I will be."

"Ah, here we are." Tristan's father returned with six leather-bound journals. He set them in the middle of the table. "We'll go through these together and see what we can find."

After dinner, Tristan took two of the journals while his father and McKenna split the rest. His grandfather's scratchy handwriting was hard to decipher at times, but it was a more interesting read than he expected. Detailed notes described his grandfather's visions and how he struggled to separate himself from what he was seeing. Tristan related to that battle. Other paragraphs described how his grandfather thought the visions worked. He mentioned "energy" several times. The most fascinating paragraphs, however, detailed his days working for The Greene Institute.

Daniel Johnson had been the leader of a group of psychics who had apparently investigated ghosts and other mundane matters in the state. They didn't seem to be widely known, but the local police often hired them to help solve strange cases. Tristan wondered why he hadn't taken the time to find out more about his grandfather's past.

"He knew my grandmother." McKenna broke the silence, pulling Tristan back to the present.

"How do you know that?" he asked.

She showed him a paragraph in the journal she was reading. "Lauren McKenna. That's my grandmother. He talks about working with her, saying she was one of the most controlled empaths he'd ever worked with." She lifted her head. "Is he still alive?"

"Yeah. Grandpa lives in Gatlinburg, Tennessee, in a log cabin on top of a mountain."

"Keeps to himself a lot since my mother passed away," Tristan's father chimed in.

McKenna ran a hand over the page. "I'll have to ask my grandma about him."

The afternoon turned into evening. Tristan yawned as he started into the last book. Maybe his dad only imagined seeing a mention of a ghost taking energy. He rubbed his eyes. He was getting nowhere.

He ran across a paragraph that started with the sentence, "A ghost grabbed her shoulder." Tristan straightened. Up until that point, his grandfather had done nothing but wax on about his visions and working with a team of other psychics. This was one of the first mentions he had seen about a ghost touching someone. "I think I found something."

McKenna set her book down and moved closer to him. His father peered at him from across the room.

Tristan began to read. *"Lauren couldn't move. She and the ghost faced off, and none of us could pry them apart. I was worried. The ghost grew brighter while she grew paler. She dropped to her knees, and the ghost let her go. He was more solid than any apparition I had ever seen. I caught Lauren before she fell to the ground."*

"Grandma never told me," McKenna said.

He skimmed through the rest of the passage, searching for a reason or an explanation. He found it at the very end.

*"Lauren said it felt like all the energy was drained out of her. I told her it made sense. Ghosts were pure energy. This one may have figured out how to grab more. It took Harvey, Sam, Betty, and me forever to track down the ghost while Sharon stayed with Lauren. It was able to throw objects and crash through walls. It could affect the physical world like nothing I had ever seen.*

*"A week later, Lauren worked on her shields, trying to make them stronger. She asked me to practice with her until she reached a point where I couldn't read her. She told me she refused to be used like that again."*

Tristan flipped a page. *"With nothing to go on, Lauren's methods were effective. She explained it to me like this. Picture your shield the way you normally do – brick wall, tower wall, whatever. Now add another wall around it, and then another. It takes more concentration than a regular shield and isn't second nature to her. We all tried and practiced and every one of us felt like we had climbed a mountain while carrying a house on our backs."*

McKenna brought her knees to her chest. "No wonder nothing ever seems to faze my grandma. I wonder why she didn't teach Jason or me how to do that?"

"My father never mentioned any of this to me either."

Tristan's father scratched his chin. "That's why I never told you, son."

"Well, no time like the present to try." Tristan took her hand, but he didn't feel as reassured as he sounded.

"Well, kids." Tristan's father climbed to his feet. "We've got some time."

17

C oming back to his apartment left a cold numbness in Tristan's gut. Two deaths already, and no one knew why. He entertained the idea of paying for a hotel room, but that was money he didn't have and there was no telling how long he would have to stay. No. He wasn't running this time. It was his apartment, and he wasn't leaving. Nor was he going to let The White Lady make her third kill.

His head still had a dull ache from strengthening his shield with McKenna and his father. He would hide somewhere in the house or around it, and they had to find him using only their psychic powers. At first, McKenna and his father found him easily, but by Sunday night, it was getting more difficult. He couldn't block them out completely, but he was making progress. Hopefully, it was enough to keep the ghost from using him.

He bit into an apple as he headed into the history building that morning. His first class wasn't until eight a.m. so he had an hour to start asking around. He opened his email to find

McKenna had sent him pictures and information on the young women who had gone missing from the area.

Tristan studied them, searching for familiar characteristics. The White Lady's features weren't defined enough for him to recognize her. When she glowed, they became more obscure. But he hoped he would see something familiar. It didn't help that the pictures were black and white, but the descriptions listed eye color. At least four of the young women had green eyes. He moved slowly, studying each picture, each profile. When he finished with one, he clicked the mouse to move to the next one.

At the third one, he froze. A young woman with long, dark hair smiled at him. She leaned against the railing of a deck, the wind tossing her hair around her. A big hair bow held one side of her hair in place. There was something about her. Something familiar. His vision clouded over and the picture disappeared.

*She stood at the window, her expression thoughtful. Her curtain of dark hair fell past her shoulders, a bright yellow bow clipped on the right side. She fiddled with a gold necklace. When she turned to face him, her eyes glistened with tears. His heart seized.*

*"But why can't anyone know? You're the best thing that's ever happened to me."*

*He walked into the room and pulled her into his arms. It killed him to see the pain in her eyes. But this was for the best. He knew it was.*

*"Because you're eighteen, and I'm thirty, and I'm your teacher. If anyone ever knew, I'd lose my job. You'd be kicked out. I can't risk it." He stepped back and held both of the girl's hands in his.*

*The girl smiled a little. She wiped her eyes. "Tell me you love me."*

*"I love you."*

*The door banged open behind him.*

*The girl's green eyes widened. "Oh, no!"*

*"So, this is why you keep staying so late," a male voice said.*
*He jumped. Someone knew! He started to turn.*

Someone shook Tristan's shoulder. The vision melted away, and the office returned to normal. Jaime appeared in his line of sight.

"Are you okay?" Concern was written all over her face.

Tristan shook his head. The girl! She was the same one in the picture! He pushed Jaime away and studied the picture on his screen. Her features seemed like they could fit. Was she The White Lady?

"Tristan, what is it?" Jaime grabbed his chin and forced him to see her. "You're scaring me."

He pulled away, barely registering her. He thought back to the day he lost control in Kayla and Zack's apartment, all the visions that assaulted him. There was one of a girl in the woods. One he thought may have come from the ghost. Was it the same girl? Possibly. He gritted his teeth. Why couldn't he remember?

A hand snapped in front of his eyes. He blinked, his brain sluggishly moving back to the here and now. Jaime's brown eyes swam into view.

"I knew it," she said.

Confusion pushed him back to the present time. "What?"

Jaime slid off his desk. "The weird blank stares, you mumbling about random things not in this office. You, sir, have the sight." She crossed her arm over her chest.

All thoughts of the girl and the ghost flew out of his head. "I'm sorry, what?" It took a moment for his brain to catch up with the conversation. When it did, he started to panic. "I don't know what you're talking about."

Jaime's features brightened. "You know, I feel a lot better now. I was worried you were having a stroke."

Cool sweat beaded at his brow. "Really, Jaime. I'm not..."

She cut him off with a wave of her hand. "Don't worry

about it. My mom has it, too. She tends to know what you're going to do before you do it. It can be a little unnerving, but I'm used to it."

"You don't think I'm weird?"

Jaime dropped down into the chair across from him. "Well, you are weird, but not because you get visions. You just need to stop zoning out randomly."

"Believe me. I'm trying." He let out a breath. "You won't tell anybody?"

"Who the hell am I going to tell?" She laughed. "Don't worry. Your secret's safe with me. Now." She scooted forward. "What have you been seeing?"

He told her about the young woman and the affair in the office. He pointed to the picture on the screen. "Her name seems to be Lily Comer, but I have no idea who she had an affair with."

"Juicy. A mystery. I like it. Where do we start?" She propped her heels on the edge of his desk.

"We?"

"I share this office, too. I'd like to know who had an affair around here. How long ago was it?"

Tristan glanced at the picture again. "I know it was at least twenty years ago. It had to have happened before she went missing."

Jaime's mouth fell open. "Missing? This gets better and better."

An insistent knock rapped at the door. Without waiting for an answer, it creaked open. Dr. Cameron's well-dressed form stepped through. "Mr. Johnson, Ms. Liu, I hope I'm not interrupting."

"No, sir. Come in."

Jaime jumped to her feet. "We'll talk later," she said with a wink as she made her way back to her own desk.

Cameron took the seat Jaime vacated. His expression was serious.

"How can I help you, sir?" Tristan gripped the edge of the desk. He wasn't getting fired, was he? He forced a smile, hoping to ease the situation.

Cameron did not smile back. He fidgeted with his shirt-sleeves, his eyes full of worry. He wiped his brow as he shifted his weight. His feet tapped out a rhythm under the desk. Puzzled, Tristan's smile faded.

"Dr. Cameron, are you okay?" Tristan asked.

The older man took a shaky breath. "Yes. No." He shook his head. "On Friday night, someone else died in your building, didn't they? Paul Martin?" Cameron's voice quivered.

"Yes, sir. Did you know him?" All of Tristan's worries about his job security melted away.

Cameron wiped at his eyes. "I did, yes. We hadn't spoken for many years, but he had been a very good friend." He rubbed his mouth. "Did...anyone...see what happened?"

Tristan opened his mouth and closed it. How could he answer that question? He entertained the idea of telling Cameron the truth. After all, the man did know about The White Lady legend. However, Cameron didn't believe in it. Tristan settled on the same half-truth he gave the police detectives. "I saw him fall down the stairs when I came home."

"Oh, God." Cameron closed his eyes. His face went white as a sheet as he slumped forward. Alarmed, Tristan jumped to his feet.

"Sir, do I need to call somebody? Get you a glass of water, maybe?" Tristan glanced at Jaime. Her phone was in her hand.

"Do I need to call someone?" she asked.

"No, no. I'll be all right." Cameron inhaled deeply, held the breath, and let it go. He took another breath, and another, until he breathed normally. "Paul and I were friends for a long time, ever since high school. We both grew up here in Asheville. We lost touch when I went away to college, but we met up again when I got an assistant professorship here. We were part of a whole group of friends who used to hang out together before most of us got married. I guess his death was more of a shock to me than I thought." Cameron wiped his face as he leaned against the back of the chair. "Do you know why he was in the building, or how he fell down the stairs?"

"I don't know." Tristan hated how smoothly the lie came out. "I heard he was pretty mad about the paranormal investigators." Maybe it wouldn't hurt to mention that much.

"Paranormal investigators?" Cameron's brow wrinkled.

"Investigating The White Lady legend."

Cameron shook his head. "Possibly. I didn't think he believed that legend when it started ten years ago."

Tristan shrugged. "Maybe he did." He stood, balancing against the desk. "Sir? Did he ever mention anything about seeing a girl from this school? Maybe in secret?"

Cameron's eyes widened for a second before he chuckled. "Paul Martin? No. He's been in love with his wife for years. They've been together since high school. I can't imagine him with anyone else. Why?"

"The legend again. The investigators have a theory the ghost was a student who went here twenty years ago, but they haven't been able to narrow down who she was." Not bad for a guy who was flying by the seat of his pants.

A strange look came into Cameron's eyes, but was gone in a second. Tristan wasn't sure he saw anything. "That silly legend. Getting everyone worked up."

"Sir, you don't look so good. You should probably go home and rest." Tristan wasn't sure how to comfort the older man. Even though Cameron was his superior, he didn't know the man that well. Again, he looked to Jaime for an answer. She merely shrugged.

Cameron nodded. "Yes, yes, you're right. I just…I knew you lived in the building and had lost your friend. I wanted to know if you knew anything."

Tristan swallowed. The urge to tell him the truth bubbled up. He kept it in check. "I don't know what the police found out. You might want to ask them."

The older man straightened, his shoulders back. "Thank you. If you hear anything, will you tell me immediately?"

"Yes, sir." Tristan didn't hesitate with his answer. He understood how it felt to lose a friend, especially to lose one the same way. He wanted to find the answers not for himself, but for Dr. Cameron, too.

Appearing steadier, Cameron got to his feet. He shook Tristan's hand. "Thank you," he said again. Picking up his briefcase, he continued on his way down the hall.

Tristan sank into his chair. How had everything become so complicated in the past couple of weeks? He had helped bury his best friend one day ago. He had witnessed another man's death, a man who had the same hair color he did. Had The White lady planned to kill him that night, or had Paul been an unexpected opportunity? He ran a hand over his face.

Lily Comer smiled at him from his screen. How did she fit into this? Was she the ghost? Or was she simply an unfortunate girl who was missing?

Another door clicked open. Tristan peered out into the hall to see Dr. Jonas Knight, the professor whose office was located across the hall, step out and freeze when he saw Tristan. He stared for a moment, almost like he expected Tristan to say something. When Tristan didn't, the skinny man locked his door and scurried down the hall. Tristan shook his head.

He had seen Dr. Knight a couple of times since the first day. The man never said anything. He studied Tristan every once in a while, and the attention would make Tristan's skin crawl. He couldn't figure out what Knight found so fascinating.

Tristan checked the clock. He still had twenty minutes before his first class of the day. He waved to Jaime as he walked out of the office. He passed Dr. Smith's office and stopped. The robust professor had made a point to check in on Tristan every other day when his schedule permitted. When he saw Smith coming, Tristan prepared for at least twenty minutes of his day to disappear. Smith loved to talk. He not only asked about Tristan's semester and how he was doing after his friend passed away, but he also gossiped about students and fellow professors alike. It was never mean-spirited, only a few tidbits here and there. If anyone knew anything about an affair twenty years ago, it was probably Smith.

Smith's door stood wide open. The older man sat at his desk, glasses perched on the end of his nose, reading one of his students' papers. Clutching a red pen, he marked it every few seconds with a groan.

Tristan knocked on the open door. Smith lifted his head, his eyes blinking owlishly. His face broke into a smile when he recognized Tristan. He pulled off his glasses.

"My boy, what brings you to my doorstep this morning?" Smith leaned back in his brown leather chair, his fingers laced behind his head.

Tristan crossed the room, taking in the medium-sized office. He had never been inside before. Old textbooks and some newer history books filled the wooden shelves on either side. One shelf was dedicated to all the books Smith wrote. Tristan recognized a few of the ones about the local history of the area. He reached the large black desk, which rested in front of a long, narrow window with the blinds drawn. He sat down in the hard chair across from the older man.

*How do I start this conversation without Dr. Smith thinking I'm crazy?* he wondered. He cleared his throat and jumped in. "Sir, I have a couple of strange questions to ask you about my office."

"Your office?"

"Yeah, did anyone, maybe, have an affair in there?"

Smith threw his back and laughed. "Many a young student has had a tryst in there. Why? Do you want to have an affair in there?"

"No, no. I just…heard about one twenty years ago. The girl went missing. Her name was Lily?"

"Twenty years ago?" Smith rubbed his beard. "That's going back a ways, son. What brought this up?"

Tristan tried to appear nonchalant about the whole thing. "Oh, you know how students are, telling each other stories about the place." His mind churned as he searched for a reasonable lie to explain his interest. He hadn't thought this conversation out very well. "Um, an older sibling of one of my students knew her." Crap! That sounded forced even to his ears.

Smith made a thoughtful noise as he rocked back and forth in his chair. "Like I said, a few professors have had affairs in several of the rooms around here. It's hard to remember one, especially from twenty years ago."

"Ah, well, thought it was worth a try." He gathered his satchel and headed to the door. Wait! Hidden Forest! Maybe he could try another tactic. He stopped halfway across the room. "Sir, I think she may have been connected to the Hidden Forest apartment building. Do you know anything about that building?"

Dr. Smith dropped his smile. "Such a tragic place. Ian just told me about Paul's death last Friday."

"You knew Mr. Martin?" Surprise leapt into Tristan's voice. He sauntered back to the desk and sat down.

"I did." Smith picked up a framed picture that sat on his desk. "I knew him fairly well. We became friends when I started working here, but we hadn't spoken in a long time. His father's company built many of the newer buildings on campus. I suppose he took over that business after his father died a few years ago." He handed the picture to Tristan. A group of seven men stood on the edge of a lake, fishing rods held high. Smith pointed to the man on the left. "That's me." He pointed to the man next to him. "And that's Paul."

Tristan studied the picture, noting how most of the men wore bucket hats. Did any of them help Paul Martin kill a college girl? If he had indeed killed her and that was why the ghost went after him. "How old were you?"

Smith took back the picture. "We had to be about thirty, maybe?" He pointed to another man on the right. "That's Dr. Cameron." Cameron smiled at the camera, holding a large fish on the end of his hook. "And the one in the back who looks like he's not having a good time is Dr. Knight." Dr. Knight stared stone-faced at the camera. Smith chuckled. "Knight hated the whole idea of fishing, but Ian felt bad if he didn't invite him." He set the picture back on his desk.

"What happened between all of you?"

"Life, Mr. Johnson. Things happen and they take up more time than you think they will."

So, his original plan wasn't going so well. He decided to try another tactic, and appeal to Smith's knowledge of local history. "Have you ever heard of the legend of The White Lady? She haunts Hidden Forest." Tristan sat up straighter. "Before my friend Zack died, and especially after, people told me different versions of the legend."

Smith nodded. "Yes, I have. I'm not surprised a story like that would spring up. No one ever did find out who killed those boys ten years ago, did they?"

"No, sir." Tristan paused, and then decided to tell Smith the truth. "I have seen her, though."

"You've seen a ghost?"

"Yes, sir. I know it sounds crazy, but I think there's some truth to the legend." He stopped short of telling Smith how he had seen The White Lady hurl Martin down the stairs like he weighed nothing. He scooted forward. "You've been here a while. Have you heard of any women dying in those woods? Maybe before Hidden Forest was built? Maybe during it?"

Smith's blue eyes studied Tristan for a long moment. Tristan shifted, his left leg shaking. This was it. This was how he was going to get fired from his job and kicked out of school. "Son, maybe you should take a few days off. It sounds like you've been through a lot. Take some time to grieve and clear your head."

"You don't believe me?"

"I believe you believe it."

Smith pushed back his chair and stood. He pulled a dusty black binder off his right shelf. He set it in the middle of the desk with a thud, right on top of the papers he had been grading. He reclaimed his seat as he flipped it open to a page near the back. A black and white picture of Hidden Forest was at the top of the page with statistics listed underneath it. "My boy, this book lists all the buildings in and around the Blackwood campus. Hidden Forest has only been around for twenty years. It was originally part of student housing, but was converted to regular apartments a few years ago. As far as I know, no woman has died in the building or the surrounding area." He turned a few pages to reveal the history building. "If there were such a thing as ghosts, this building would more than likely be haunted. It's much, much older than Hidden Forest."

Tristan regarded the page in front of him. "I don't think a ghost would care how old the place was, but I understand your point, sir." Part of him wanted to throw the binder across the room. This conversation wasn't getting him anywhere. Dr. Smith was telling him things he already knew. But he knew the ghost was real. Every time he closed his eyes, he could see Zack fall backwards out of a window or Mr. Martin thrown down the stairs. Someone knew who this ghost used to be and why she was so angry. Someone also had to know if Lily Comer was connected to her or not.

He shook Smith's hand. "Thank you for your time, sir. I should probably get to class."

Smith cracked a smile. "Don't mention it, son. I'm here anytime you want to talk history." He patted Tristan's arm. "And think about taking that time off. It'll do you a world of good."

## 18

"Coffee for everybody!" McKenna set a foam tray of coffee cups on her desk. The dark, warm aroma filled the small space in a matter of seconds.

Tabitha left one of the desks in the back of the room. "Caffeine. Thank God."

Drew stepped out of the equipment room, his nose in the air. "Pumpkin spice. I love this time of year." He grabbed the giant cup with his name on it.

Aaron appeared out of his office. "About time you came back to work." He found his cup and took a sip from it. "Off gallivanting all over the state." His mood lifted as he enjoyed the coffee. He grunted. "I guess I can forgive you."

Drew slurped.

Aaron side-eyed him. "I don't know why you put all that frou-frou stuff in your drink. Coffee should be served plain and black."

Tabitha bumped his hip. "With a hint of chocolate."

He rolled his eyes and continued drinking.

McKenna dropped a straw into her Mocha Frappuccino. "I wasn't off gallivanting. Tristan and I went to his parents' house to find out more about why the ghost pulled energy from us."

Drew wiggled his eyebrows. "Sure you were." He sucked in air when McKenna kicked his shin.

Aaron grabbed a chair from his office. "What did you find out?"

She told them about Tristan's grandfather's journals. "Neither he nor his team understood it, but my grandmother apparently figured out a way to stop it." She sipped more mocha. "Did you know my grandmother worked for The Greene Institute, too?"

Tabitha perched on the edge of the desk. "She did?"

"Lauren McKenna."

Aaron and Tabitha exchanged a look.

"I've heard the name. Didn't think about that McKenna being connected to our McKenna," Tabitha said.

McKenna waved her hand. "Anyway, after she was attacked, she learned how to make her shield stronger." She chuckled. "No wonder nothing ever seemed to get to her." She stirred her drink with the straw. "Mr. Johnson apparently wrote down her instructions. Tristan and I tried to follow them and worked on strengthening our own shields."

Aaron propped his feet on the desk. He closed his eyes, savoring the hot liquid. "Any luck?"

"Not yet. My head was pounding by the time we had to go home, and Tristan was so tired. It's a miracle we made it back." She still felt some of the effects from working on her shield. The caffeine helped steady her. "How about here? Find anything we can use?"

Drew cleared his throat. "Well, we did get some interesting footage. I've got it cued up in the back if you'd like to see it." He jammed his free hand into his pocket. "I still need to clean it up and study it, but a fresh pair of eyes will be nice."

McKenna nodded. Setting her coffee on her desk, she followed him into the cramped equipment room. Filled to the brim with hard drives, cameras, monitors, and other ghost hunting gadgets, two people barely fit into the small space. Two chairs and two small desks were located along the back wall. Drew led her to one. His fingers flew over the keys, and the voice-recording program appeared on the screen.

"Our first piece of evidence," he proclaimed. He clicked one of the keys.

McKenna's voice cut through the quiet, asking if the ghost was there.

"He has to pay," was the answer.

She gasped. "You got it! That's the sentence I heard."

"Yeah, she was there. Didn't bother answering any other questions, though."

The door creaked behind them. "Show her the video." Aaron pushed his way in with Tabitha right behind him.

Drew cued up the video. "You ready?"

"Just play it, Keane," Aaron grumbled.

The black and white image of an empty bedroom appeared. It took McKenna a moment to realize it was Tristan's.

Drew faced her. "Okay, this happened before we walked into the apartment." He clicked the mouse.

The room was quiet and still with faint white noise in the background. Then the image jumped and rippled. To the left of the monitor, a white figure appeared. She was faint and fuzzy, but McKenna made out the outline of her dress and her long hair. Her heart jumped into her throat as she took an involuntary step back. The ghostly woman turned in a circle before peering at the camera. The image cut out.

"Did we get her attack?" McKenna's voice was high and tight.

"No." She felt Drew's regret. "It's like she took out all the cameras. Probably pulled the energy from them, too."

"But the regular energy wasn't enough." McKenna steadied herself against one of the equipment shelves behind her. She covered her chest, remembering the ice as The White Lady plunged her hand inside. She swallowed. "Rewind it one more time. I want to make sure I saw what I think I saw."

"Are you okay?" Tabitha touched her arm.

McKenna pushed away from the shelf. "I'm fine."

"No one blames if you want to take some more time after what happened."

She set her jaw. "I'm fine. I'm not going to let her get to me." She pulled out the extra chair and sat down.

Aaron and Tabitha leaned over Drew's shoulders as he scrolled the video back frame by frame. Drew clicked play, and the images replayed on the screen.

This time, McKenna shoved her emotions to the side and focused on the details. "Stop." She narrowed her eyes, taking in the fuzzy image.

Aaron cleared his throat. "Can we clean this up enough to identify her?"

"I'm going to try, but her features aren't real defined up close." Drew readjusted his hat. He shook his head. "I can't believe this small thing killed Zack, a man twice her size."

"All that's left of her is energy," Tabitha said. "With the extra power she pulls from around her, and the boost she got from Tristan and McKenna, she can affect the physical world."

"That plus her anger makes her stronger." McKenna hooked a strand of hair behind her ear. "She'd probably kill every year if she had a permanent psychic to feed off."

"Then why didn't she keep Jason around?" Drew asked. "No offense."

"He fit one of her types." A sense of dread filled her. "We need to pull Tristan out of there and make sure I'm not there to take his place."

Drew pulled up another program, opening the video images into it. "He can always crash at my place. Now, all of you go away. I need some room to work here."

Tristan stood in front of the Restless Spirits office. Part of him wanted to know if there was a connection between the ghost, Lily, and the visions in his office. He glanced at the picture he had printed one more time. Her face definitely matched the girl in his visions, and the eyes matched the ghost. The only way to find out lay through the office door.

When he got the message McKenna had left describing the footage the team had recorded, he couldn't believe it. Proof that they all weren't crazy and that The White Lady did indeed exist. It was one thing to see her himself, but it was another to have video evidence. Then she had told him Drew was cleaning up the image, hopefully bringing out The White Lady's features. The ghost was either so transparent or so bright it was hard to focus on her face. Her eyes were the only features that stood out.

With that promise lingering in his mind, he decided to drop by the office after work instead of calling McKenna back. If this could be over in the next few days, Tristan would have his life back. And possibly a chance to start a relationship with the gorgeous empath.

He pushed open the glass door, the bell ringing in his ears. The front desk was empty. Not a soul greeted him. He let the door close behind him as he walked farther into the room.

"Hello?" he called. No answer. "Hello!" he raised his voice.

The door on the left of the back wall swung open. McKenna stuck her head out of the open doorway and smiled when she saw him. It brightened his day. She walked all the way out, the door clicking closed.

"Tristan, what are you doing here?"

"You said you caught her on tape." He handed her the picture. "I think I might know who she is."

Her blue eyes sparkled. "This is one of the missing girls, isn't it?" She rushed to her desk to bring up the matching file. "Lily Comer. How do you know it's her?"

"I don't. Not really. But she keeps turning up in my visions."

"Visions? As in plural?" She whirled around. She reached for his hand, and in that moment, Tristan welcomed the warm connection. Her expression turned to concern. "You said you can't control it. Are you okay?"

"Yeah." He tapped his temple. "Scenes tend to sneak in every once in a while. I never know what they'll be, and I can't call them up on command." He indicated the picture. "She's been in all the ones I've had in my office, and I think I saw her in one of the flashes in the apartment. The girl in the woods."

"What do you see in your office?"

He told her about each vision of the girl and the mystery man. "I always see it from his point of view so I never see his face. I think he's a professor, and he had an affair with her, a student." He told her how he had originally thought they were random, but they kept pushing through his walls. "Today, I saw her face, every feature. I'm almost positive it's the same girl, and her features resemble The White Lady's."

McKenna chewed on her bottom lip, processing the information. "I was helping Drew clean up the image. He may have something to show us."

She turned on her heel, heading for the back, and indicated Tristan should follow her. Tristan followed her into a cramped room stacked with electronic equipment. It was Drew's version of paradise. He spotted his friend sitting in front of one of the computers, playing with an image on the screen.

"How's it coming?" McKenna asked as she settled into the empty chair beside him.

Drew moved his headphones, a tinny version of "Paranoid" playing through the speakers. He glanced up. "Hey, man. Come to see the ghost in digital format?"

"Something like that." Tristan came around the other side of Drew, resting a hand on the edge of the table.

"Well, I think this is the best I could do. Any larger and she starts pixelating." Drew hit a button and the cleaned footage began to play.

Tristan regarded the image on the screen. The White Lady circled and eyed the camera. His eyes widened as he studied the curve of her jawline and the shape of her eyes. It was the best look he had gotten of her since the first day she appeared. "Still have the picture?" he asked McKenna.

She nodded and held it up to the screen.

Tristan felt like someone had knocked the breath out of him. "That's her. That's the girl I've been seeing. That's Lily."

"You're sure?" Drew's voice rose an octave with excitement.

"Absolutely."

"Tristan, are you willing to go back to your office with me? Maybe try to see something?" McKenna beamed.

Tristan shoved his hands into his pockets. "I don't know. You saw what happened last time."

She held up her hand. "I won't push you. But maybe I can pick up emotions from your coworkers or maybe a general impression of the place. If the energy is strong enough to break through your barriers, there might be some residual emotional energy for me to read."

She seemed so hopeful that he could say no. Tristan nodded. "All right."

Twenty minutes later, he found himself back at the history building. The halls were quiet since most people had already gone home for the day. A few professors still lingered, preparing for their night classes. Most of the offices were empty.

"It's a little creepy when no one's here," McKenna muttered.

Tristan laced his fingers through hers as they climbed the stairs. When he turned the curve at the landing, he smiled back at her. At that moment, he slammed into someone. A briefcase dropped and papers went flying. Tristan let go of McKenna's hand.

"Watch where you're going," a man said tersely.

"I'm sorry." Tristan held out his hand to steady the other person and found himself looking into the face of Dr. Jonas Knight.

Knight glared. "Mr. Johnson." Once he was on his feet, he dusted his dark pants and groaned when he saw the mess around him. "I suppose I'll have to spend another hour putting them back in order."

"I'm really sorry, sir. I wasn't watching where I was going."

Knight waved at him as he corrected the glasses on the bridge of his beak-like nose. "I'm not surprised." His gaze flickered to McKenna.

"Why don't you let us help you?" She crouched down and started collecting papers.

Tristan and Dr. Knight joined her on the floor.

"Where were you going in such a hurry, Mr. Johnson?" Knight stuffed a group of papers into his briefcase.

"I left something in my office." Tristan collected the last of the papers, placing them into the briefcase.

Knight glanced from Tristan to McKenna and back again, his gray eyes taking in the scene. "I see the tradition continues," he sighed.

Tristan helped him to his feet once again. "The tradition? What tradition?"

"Young professors and their office romances. I've seen it happen during the many years I've been here." He checked his pockets, making sure he had everything with him.

Tristan shook his head. "No, sir, we're not…"

"I'm not stupid, Mr. Johnson. I also don't care. Just make sure no one catches you." He started for the stairs.

"Wait, sir. Who else have you caught?" Tristan paused and exchanged a glance with McKenna. "Doing this?"

Knight straightened, his shoulders back and his chest puffed out. His eye level came to Tristan's chin. "I do not tell on people. When someone entrusts me with a secret, I keep it. Now, good evening, Mr. Johnson." With that, he turned on his heel and headed down the stairs.

"He knows something," McKenna said. "He was calm until you asked him about other affairs. And then he became guilty and sad."

Tristan watched the professor disappear down the stairs. "I wonder what he could be guilty about. He never talks to anybody."

"I guess he wants to keep his secrets." She watched him make the turn and disappear down the last flight of stairs.

The office was dark and silent when Tristan opened the door. Jaime had already gone home for the night, so he and McKenna were alone. He flicked on the light.

"Here we are, center of everything. Do I need to walk outside?"

McKenna walked into the middle of the room. She held

out her hands as if she were feeling her way around. "No. I've been around you long enough that I can filter out your emotions."

His lips quirked. "Know how I feel, do you?"

"Yes, and you need to stop feeling that particular emotion right now. I'm working here." She stood still and closed her eyes.

Tristan sat on the corner of his desk. "Need me to do anything?"

"Just stay there and be quiet."

He nodded but didn't say another word. Watching her work, he noticed how pretty she was when the expression on her face was serious. She wrinkled her brow in concentration, and Tristan couldn't help but smile.

He didn't know what to make of this strange woman. She understood him and seemed to believe in him. He had never really been with anyone who had believed in him that much before. Actually, he had never been completely honest with anyone he had ever dated before. It took all of his effort to keep the psychic part of himself hidden. But with McKenna, honesty came easily. He wasn't afraid to show all of himself. That realization was terrifying.

She didn't say a word as she turned a slow circle, her eyes still closed. He wondered how she felt about him. If he tried to see the past again, would she be there to ground him? He hadn't wanted to admit it to himself, but he felt a stronger connection to her since she had brought him back from the brink of insanity.

Insanity. Was The White Lady insane? What had happened to that young, smiling college girl? How had she gone from a sweet girl who believed in love to a cold-blooded killer? What would drive a spirit to that kind of madness? Who was the man she was seeing? What happened to him?

Lost in thought, Tristan hardly noticed the room change around him. Lily's voice echoed in his ears.

*"Tell me you love me." He turned and saw her standing next to him. Her light green eyes bore into his as she fiddled with the yellow bow in her hair. She unclipped it, her hair falling to her shoulder. His pulse jumped at the beauty of it. Pressing it into his hand, she smiled. "Even if you can't say it out loud, you can keep this. That way, I'll know you have a piece of me."*

*The scene changed before him. The bright happiness changed to the gray of melancholy. She was missing, gone. No one could tell him what happened to her. He held the yellow bow tight in his grip, grief overwhelming him. He only wanted to keep her safe. The breakup wasn't forever, only until she graduated. One more year, and she would be his. He wanted to toss the bow off one of the mountaintops so no one would ever find it again, but he couldn't let go of it. It was a piece of her. He opened the top drawer of the desk and unlocked a secret compartment. He placed the bow inside and locked it.*

*"Why?" he asked.*

"Tristan?" McKenna's face swam into view, but it was like he saw her through a curtain of water. She wiped his cheek with her thumb. He blinked. His cheek was wet. "Tristan, what happened? You hit me with a tidal wave of grief. What's wrong?"

He blinked again and wiped his eyes. "I loved her."

"Who did you love?"

Tristan shook his head. "No, that's not right." He slid off the desk. Seeing the familiar surroundings of the room brought him back to himself. He moved away from McKenna. "I'm sorry. I think I saw something."

"You did more than see something. You felt it." She leaned against the desk. "I wasn't picking up anything but you, and then all of a sudden, your feelings changed. Love, and then, the grief. Tell me what you saw."

Tristan swallowed. "I saw her again, Lily. She stood right beside me." He indicated the spot to his right. Taking a deep breath, he tried to steady his nerves. The grief he experienced was fading like a dream. "She handed me a yellow hair clip, one she wore all the time. And then the scene changed."

"That was the moment you were sad."

"Not me, but the guy I was seeing this past event through. I...he put the clip in the top desk drawer." Tristan touched his desk. "I think it's in here."

"Tristan, that was years ago. Don't you think he would've taken it with him when he left this office?"

"Only one way to find out." Tristan pulled open the top drawer. At the bottom was the outline of a small door with a lock on it. He yanked it out, placed it on the desk. After he removed all of the stuff from inside, he shook it. Something rattled in the bottom.

McKenna's mouth formed an O shape. She stepped closer to the desk. "Do you have the key?"

Tristan pulled out more drawers. File folders, pens, sticky notes, but not one of them had a key. "No." He blew out a breath. A connection to her was so close, yet so far away.

McKenna bent over it, her hair brushing the wood. "Know how to pick a lock?"

"No clue."

She dropped into his chair, booted up his computer. "Well, let's do a little research." She googled the steps to picking a lock with a paper clip. She grabbed two, giving one to Tristan. "Start shaping this like the picture."

"Who knew picking a lock would be an important skill when battling killer ghosts." Tristan grunted as he pulled his paper clip straight.

"You never know," she panted, "what you're going to need." She gritted her teeth and yanked the bottom of her clip straight. She then curved the top. Collecting the two clips, she followed the rest of the instructions, gnawing on her bottom lip as she tried to unlock the secret drawer.

Her face red with frustration, she continued to work.

"Want me to help?" Tristan offered.

McKenna waved him off. "I've got this." She groaned. "I will defeat this."

True to her word, the lock clicked and the tiny door sprang open. The same small yellow hair clip he had seen rested on the bottom. Shaped like a bow tie, it was unassuming and delicate. His fingers brushed the satiny hair accessory.

He showed it to McKenna. "Looks like someone forgot it was here."

"Maybe. The question is, who is he?"

## 19

Tristan spent the whole night studying the hair clip. It was such a small thing, with a satiny feel and shaped like a bow tie. Why would the mysterious man hide it in a compartment and then forget about it? He tried to picture The White Lady wearing a yellow bow, but it was a hard image to conjure. He left it lying on his side table to see if it would attract the ghost. He didn't see her or feel her, but the next morning, it was sitting on the kitchen table.

He chose to go back to Smith's office to see if the older man recognized the hair clip or if he knew about the possible affair. McKenna wanted to go with him.

"Wait for me. I can read him and see if he's lying," she said.

Tristan cradled his cell between his cheek and his shoulder as he locked his apartment door. "Can you make it to the college this morning?"

"No. I have to meet a potential client this morning. Why can't we do it this afternoon?"

"Because I have class, and Dr. Smith leaves at noon."

McKenna heaved a sigh. "Okay, but if you find out anything, you let me know."

"You'll be the first one I call."

~

"Dr. Smith, can I talk to you?" Tristan knocked on the open door of the office, peering inside.

The boisterous professor peered over the rim of his glasses, giving Tristan a long look. "My boy, you're back again. What can I help you with this time?" He closed his laptop, placed his morning coffee on the desk, and settled back into his chair, much like he had the last time Tristan visited. He rested his joined hands on his stomach.

"Well, sir." Tristan walked inside. "I found this in a drawer in my desk." He set his bag on Smith's desk and unzipped it, retrieving the yellow hair clip. "You wouldn't happen to know the girl this belongs to, would you?"

When Tristan set the bow between them, Smith raised an eyebrow. "How did that get into your desk?" He examined it as if it were a rare artifact.

Tristan kept his demeanor relaxed. He didn't want Smith to know how anxious he was for the answers. "I don't know, sir. I heard something rattling around in there so I searched the whole drawer. Finally found a hidden compartment. Took me forever to break into it." Not completely a lie. "I hope I didn't damage the desk."

"Oh, I'm sure you didn't, son. I'm surprised those old desks are still holding together." Smith's eyes stayed glued to the tiny yellow treasure. "You know, I've taught a lot of students in my day, and many of the girls wear hair things like this." He handed it back to Tristan. "Did you ask Ms. Liu if it was hers?"

"No, but why would she put a hair bow in a secret compartment in my desk?"

Smith was quiet for a moment. "Good point. Perhaps it belonged to a graduate assistant before you. Yes, that's probably the explanation."

"Maybe." Tristan pitched it back into his bag. This line of questioning wasn't giving him the answers he wanted. Smith knew everything that went on in the department, why didn't he know about the hair clip or the affair?

Smith's face was neutral. He wished McKenna could have come. The professor was a hard man to read. Maybe he was expecting too much. Smith probably really didn't recognize the bow. The older man was right. Other students had used that desk before Tristan came along. Time to try a different tactic.

Tristan zipped the satchel. "Sir, who had my office before I did? Maybe I can find the grad student and give this back to her?"

Smith scratched under his beard, his eyes thoughtful. "That's going back a ways, my boy. Lots of different people have passed through there. Why do you want to know?"

Tristan shifted from foot to foot. Smith would probably send Tristan off to the looney bin if he talked about the ghost and being psychic. So, he angled for a simple approach. "Curious, I suppose. I found something in my desk that wasn't mine, and I'm a sucker for the history of a place." He grinned. Smooth, Johnson. He even believed the lie himself.

"Well, it started out as one of our classrooms, but was turned into the graduate assistant office about twelve years ago." Smith walked to the farthest shelf and plucked a binder from it. He tossed it across the room. Tristan fumbled it, but kept it from falling to the ground. "You'll find some of the old grad students' names in there. I kept in touch with some of them after they left."

Tristan opened it up to find twelve years' worth of names, phone numbers, and addresses. His brow furrowed in concentration. It was possible the man he kept connecting with had been a graduate student, but was that the same kind of teacher/student relationship a professor would have? "Thank you, sir. This will give me a place to start." He paused as if he were thinking about his next words. "What if this bow is older than that? I don't know much about fashion, but I think I saw a picture of one of my cousins wearing something like this a few decades ago."

Smith pressed his lips together. "Let me think. A lot of professors used that room. That's a long list." He stroked his beard. "A few decades, you say? That's pretty specific." He drummed his fingers along the side of the shelf. "What are you not telling me, Mr. Johnson?"

Tristan swallowed. "Nothing." He gave a nervous laugh. "Just want to find out who this belongs to."

Smith's face softened. "Son, I can't help you if I don't know the whole story."

Tristan stared at the ceiling. "You'll think I'm crazy." His stomach rolled at the thought of resorting to the truth.

"Try me."

"It's a long story, but I think it belongs to the ghost in my apartment building." He lowered his head to meet Smith's gaze. "The White Lady."

Smith threw his head back and laughed. The boisterous sound echoed off the walls. "Why would you think that?"

Tristan shook his head. "I told you, it's a long story." He set the binder down on the desk. "I want to learn who put this bow in my desk. I just need a name."

Smith crossed the room and patted Tristan's shoulder. "I don't know where you got these crazy ideas, but I'll answer your questions as best I can. What are you looking for?"

"Is there any professor still here who used my office as a classroom?"

Smith was quiet for a moment. "Three of us, Mr. Johnson – Dr. Cameron, Dr. Knight, and myself. You think a professor put it in your desk?"

"Yes, sir. I'm hoping it's someone who's still here. Somebody who can tell me more about the girl who used to wear this."

Smith sighed. "A girl who you think is a ghost now?"

"Yes, sir."

Smith patted Tristan's back as he leaned against the edge of his desk. "I'm sorry to say it wasn't me, son. But I wish you luck on finding out more about it. It sounds like a fascinating search."

Relief flooded through Tristan. Smith wasn't going to fire him and recommend him for therapy. "Thank you, sir."

"If you need anything else, Mr. Johnson, please let me know." Smith gave Tristan a jovial smile before returning to his laptop.

Tristan adjusted the strap across his chest as he headed out of the office. If Smith didn't know anything about the hair bow, then that left Dr. Cameron and Dr. Knight. Dr. Knight scoffed at the idea of having an affair in the office, so that left Dr. Cameron.

Cameron's office door was closed, which meant he was still out of the building. Tristan knocked anyway, in case the head of department was hiding behind it. No answer. He would have to come back to Cameron.

Tristan checked his watch, realizing it was time for him to teach a class. He took the stairs two at a time.

Later that afternoon, Tristan decided to track down Knight. Even though the abrasive man had refused to tell him anything the night before, maybe he would open up after seeing the yellow bow. Talking to him wouldn't be easy, but finding him wouldn't be particularly difficult. If Knight wasn't in his office, then he was in the rare book section of the library. Tristan had learned that bit of trivia from Smith on his first day. He followed that knowledge and found Knight sitting at a desk in the back of the small, dusty room, poring over an old, decrepit book.

When he was only a few feet away, Tristan cleared his throat to announce he was there. Dr. Knight turned around.

"Mr. Johnson. We meet twice in one week. If you have a question, my office hours are posted clearly on my door." He then returned to the book he was studying. Tristan peered over his shoulder to see what book it was. STRANGE STORIES OF THE SOUTH was printed across the top.

"A little light reading, sir?" he asked.

Knight raised his head, an eyebrow lifted. Tristan settled into the chair across from him. He wasn't leaving until he got some answers. Closing the book, Dr. Knight adjusted his glasses and peered intently at Tristan. "Is there something you wanted, Mr. Johnson?"

Tristan pulled the hair bow out of his bag. "I hate to interrupt you, sir, but I was hoping you could help me out." He placed it on the table between them. It was a bright speck in the middle of the dark browns and blacks of the room. "I found this in one of my desk drawers. Dr. Smith said you used to teach in that room. Do you recognize it?"

Dr. Knight picked it up, studying it as if it were a strange object left in his midst. His features seemed to soften a little. "How do you know it was from that period? It could have been from a grad student who had that desk before you."

Tristan squirmed. He really should have come up with a lie that would back up his assumptions. "It looked rather old."

"Anything stuffed in a drawer can look old after a while, Mr. Johnson."

Tristan ran a hand through his hair. "Last night, you thought I was bringing my girlfriend to my office. You've seen other people do that. Something tells me you know more than you're telling."

Setting the hair clip back down, Dr. Knight pushed a strand of light brown hair out of his face. "I don't like to talk about things. I am not a gossip." He drummed his fingers on the table, considering his next answer.

"Please. I think something terrible happened to the girl who used to wear this." Tristan leaned forward. "I want to help her."

Knight took a deep breath. His gaze was level. "Are you sure you can't just see the answer? It would be a lot easier."

Tristan's mouth dropped open. "Sir?"

Knight waved his hand. Dust flew off the table. "Cut the crap, Johnson. I knew your father."

"You did? How?"

"I worked with the Boone police from time to time. I watched your father work and put the pieces together." A rare smile crossed Knight's face. "Don't worry. Your secret is safe with me." He spread his hands. "Who am I going to tell?"

Tristan let out the breath he didn't realize he was holding. "Thank you, sir, but you just watched my dad?" None of this made any sense.

"No." Knight took off his glasses and rubbed his eyes. "I needled him until he finally told me. He saw the present; your grandfather saw the past. So if it alternates like that, you must be able to see the past as well."

Tristan pulled away from the table. His mouth worked, but no sound came out.

Knight pushed his glasses back onto his nose. "Stop looking at me like a fish, Mr. Johnson."

Tristan shook his head. "I'm sorry, but why didn't he tell me?"

"You'd have to ask him that."

"Why didn't you tell me?"

Knight's mouth formed a straight line. "Are we going to talk about this or the hair bow? I have a class to teach in twenty minutes."

Tristan shook himself out of the shock. Knight was right. Find out about the bow now, and worry about the rest of it later. So Tristan told him about the visions in his office and the ghost in his apartment, and how he thought they were the same person. "She had long dark hair and green eyes. She wasn't very tall, maybe came to here." He rested the side of his hand at the middle of his chest. "I know her name was Lily, but I don't know who the man she dated was. I see through his eyes and never see him."

"Hence the questions." Knight picked up the bow again. "My office used to be right next to that room, and I remember hearing things when no one was supposed to be in there. Ian Cameron used that room quite often instead of his office." He set down the bow, pulled off his glasses, and wiped the lenses with the edge of his tie. "He was the charming professor. The one whose classes the students always wanted to take." He replaced his glasses. "The one the graduate assistants wanted to work for." Taking the old book back, he carefully opened it. "He had students going in and out of that room."

"Did any of them own anything like this?" Tristan asked.

"Yes." His resolve crumbled. "Lily did. I remember her, Mr. Johnson. She had a job with the college through a work-study program, and most of her duties were in the history department. She ran errands for all of the professors, but she spent most of her time with Ian."

Tristan nodded, his suspicions confirmed. "What happened to her?"

"That, I don't know, Mr. Johnson. I know she disappeared

twenty years ago, but I assumed she quit school and went somewhere else. At least until the news started calling her a missing girl." Knight shook his head. "Such a shame. But I've known Ian for almost thirty years. I don't believe he would ever hurt her."

*But someone did*, Tristan thought.

∽

D r. Cameron and Lily Comer. Connecting the man to the visions wasn't easy. Cameron appeared to be an easygoing man, a family man. Tristan didn't miss the ring on his finger or the pictures of Cameron's wife and kids in his office. But it had been twenty years ago. It was possible Cameron was the man Lily had loved. The question was, was he the man who killed her? And if not, who was?

Tristan dropped his keys and his bag on the kitchen table. He grabbed the yellow bow from the front pocket of his bag, twirling it in his hand.

Maybe Mr. Martin had been the one to kill her? Tristan didn't know much about the construction of the building, but surely Martin would have access to it. McKenna had said she felt the man was hiding something, and he seemed nervous about the investigation in the first place. But was he a killer, or only an accomplice? With the viciousness Lily had used while throwing Martin down the stairs, Tristan had no doubt the man had been involved.

He stretched out on the couch, holding the bow up to the light. Such a small, delicate thing, almost like the ghost herself.

Tristan set it on the coffee table and stared at the ceiling. Finding the man who had hidden it was proving to be harder than he thought. Giving up and moving out would be the easiest course of action. Crashing at Drew's place wouldn't be a problem. Or maybe McKenna would let him stay with her? His lips curved into a smile at the thought.

No. He didn't want to run away this time. What if The White Lady found another source of psychic energy? He didn't know his neighbors. One of them could have the power to let the ghost kill one more person. And neither one would know how to protect themselves. He frowned, the guilt weighing on his conscience. He didn't wish that feeling of helplessness on anyone else.

The lights blinked. Tristan's body tensed.

The air around him cooled. Goosebumps prickled his skin.

He jerked upright, his muscles taut. His whole body was alert. She was coming.

The lights cut out. The setting sun cast the only available light through the slats of the closed blinds.

Tristan gripped the edge of the couch. His breath puffed out in small white circles as his arms started to shake.

The White Lady appeared beside the coffee table. Her face held no expression, her eyes their usual impossible green. She stared at him before brushing her fingers over the bow. Now that he had seen the picture and put the pieces together, he could make out the young woman she used to be.

"Do you recognize this?" His voice was strangled.

Her green eyes flashed to red. CDs and DVDs flew off the entertainment center. Their sharp corners stung as they nicked his arms. He jumped off the couch. The door was only a few feet away.

His fingers touched the knob. He had left it unlocked; he could make it. Everything went still.

He pivoted a slow circle. The White Lady's attention was no longer focused on him. Her hand passed through the bow.

"It used to be yours." Tristan took a tentative step

forward. "You can stop now. We're close to finding the people who killed you." He reached out a hand. "Let me help you."

Her head twisted in his direction. "You will pay!" She flung out her hand. Tristan slid back into the wall, sticking to it like a fly in a spider's web. His muscles froze as his feet left the ground. The ghost was on him in seconds, her hand at his throat.

The White Lady whipped her head to the door when three sharp knocks sounded.

"Tristan?" McKenna! No! What if the ghost went for her?

The bitter cold started at his throat and seeped into his head. "Mac! Run!" He kicked, but his legs passed through air.

The knob clicked. "What's wrong? I'm coming in."

The White Lady pulled at his energy, slow and deliberate. This was it. She wasn't going to wait for Friday. Bit by bit, her body solidified.

Ice filled every part of Tristan's body. His arms and legs were limp. Was she going to suck him dry instead of throwing him out the window? His vision blackened at the edges.

"If you're going to do it, just do it."

## 20

Her breath escaped her lungs when McKenna raced into the apartment. Tristan's head was a couple of inches from the ceiling, the ghost's hand at his throat. He hung there like a dead wind-up toy. The ghost glowed, but her body was still transparent. McKenna searched for Tristan's emotions. The dullness of resignation came back to her. No! He couldn't give up.

Salt! She needed salt. Her feet moved into action. The light from the hallway streamed in through the open door, giving her enough to see. Her hands searched the kitchen, hitting the sharp edge of every corner. Cabinet doors squeaked open and slammed shut as she hunted for the one household tool she knew would chase The White Lady away. She crumpled the top of a bag. Bringing it into the light, she made out the S and the A. Perfect!

She tore it open and reached inside. Small rocks sifted through her fingers. She clutched a handful and threw it at the ghost. Her aim was true. The ghost screamed. Tristan tumbled to the ground, landing with a loud thud. McKenna threw more salt at The White Lady. The ghost broke in half and disappeared, wisps of white trailing behind her.

The lights blinked on as the air in the room warmed.

McKenna set the bag on the table, her hands shaking. She took a deep breath as she tried to steady her racing heart. She swayed a little as the adrenaline left. The nearby chair invited her to sit down, but she fought the urge. She still didn't know if Tristan was all right.

Tristan groaned. She ran to him and lightly tapped his cheeks. His eyes were open, but they were staring at nothing. "Tristan? Can you hear me?"

She felt for an emotion, any emotion. There, faintly, was a flicker of resignation. Then relief and gratefulness pushed it aside. McKenna grabbed Tristan's chin, forcing him to look at her. "Tristan, please."

Confusion seeped in. He slowly blinked as the color came back into his face. His skin was freezing. McKenna retrieved a blanket from his bed, draping it over his shoulders. She wrapped her arms around him, her hands rubbing his upper arms.

Her heart rate slowed down as she watched the life return to those soft green eyes. Eyes that focused on her. She sank to the floor, all of her fears floating away.

"Oh, thank God. Your color is coming back," she breathed. He was alive, whole.

Tristan licked his lips. "You got rid of the ghost with salt?" His voice cracked.

"A temporary solution. She'll be back, but it won't be for a while. What happened?" *Concentrate on him. Get him to talk. Don't dwell on the image of Tristan half dead in The White Lady's grip.*

"Don't know." He licked his dry lips again. "Was looking at the hair bow and she showed up." He struggled to move, but McKenna held him still. "Could use something to drink and eat."

McKenna relaxed. He was all right. He was going to be fine. "I'll take care of it. You just lay there."

He gave her a lazy thumbs-up. "That I can do."

She reluctantly pulled away from him, closed the front door, and walked into the kitchen. Resting her hands on the small counter, she took a deep breath. And another. What if she hadn't come by? What if the door hadn't been unlocked? The mere thought of Tristan dead cut through her. Her hands shook. Raking them through her hair, she continued to pull in a breath of air and let it go. He was fine. He was whole. He was alive.

Food. It would keep her mind off Tristan almost dying. Cabinets creaked open and thumped closed as she gathered ingredients for a meal. He didn't have much in his apartment, but she did find bacon and eggs in the refrigerator. Her grandmother used to make her breakfast for dinner when she'd had a bad day. Today certainly qualified.

She took off her jacket and draped it over the nearest chair. Pulling her hair back into a ponytail, she went to work.

Tristan broke the quiet. "Why are you here? Did we have a date?"

"No. I wanted to come by and see what you found out about the hair bow." The bacon sizzled on the griddle. "I called first, but your phone was dead." *Stick to the facts. Don't think about the dread that settled in your stomach*, she told herself.

Tristan grunted. She glanced over to see him push to his feet. It took a moment for him to stand without swaying. "Weird." He picked up the phone. "It had half a charge when I got home."

"The ghost must have drained it." More sizzling as the rich, savory smell of bacon filled the air.

Tristan wrapped the blanket tighter around his shoulders as he walked into the kitchen. "Breakfast for dinner?"

McKenna's mouth turned upwards. "It's comfort food for me."

"Can I help?" His voice was stronger, richer. Calm and determination filled the air between them. He felt more like Tristan. The ghost must not have taken as much as McKenna had thought.

It felt good to laugh. "No. Go sit down on the couch and rest. I'll bring you something to drink in a minute."

He shuffled over to couch, his shoes swishing against the hardwood floor. She chewed on her bottom lip as she watched him go. He must not have had time to take them off.

She poured a glass of Pepsi and set it down on the coffee table. "So Lily recognized her bow?"

Tristan tossed his shoes onto the floor. "She did. I guess she decided I was officially one of her killers if I had it. She was pretty pissed about it." He sipped the cold drink.

"That would explain why she was trying to kill you ahead of schedule." McKenna went back to the kitchen.

"Unfortunately, no one else at the college recognized it."

She cracked an egg. "Or someone is lying." The yolk plopped into a bowl. "You talked to everybody?"

"Except for Dr. Cameron. He won't be back until tomorrow. But I think he might know something about it."

McKenna slid the finished bacon onto a plate and started cooking a few more strips. "Why do you think that?" She cracked another egg and whisked the yolk in the bowl.

"Dr. Knight mentioned something that made me think so." Tristan stretched out across the couch as he pulled his shirt out of his pants. Heat rose in McKenna's cheeks as she thought about his pants. "What about you? Any luck on Lily herself?"

"No." McKenna yanked her thoughts back to the case. She

scrunched her nose. She had spent the whole day trying to piece the girl's life together but didn't get far. "No one in her family called me back, even after I left several messages. Her old roommate Sarah did, though. I'm driving out to see her tomorrow."

"Need some back up?" Tristan offered.

McKenna scrambled the eggs. "No, you have to talk to Dr. Cameron, remember?"

"Oh, yeah." He rapped his knuckles on the side of his head. "Brain is fuzzy after having a ghost pulling it out of me."

"I understand." The memory of having her insides turned outside was fresh in her mind.

She finished cooking a few minutes later. She handed Tristan a plate and sat beside him with one of her own. He shoveled eggs into his mouth. Her heart soared. He really was going to be all right.

"These are fantastic!" he said around a mouthful. "Could use some ketchup, though."

She rolled her eyes before grabbing the ketchup and bringing it back to him. Yeah, he was going to be all right. She just wanted him to stay that way.

"I think you should come home with me tonight," she said after a few bites.

Tristan's eyes twinkled. "Maybe you should stay here."

She felt his interest and smiled. "I mean for your protection."

Tristan set down his plate and scooted closer to her. "We can do both." He took the plate out of her hands, setting it on the coffee table. He tucked her hair behind her ear. Bending down, his teeth nipped at her neck.

She laughed as she pushed against his chest. He didn't budge an inch. "I'd feel better if we were at my place. Lily seems hyper focused on you right now. If I had lost…" Her throat closed as she thought about the scene she walked into.

"Hey." Tristan cradled her jaw. "I'm okay. You saved me. I'm okay."

"I know." She tried to get her emotions under control. "But I'd still like you to come home with me."

A smile slid across his sexy mouth. "Okay. Let me pack a bag."

MᶜKenna fumbled with her apartment key. Her skin flushed with heat, and her hands shook with nerves. Was she really doing this? Seeing Tristan near death brought home the fact she may not have another chance to be with him, especially since he didn't want to move out of his place. But initiating was a whole new thing. She was reserved when it came to relationships. She had a tendency to date and draw the relationship out. She kept her powers a secret until her boyfriend found out she could read their emotions. The relationships usually ended at that point.

Her keys slipped from her hands, jangling as they hit the ground. She took a deep breath and rested her palm on the door, willing herself to calm down. Tristan already knew about her empathy. Even though he denied his own abilities, he never once shied away from hers. After all, he understood what it was like to be different. The moment was right. This relationship, flirtation, or undefined feelings they had felt right. She was thinking too much.

She picked up her keys and stuck the right one in the lock. Tristan's strong arms enveloped her. She warmed at his touch as he cradled her hands in his. "Need help?"

The lock clicked. They stumbled into the apartment, shut the door. McKenna pushed Tristan against it and crushed her mouth to his. Every part of her body tingled as she drank him in. Her hands fisted in his curls. He dropped his bag on the floor.

She came up for air. "You're not sleeping down here this time." She barely registered Oscar's meow of protest as she dragged Tristan up the stairs.

A rush of excitement made its way up her spine like a white-hot lightning bolt. Tristan's breath was hot on her neck. His tongue stroked her neck as his hands reached under her shirt. "Your clothes are in my way," he mumbled. He pulled her shirt over her head and tossed it on the stairs. Her bra soon followed. She gasped as he cupped her breasts and caressed them. She leaned into him and moaned. Laughter bounced off the walls as she pulled him into the bedroom.

She took his mouth again. Spicy cinnamon danced on her tongue. She craved the taste, and pressed her body against his. She pulled back, grabbing his shirt. "This is in my way." Her fingers undid the buttons, but it was forever before she peeled off the shirt. Her eyes widened at the muscles underneath. Not what she expected from a bookish history teacher. She traced the bends and curves. She had to see more. Her hands tugged on his pants.

His eyes sparkled as his lips curved into a smile. McKenna unhooked the button and slid them off. More clothes followed. She pushed him onto her bed and straddled him. His fingers tangled in her hair, pulled and teased. His burning lust echoed inside her mind and her heart.

McKenna tossed her head back and laughed. Bending over, she nibbled on his neck. She cupped all of him and stroked. His back arched as a moan escaped his lips. She trailed kisses down his chest and stomach. He trembled under her touch.

Tristan flipped her over, her back pressing into the soft

mattress. She bit her lip, wondering what his next move would be. His curls brushed her face as he nibbled at her neck, drawing a moan from her throat as his lips and teeth toyed with the thin flesh. He growled, a low rumbled in his chest.

Taking her face in his hands, he brought her lips to his. Her lips slightly parted, welcoming him in. She melted in his arms. Everything disappeared in that moment—the ghost, the fear, all of it. All that mattered was the man in her arms. She dropped her walls, letting his emotions flood through her. Lust, love, want, confidence. They washed over her, drowning her in him.

Goosebumps prickled her skin. Her whole body tingled as her breath quickened. Her legs parted, welcoming him. He caressed her stomach, his touch light and soft. He traveled down, tracing her curves. He took a breast in his mouth, his tongue playing with the nipple. Heat raced over her body as he moved to the other breast.

She wrapped her arms and legs around him, hanging on for dear life. He slid inside, the movement becoming a rhythm. She followed the beat, clutching his curls. The beat rocked faster. She vibrated, tingles becoming intense. She climbed to the edge, hardly able to catch her breath. His name fell from her lips as each dive brought her closer and then tipped her over. Her eyes rolled back into her head. Her body shuddered as her heart quickened. Intense desire washed over her, doubling in force.

She focused on Tristan, drops of sweat on his brow. His eyes were the most vibrant green slits. They closed as he emptied into her. His need joined hers, and she had no doubt about how he felt. Love and lust drifted from him in a heated wave. She brushed his hair back, and he opened his eyes.

She snuggled in the crook of his neck while he played

with her hair. Every one of her muscles relaxed. She could hardly move. Sighing, she pressed into him.

"I like you when you lose control," McKenna said.

Tristan chuckled. "Maybe I should lose control more often."

Between his steady heartbeat and the heat of his skin, she drifted off to sleep.

## 21

Tristan awoke to an empty bed. He rolled over, breathing in the salty scent of the ocean. He smiled as he remembered the night before. He wanted to do it again, but the woman was nowhere to be found. Groaning, he glanced at the clock through bleary eyes, amazed he was awake so early. He rose up on his elbows to see the judgmental green eyes of McKenna's large gray and white cat.

"Morning, Oscar." The cat stretched out his head and allowed Tristan to pet him. He stroked the soft fur before peeling back the covers.

The warm, buttery smell of pancakes greeted him as he trudged downstairs. He found McKenna standing in the kitchen, flipping cakes on the griddle. Her hair tangled at the ends, and her faded blue t-shirt had small holes in it. She looked like a goddess. Sneaking behind her, he wrapped his arms around her waist. She giggled.

"I'm getting another home cooked meal?" he asked.

"As long as you don't mind breakfast food again. Breakfast is my specialty." McKenna gave him a quick kiss on the lips.

"I think I can live with that."

This time, they sat at the table. Tristan drenched his stack of pancakes in syrup and savored the first gooey, sweet bite. "Best I've ever had."

McKenna smirked at him. "I bet you wouldn't say that to your mother."

Tristan popped in another bite. "Not if I value my life."

She studied him while she munched her breakfast. "Tristan, I have a theory about you."

"A theory?" Tristan froze in mid-chew. Her tone had a 'we need to talk' vibe. He sat back and carefully finished eating.

"Yeah, a theory." She sipped from her coffee mug. Leaning back in her chair, she continued, "I think you can control your powers better than you think you can."

Tristan set down his knife and fork. He swallowed the first flash of anger. No use in getting defensive. "Where did you get that idea?"

McKenna smiled. "It's something I've been thinking about since you found the bow."

Tristan raised an eyebrow but didn't say anything. He rubbed the back of his neck. Change the subject. Talk about the weather. Compliment her pajamas. Anything!

McKenna continued. "You found the bow using your powers." She pointed at him with her fork. "You saw Lily in your office. Yet, you didn't lose control, not like you did at the apartment. You can do it on instinct."

Tristan's appetite vanished. Discussing his powers was something he definitely didn't want to do after the fantastic night they had had together. *Distract her*, he thought, but his mind was blank. He tore tiny pieces off the top layer of his pancakes. "Yeah, I can only do it for a little bit, though." Admitting that was harder than he thought, especially since he didn't want to acknowledge anything about his powers. His right leg started to bounce under the table. "I try to keep my shields up all the time, but sometimes, past events sneak in, and I can't stop them. But they come in bits and pieces so I guess they don't overwhelm me." He shifted. "Can we talk about something else?"

McKenna moved her chair closer to him. "You get scared when you drop your shields all the way." She touched his arm. "You don't have to be afraid anymore."

"Mac, I put my cousin in the hospital." His jaw twitched.

She sighed. "Is that the only time you lost control?"

He wiped his sticky hands. "No. It happened the first time when I was eleven."

"And you've carried that with you for fourteen years. I think if you practice with me, you could learn enough control to see something." She touched his cheek, turning his head.

Tristan jerked away. "I bruised you and kicked Kayla, Drew, and Tabitha. It's too dangerous."

She straightened. "Doesn't matter. I brought you back. Together, we can do this."

Tristan pushed away from the table and sprang to his feet. "I know, but what if you're not there the next time?" He gripped the back of the chair. "My focus is terrible. I can't see what I want. I can only see what it wants to show me." His knuckles whitened.

McKenna jumped up. "It's not an 'it.' Not a separate entity. It's you, a part of you. A part of you that you can learn to control. Why are you fighting me on this?"

Tristan knocked the chair forward. It hit the edge of the table with a loud thwack. Everything inside him told him to run, and he listened. He grabbed his bag from the couch. "I've got to go. I'll be late. What do I do if Dr. Cameron knows anything?"

"You're changing the subject on me?" McKenna jutted her chin out. Her eyes flashed.

"Mac, I'm going to keep ignoring *it* like I've always ignored *it*." He stuffed his clothes from yesterday into the open bag. "Now, Dr. Cameron."

McKenna stared at him, an expression of disbelief evident on her face. Her mouth drew a thin line as she ground out her reply. "Ask him to come to your apartment tonight. Maybe he can reach Lily and send her on."

"Thank you." He stalked up the stairs to change.

Footsteps pounded behind him. "Oh, no, you don't." McKenna grabbed his hand and held on tight. "I won't let you give up on this."

He whirled on her. "Why do you care? Is it so you can avenge your brother's death faster? What?"

The slap was quick and sharp, a loud pop in the quiet room. Tristan stumbled back, his mouth slightly open. McKenna's eyes were blue ice. She turned away from him and marched back down the stairs.

He swore under his breath as he cradled his stinging cheek.

～

McKenna gritted her teeth. Last night had been a mistake. The whole thing had been a mistake. She had shared all of herself with him, trusted him as she wanted him to trust her. But it wasn't meant to be. He couldn't even trust himself and his power. She yanked the wheel to the right, narrowly missing her turn.

*The ghost can have him*, she thought. The angry part of her wanted to turn the car around and head back to her apartment. If he didn't want to help her, then why should she help him?

A memory of her brother chasing her through the woods near their childhood home sprang into her mind. She wasn't doing this solely for Tristan. Condemning the other men in that apartment because she was pissed off wasn't the answer. Her grip tightened on the steering wheel. One selfish untrained psychic wasn't going to stop her.

She focused her attention on the upcoming interview as she pulled into Sarah Bell's driveway. She gathered her things, straightened her back, and climbed out of the car. So much more was going on than her relationship with Tristan. She had spent the whole drive stewing and her shoulders tightened painfully as a result. She rolled her head back and forth.

"Forget about him," she mumbled. "You've got more important things to do."

Mrs. Bell's house was bigger than she imagined. It was a three-story cottage that hung off the side of the mountain. A clear view of Grandfather Mountain added to the breathtaking beauty of it. The shape of a nose and a beard in the distance was visible even on a cloudy day.

McKenna knocked.

A short woman with chopped, chin-length dark blonde hair greeted her. Her hazel eyes shone as she led McKenna inside. "Welcome!" she exclaimed as she introduced herself. "Let's sit in the sunroom."

McKenna relaxed as she followed Mrs. Bell through the organized and neat house. She felt like she had stepped into the pages of *House Beautiful*. Pictures of family and paintings of the mountains lined the short hallway. Mrs. Bell made a left turn, and McKenna found herself in a room full of windows. The Blue Ridge Mountains spread out before her.

She gasped. "This is amazing." Her fight with Tristan was forgotten.

"Thank you." Mrs. Bell beamed. "I designed it myself."

McKenna sat in a cushioned white wicker chair. A pitcher

of sweet tea rested on the small coffee table in front of her. Mrs. Bell took the other chair.

"I have to say I was rather surprised when you called." Mrs. Bell poured a glass of tea. "I haven't thought about Lily in years. That must make me a terrible friend." A hint of sadness settled over McKenna as the older woman held the glass out to her. "Would you like some?"

"Thank you." McKenna drank some before placing it in front of her. "And, no, I don't think it makes you a terrible friend."

Mrs. Bell chuckled. "I hope not. I spearheaded most of the searches after she disappeared. We never did find any evidence of what happened to her." She stared out at the mountains, the melancholy hovering in the air.

McKenna leaned on the arm of the chair. "Do you remember anything about the day she went missing, Mrs. Bell?"

"Please, call me Sarah." She took a deep breath. "As if it were yesterday." Sarah fiddled with the end of her dress. "Lily had been depressed for a couple of weeks. She wouldn't talk to me or go to class. I threatened to make her see a counselor. She ignored me." A corner of her mouth curved up. "But that night, she seemed to come alive. She had a piece of paper in her hand, and she was dressed and ready to go. I had a part time job at K-Mart at the time and was coming in from my shift. All she said was, 'Bye,' as she ran out the door."

"Did anyone find the piece of paper?"

"No. I didn't even know where she was going. She was just gone." Sarah raised her hands helplessly.

McKenna sipped more of her tea, letting the information sink in. It was clear Lily was meeting someone that night, but who? "Did she ever mention a boyfriend?"

Sarah smoothed her skirt. "She told me she met someone

over the summer while she was taking summer classes, and that it was a big secret."

McKenna leaned forward. "Did she tell you his name?"

"No. Apparently, I wasn't allowed to know the secret. But she said she was going to marry him, and they were going to live happily ever after." Sarah's eyes found the mountains again. "I tried to get her to tell me, but she wouldn't. Said she would when we graduated."

"Was she ever scared of anybody?"

Sarah fidgeted in her chair. Unable to stay still, she walked to the window. "You're asking the same kind of questions the police did years ago." She turned. "What new information have you found? Why is an investigator interested in a twenty-year-old missing person's case?" The color drained out of her face as her fear smacked into McKenna. "Oh, God. Did somebody find her body?"

"No." McKenna joined her at the window, projecting calm. "It's nothing like that." The truth was on the tip of her tongue. A laptop with the footage sat in her bag, waiting to be shown. But feeling Sarah's devastation made McKenna hesitate. What good would it do to share footage of a soul who wasn't her best friend anymore? It would be cruel.

She chose a different tactic. "There's an apartment building near the Blackwood campus. It was built in the woods where everybody used to hang out."

Sarah nodded. "I remember them building it."

"Well, someone found a bow that might have belonged to Lily on the ground." McKenna stumbled through the lie. Even though she knew it was wrong, she projected as much trustworthiness as she could.

Sarah's shoulders relaxed. Her face beamed. "Evidence that she didn't run away?"

"Possibly."

"But why are you here instead of the police?"

Good question. McKenna nibbled on her bottom lip. "I'm...I'm one of the investigators. Like I told you on the phone." Thank goodness she hadn't told Sarah she was a paranormal investigator. There were times to tell the truth and times to omit it. She changed the subject. "Sarah, what do you remember about Lily's personality?"

Tears pricked the corners of Sarah's eyes. "Lily was great. She was wild, open, friendly. Funny." She laughed a little. "I was the shy one, always wanting to stay in my room. Lily wouldn't let me. We spent three years tearing through campus like we didn't have anything to lose."

With Sarah back on topic, McKenna went back to her original question. "Did anyone scare Lily? Make her nervous?"

"You mean, did anyone want to hurt her?" Sarah sat back down and rested her hands in her lap. Her brow wrinkled as she tried to remember. "A week after we started our senior year, she did seem jumpy. She was happy about the guy she was seeing, but flowers came to our dorm, and they didn't seem to be from her mysterious boyfriend. They were never signed."

"Anything else?"

Sarah shook her head. "That's about it. I'm sorry. We didn't talk that much the last year." McKenna recognized regret coming from the older woman. "I wish I had made more time."

McKenna held out her hand. "Her disappearance wasn't your fault. I hope you know that."

"I know. I only wish I'd had more time with her."

McKenna shook her hand. "Thank you for your time, Mrs. Bell."

Sarah led her back to the door. "Let me know if the evidence leads to something. Twenty years is a long time not knowing what became of your best friend."

∾

W hy did she have to push? Tristan groused, replaying the conversation in his head. He had a tentative grip on his sanity as it was. He'd been lucky to come back the last few times. What if this vision shoved him over the edge?

Find out more about Lily and her affair at the college? Sure. Pay attention to any psychic images that might push their way through? Yes. But trying to will a picture of the past and letting everything in at once? No. He wasn't going to try again, not after the last time. His ability was too erratic.

The look of disappointment on McKenna's face almost did him in. He wanted to be with her, to touch her, to have her believe in him, to turn those beautiful blue eyes his way. He wouldn't let it cost him his sanity, though, and that was a problem.

He rubbed his cheek. It was still red from where she hit him. He deserved that, and he wished he could take back those words. He let out a breath. Maybe starting something with McKenna was too much. She wanted a part of him that he couldn't give. Maybe it was the only part of him she cared about. It would probably be easier to say good-bye once all of this was over.

Tristan ignored his fight with McKenna as he tracked down Dr. Cameron. He found the department head settling into his office. Thank God the man was back. If he was connected, he might be able to stop Lily. And then Tristan could put both the ghost and the empath behind him.

"Dr. Cameron?"

Cameron glanced up from his desk. He smiled when he saw Tristan standing in his doorway and waved him inside. His eyes had dark circles under them, but he seemed to be in better spirits than he was several days before. "Mr. Johnson, what can I do for you?"

Tristan stepped inside and closed the door. His heart pounded in his ears. If Cameron didn't recognize the bow, then he was out of leads. And he had to find a way to stop The White Lady before she killed her next victim. He slid into the chair in front of the desk, sucking in a deep breath.

"I need to ask you something, sir." Tristan retrieved the yellow hair bow, placing it on the desk between them. "Do you recognize this?"

The air in the room went completely still. Cameron rubbed a hand over his face as he studied the hair accessory. Tears shone in his eyes. He picked it up, turning every angle to the light.

Tristan didn't know what to say. He had never seen such a tender expression on the older professor's face. His legs bounced under the desk.

Cameron glanced at Tristan. "Lily Comer."

"You knew her?" His legs stilled as he straightened.

"I did." Cameron sat back in his black leather chair. "I forgot all about this. Where did you find it?"

Tristan sank back into his seat. "In my desk, sir."

"It was locked in a secret space in one of the drawers. I remember now." Cameron shook his head. "I should've come back for it, but life got in the way."

Tristan chose to stick to the lie. "The drawer kept rattling and I got curious."

Cameron heaved a sigh. "Lily was one of my students. She was bright, beautiful, had such a future ahead of her. Even though I knew it was wrong, I fell in love with her the summer before her senior year. We started meeting out in the woods, right in the area where they were building Hidden Forest. At night, hardly anyone went near the construction site, so it was perfect. It would've been bad for both of us if someone had seen us. Teachers and students aren't supposed to have affairs.

"Then as the weeks went on, we became more daring. Started meeting in the classroom that became your office. Everything would have been fine if Dr. Knight hadn't caught us. He was working late that night, and tore into me. Said it wasn't professional." Dr. Cameron's fingers caressed the hair bow. "He was right, of course.

"I begged him not to tell anyone. My career meant the world to me, and if Lily could just hang on, we could go public when she graduated." He set the bow down. "I broke it off with her. Told her to wait until graduation. She was so angry, said she never wanted to see me again." Cameron's eyes were solemn.

"I heard she disappeared."

Cameron ran a hand over his face. "I heard that, too. One day, she stopped coming to class. No one could find her. Her stuff was still in her dorm room so I don't think she left school."

Tristan shifted. He ignored his nerves and asked the direct question. "Do you know what happened to her?"

"No." Cameron shook his head. "I kept expecting the police to show up at my door at any minute to ask questions, but they never came. She must have hidden our secret well." He wiped his eyes. "I loved her and would have made her happy."

If McKenna had been there, she would be able to tell if he were lying. But Tristan was there alone. He didn't expect Cameron to come out and say he killed her, but part of him wanted to believe the man was telling the truth.

"Thank you for telling me." Tristan cleared his throat and launched into the next part. "You're going to think I'm crazy, but I think Lily is The White Lady of Hidden Forest."

Cameron lifted an eyebrow. "The ghost the students tell stories about?"

"Yes, sir. You might be able to help stop her."

"Mr. Johnson, I don't think…"

"At least meet the paranormal investigators who are looking into her. We could use your help." Tristan winced. It sounded crazy even to his ears.

Cameron touched the bow one more time. He was silent so long that Tristan gathered his bag, preparing to be thrown out. The older man lifted his hazel eyes. "Fine. I'll hear you out."

## 22

The end was near. Tristan felt it in his bones. If this worked, and he really hoped it worked, The White Lady would be gone forever. No more random deaths. The tenants living in the building ten years in the future wouldn't have to worry about a murderous ghost. Best of all, he could put all things supernatural behind him, and possibly let McKenna go.

Activity buzzed around the apartment as the sun set outside. Drew set a tripod, a camera nestled on top of it, in the middle of the living room. He said that he wanted to catch the moment the ghost moved on. Aaron and Tabitha checked and rechecked their handheld EMF readers, ready to take measurements of the activity. Dr. Cameron told McKenna about his history with Lily.

The older man hunched his shoulders as he spoke. "I knew better than to pursue her. She was a student. I was a teacher." He beamed, lost in the memory. "But there was something special about her."

"You didn't know what would happen to her when you let

her go, Dr. Cameron." McKenna sat on the end of the couch, her hands folded in her lap.

"That's the thing." Cameron rubbed his face. "I should've never let her go." He scooted to the edge of his seat. "Don't get me wrong. I love my wife and my children. They brought me back from the black period I went through after Lily disappeared. But so many things would be different." He laid a hand on McKenna's shoulder. "If all of this is true, your brother would still be alive."

McKenna started. "How did you know?"

"Tristan told me."

McKenna narrowed her eyes at Tristan. "Some people should mind their own business." The fading light outside gave her a golden halo. Her smile was warm and genuine, but her expression went cold every time she caught Tristan looking at her.

Tristan pulled his gaze away from her and went back to helping Drew and Kayla set up the equipment.

Drew glanced from his best friend to his co-worker. "What did you do to her, man?"

"I didn't do anything." Tristan stuck his hands in his pockets, feeling like a heel.

"You did something. I've never seen Mac this pissed."

Kayla glanced from the laptop screen. She studied Tristan for a few minutes. "Stop being a dumbass and apologize."

"It's not my fault."

She sighed. "That doesn't matter. It's always your fault."

Tristan clamped down on his temper. "Let's just worry about this, okay. The sooner it's over, the better."

Drew arched an eyebrow as he snapped the camera into place and turned it on. "Ready!"

Cameron stood and wiped his hands on his pants. "I don't even know what I'm supposed to do."

McKenna touched his arm. "Just be yourself. Tell her everything you wish you'd had the chance to tell her."

"You're going to be fine, sir," Tristan added as he crossed to them.

Aaron moved to the left side of the room. "Start talking whenever you're ready."

Tabitha nodded as she took the right side of the room. She tossed a small bag of salt to each person. "Stay calm. Use these if things get out of hand."

Cameron cleared his throat. McKenna nodded encouragement, and he addressed the air. "Lily, I don't know if you can hear me or even if you're really here." He walked around the coffee table, his hands in his pockets. "I don't even know what happened to you the night you disappeared. All I know is I shouldn't have let you go."

The lights blinked.

McKenna gave Cameron's arm a squeeze. "Keep going."

"When I first met you in the hall, I thought you were the most beautiful girl I'd ever seen." Cameron's voice gained strength. "You didn't look like anybody else, and I loved that about you. I probably shouldn't have approached you, shouldn't have asked to see you after class, but I couldn't help it. I had to know you." He kicked out his foot and sauntered to the center of the room.

Tristan noticed his breath puff out in tiny clouds. He shrugged into his jacket, bracing himself for what was coming.

"I'm going to have to let you go again, Lily. It's time to move on and find peace." Cameron's voice grew stronger with every word.

Everything plunged into darkness. Cold air kissed Tristan's face. The fine hairs on the back of his neck stood on end. She was coming. He knew the signs by heart. He concentrated on making his psychic walls impenetrable.

"Should I...should I keep talking?" Cameron asked.

"Yes. Don't be afraid," McKenna answered. A reassuring calm fell over the room.

"Lily, I miss you every day. I wish to God I'd handled things differently." Cameron's voice rang through the darkness. "Forgive me and be free, please."

A white glow appeared to Tabitha's right. She stumbled back as she raised her EMF detector. Tristan wasn't sure what the numbers indicated, but Tabitha seemed pleased. The light reshaped itself into the familiar form of The White Lady. Her features were impassive as her eerie green eyes studied the room. She moved from Tabitha to Cameron in the blink of an eye.

The older man gasped but held his ground. "Dear God, it is you." He seemed to pale in her unearthly glow.

The White Lady cocked her head to the side. "You have to pay." She clutched his shirt and lifted him off the ground.

Tristan didn't think. He threw the contents of his salt bag at the ghost. White grains fell through the air. She dropped Cameron and separated into fragments. The white wisps swirled and reformed behind him. She grabbed him once again.

Cameron whirled around and held up a hand. "No." He kept his eyes on the ghost. "I always wondered where you went. Why you left. I was going to make it up to you. After you graduated, I was going to come back."

She didn't give any indication that she understood his words. Her eyes flashed red. "You have to pay."

Salt flew from all directions. The grains stung when they hit Tristan's skin. The White Lady screamed. She split apart and loosened her grip. Cameron fell to the floor.

"Dr. Cameron!" Tristan rushed forward, but the older man waved him off.

"I'm all right."

The ghost reformed at the other end of the room. Her cold eyes swept the area, landing on Tristan.

"Sir, did you have anything to do with her death?" Tristan asked. He helped the older man to his feet, but his gaze was glued to The White Lady.

Cameron watched the ghost. "No. I didn't even know she was dead. I swear."

"Sarah said Lily had gotten a letter the day she died. Did you send one?" McKenna asked.

"No. No, I never sent any letter."

The White Lady bared her teeth and blinked away. Darkness and silence were left in her wake.

Tristan searched the room, barely able to see anything. "Is that it?" Before anyone could answer, a block of ice plunged into his back. All the breath left his lungs as the cold spread through every part of his body. Walls! He had to steady his walls. His control slipped, and with it, all of the bricks of his mental shield tumbled down. She ripped through his mind as if he were made of paper. The pulling sensation started. No, *yanking*. This time, The White Lady had no patience. Tristan hit his knees, his vision going dim.

Everything happened at once. Aaron shouted orders, but the words sounded like gibberish. Small grains hit his back. No effect. The White Lady had taken most of his energy.

Tired. He was so tired. If only they'd let him sleep. Please, let him sleep. He slumped on the floor. Cold. So cold.

Out of the corner of his eye, he saw Drew charge the ghost. He tried to yell, to warn his friend. The ghost plucked Drew out of the air. She held him suspended for a moment. It seemed so much longer. She then slammed him through the coffee table with a loud crash.

"Drew!" McKenna's voice rang out. She moved to help. The ghost sent a gust of wind and pushed her back against the wall.

"More, now!" Aaron barked.

More salt rained over him, covering his back and hair. The ghost screamed. The block of ice pulled out of his back. Tristan fell forward, and his eyelids slid closed.

A steady, loud-pitched sound pushed its way through Tristan's consciousness. He blinked open his eyes and a bright, white world came into view. Objects came into slow focus. A streetlight shone through the window to his right. A machine beside him with a black screen and green squiggly lines beeped. A small instrument pinched his forefinger while a slender tube sent liquid into his arm. Inane chatter came from the TV above him. His back was nestled into a soft mattress. He pulled the sheets and a blanket up to his chin.

*Where am I? How did I get here?* He struggled to remember the events leading up to this. Freezing cold. All of his energy drained out of him. The White Lady ripping him apart and knocking down his friends with ease.

"Drew? McKenna?" He bolted upright. Pain exploded in his head and he sank back down against the pillows.

"Tristan, I'm right here." McKenna appeared beside the bed, her eyes impossibly blue. A black and blue bruise bloomed on her cheek.

He caressed it. "You're hurt."

She touched his hand. "I'm okay. She went after you first."

"Everybody else?"

"Aaron and Tabitha were able to get Dr. Cameron out. They're all fine. Drew tried to jump between you and The White Lady. She cracked his ribs." The memory of Drew crashing through the coffee table came back to him.

Dread pooled in his stomach. "Kayla?"

"She's fine. She has a few scratches that she's been showing off to the hospital staff." McKenna settled into a chair. "We used up all of the salt we brought, but we managed to take the ghost down." She laughed a little. "I've never seen anyone attack the way Kayla attacked that ghost. That woman has no fear."

As if on cue, Kayla peeked into the room. "Is he awake?"

"Yeah. His color is coming back."

Kayla walked in and pushed up the sleeve of her shirt. Scratches covered her arm. "I gave her as good as I got," she beamed.

Tristan opened his mouth to answer her, but no sound came out. The room shifted and changed around him. He sucked in a breath through his gritted teeth when images of past visitors of the hospital room assaulted his brain. An accident victim with painful head trauma who didn't make it. A little girl wailing with a broken arm. A man with something sharp stuck in his foot. He shut eyes and grabbed his head.

Cool fingers touched his forehead, and he relaxed. The people faded into the background, their voices muting. The simple touch kept the images from overwhelming him. "Think about your wall, Tristan," McKenna said evenly.

He pictured the brick wall, the familiar mental structure sliding into place. The visions receded along with the pain in his head. With McKenna keeping him relaxed, he strengthened it with ease. The shadows of the past vanished.

Air whooshed out of his lungs as he smiled. "Thank you."

"You're welcome."

Kayla cleared her throat. "Well, I'll go check on Drew. Need any coffee, McKenna?"

"No. I'm good." McKenna continued to look at Tristan.

With a wave, Kayla left the room.

Tristan held McKenna's hand, not wanting to let go.

"Look, I'm sorry for snapping at you. I shouldn't have assumed..."

"No," McKenna interrupted. "When I think about something, I tend to push. I'm sorry for beating the dead horse."

"But you're right. Tonight didn't have to happen. If I wasn't so damn afraid, Drew wouldn't be in the hospital." He took in the equipment surrounding him. "I wouldn't be in the hospital." The tube in his arm pulled as he tried to sit up. He started at the quick jab of pain. "Will the nurses let me see him?" More guilt to pile on to his conscience.

McKenna patted his hand. "I don't know. Let me ask." She stood. "And stop feeling guilty. It wasn't your fault." She touched his chin. "None of this is your fault."

After proving to the nurse he could sit without slumping over, she helped him into a wheelchair. Gripping the moveable metal pole that held his bag of fluids, Tristan settled into the seat. McKenna thanked the nurse and pushed him out.

"Now, he doesn't look so good, and I'm not sure he's awake yet," McKenna warned.

"Doesn't matter. I have to see him for myself."

A sliver of guilt stabbed him in the chest when he saw Drew lying in the hospital bed. Bruises covered his face. His right eye was swelling, and it would probably be black and blue in a few days. Tristan touched his friend's hand. His fault. Drew wouldn't be here if he hadn't been in the room. The White Lady had gotten past his shields so easily. Why wasn't he able to hold them?

The pain of losing Zack returned. Tristan fought back the tears that sprang to his eyes. With everything that had occurred over the past two weeks, Tristan and Drew hadn't had a chance to reconnect. Drew had always been there for him, always stood up to the bullies, and kept an eye on him when he started seeing visions. He was a friend who was the first to act. Hell, if he had had the psychic powers, Drew wouldn't have hesitated.

He didn't look like himself lying silently in the hospital bed. His Duke hat was missing, and he wasn't running his mouth about a computer or a piece of equipment. God, Tristan wanted him to wake up and start telling him what an idiot he was.

He glanced around at Aaron, Tabitha, Kayla, and McKenna. No one said a word, but he was pretty sure they were all thinking the same thing. How could this happen? Dr. Cameron was the key. He was the only connection they had to Lily. But the man only made her angrier. He may not have killed her, but the ghost must have thought he sent her the letter. A letter that possibly led to her death. He was one of the three men she sought.

Three men. Mr. Martin and Dr. Cameron knew each other. If Mr. Martin was one of the three that made two that were identified. But who was the third? Tristan thought back to the professors he spoke to. He remembered the picture in Dr. Smith's office. Both Mr. Martin and Dr. Cameron were in that picture. The killer could have been in that picture, too. But who was it? No more leads appeared. He was at a dead end.

He slumped in the wheelchair.

"Tristan?" McKenna's hand slipped into his. Without saying a word, he pulled her into a hug.

"You're reading me again, aren't you?" he whispered in her ear.

"Kind of hard not to. I told you to stop feeling guilty. It's not your fault."

He let go of her. No matter what she said, it felt like it was his fault. The ghost had used him to kill one of his best friends and attempted to kill another one. He had to do something. He had to stop this. No more being afraid. Dr.

Cameron had been a dead end, but someone had sent that note to Lily all those years ago. Someone had killed her. And finding that killer was the only way to stop this. He looked into McKenna's eyes. "I have to see something. Tonight."

"Tristan, you have to stay the rest of the night. It's okay. Drew is safe."

He studied the sleeping body of his best friend. "And the poor guy who could lose his life next?" He gripped the arm of the chair.

"It's better if you're not in the apartment." Aaron pushed away from the wall.

"We don't know that. She took a hell of a lot of energy. She may be ready tonight. Hell, he might already be dead."

Kayla turned away from the window. "He's right. It doesn't look like she cares about a pattern anymore."

Tristan tightened his grip on McKenna's hand. "Come with me. Teach me how to connect with the bow. You said it might work if I have an object to focus on. I'm ready to try."

They were quiet for a moment. McKenna glanced around the room, but no one protested. She tucked a strand of dark hair behind her ear. She didn't have to agree to do this. He was thankful she was there at all. It made everything a little better.

"Tonight's the night," he tried again.

"I'll make you a deal. Rest tonight. In the morning, I'll take you back to the apartment, and we can try."

"We might be too late." He took a deep breath, the fear creeping up the back of his neck.

"Tristan, it's almost morning. Rest for a few more hours. You don't have the strength right now."

He scowled. "In the morning then." Kayla's dark eyes watched him, and he nodded to her. "This has to end."

## 23

In the breaking dawn, Hidden Forest Apartments had a larger than life feel. The brick building was eerier and more intimidating than it had been the night before. It rose out of the woods, tall and imposing. A couple of people dotted the parking lot, climbing into their cars or heading into the building. No police cars were among them. Tristan blew out a sigh of relief.

He stood at the threshold of the outer doors. He rubbed the back of his neck, his breakfast threatening to spill all over the sidewalk. Both Karie's house in Wilmington and Zack's apartment sprang to his mind. What if this didn't work? What if he lost control again?

Then that would be it. The White Lady would kill someone else. Ten years would go by, and three more men would die. The cycle would keep going. If Tristan's sight failed him, then he would fail her future victims.

"Where do you want to go?" McKenna's voice was soft.

Tristan swallowed. "She died here when it was only woods." He faced her. "Let's go into the woods."

McKenna's brow wrinkled. "I thought you said your visions were weaker outside?"

"They are. But you mentioned trying to connect to an object, right?"

"I did."

"Then I'm taking the bow to the woods."

McKenna pulled the yellow hair accessory out of her bag and handed it to Tristan. He lifted his eyebrows in surprise.

She shrugged. "I grabbed it on the way out of your apartment. Thought we might need it."

Leaves and sticks crunched under their feet as they left the sidewalk and walked into the woods. Sunlight peeked through the trees, burning off the morning chill. Cars rumbled down the street behind them while birds sang in the trees. Tristan ignored the sounds and concentrated on the task ahead of him.

He clutched the bow in his hand, careful not to break it. It was a link now, a link to a scared, heartbroken young woman. He tried to recall what she looked like in the visions he had had in his office. She had been happy, intelligent, and full of plans for the future. He held onto that image when they reached a clearing.

"Here," he said.

"Okay." McKenna stood at the edge.

He squeezed her hand before stepping into the center of the small space.

"If anything goes wrong, I'll be here." McKenna wrapped her jacket tighter around herself. "Focus on the bow, nothing else."

Tristan stopped halfway across. The bow seemed to vibrate in his hand. This was right. He winked at McKenna, and then closed his eyes and concentrated on the bow. Smooth fabric rested in his palm, the ruffled edges rough to the touch. The back clip was smooth and cool, a light metal. He thought about Lily—the picture of the smiling young woman and the terrifying spirit with a blank expression. Dark hair fell past her shoulders. Her large green eyes were the same in both incarnations. Tristan opened his mental brick walls.

*He was coming. Lily read over the words in the letter one more time, her heart pounding. The circle of light from the flashlight in her hand shook.*

*'Dear Lily, Meet me in the woods tonight at 10.'*

*No signature. That was fine. She knew who wrote it.*

*She threw her hand back and laughed, a delighted sound that echoed off the dark trees. The crickets and frogs answered her with their steady chirps. She twirled, the leaves crunching under her feet. She wanted to dance, to sing, to shout from the treetops. Everything was going to be all right. She crushed the note to her chest.*

*When Ian had broken up with her, she thought she'd never laugh again. Without him, there was no joy, no love, nothing. She was a crumbled mess. But he was coming back to her. Against all the rules, he was coming back to her.*

*Maybe they wouldn't have to stay in Asheville? Maybe Ian would take her by the hand, and they would run away together. Go somewhere where no one knew them. They could start over, get married, and have a family. A fancy white dress and a big ceremony weren't important. What mattered was that he wanted her as a wife.*

*Closing her eyes, she could almost see their future. A big green house out in the middle of nowhere. Kids with Ian's hazel eyes and her dark hair running around in the yard. Maybe they would play with a dog. No, two dogs.*

*She smoothed her hair and straightened the simple blue dress she had chosen. She hardly ever wore it, only for special occasions. And this was a special occasion.*

*A twig snapped. Lily jumped, her whole body alert. She whirled, running towards the sound. "Ian!" She skidded to a halt when someone stepped into her circle of light.*

*Not Ian, but another one of the professors. She couldn't remember his name. He had started working at Blackwood the year before, but she never took any of his classes. She had run errands for him when she ran errands for the other professors, but they had never been alone together. His blue eyes brightened. She took a step back.*

*"You came?" He inched closer.*

*"You're not Ian."*

*He shook his head, shaggy blond hair swishing with the move-ment. It was lighter than Ian's. His chin was covered with blond stubble, a light trace of a beard. "No, I'm not. But you came anyway."*

*Her hope vanished. Her stomach twisted with nerves, but she refused to show it. She clutched the flashlight. "You wrote the letter?"*

*"I did. You see, Lily." He took another step towards her. His build was stockier than Ian's. Oh, who was he? "I've been wanting to talk to you since last year." He rubbed his hands together. "I watched you whenever you were in the building. I love the way you light up a room when you walk into it." He touched her hair.*

*She jerked away. His eyes were feverish, too bright. He licked his lips.*

*"Well, thank you." It took all of her effort to keep her voice steady. "I have homework to do so I'll see you around." She headed back the way she had come.*

*He grabbed her arm, squeezing it. She yelped in pain as she dropped her flashlight. "How can you love him, Lily? How can you love him and not me?" he asked.*

*Lily struggled against his hold. "Let me go." She kicked his legs, hit his arm with her free hand. He caught her other arm. Her leg swung out, kicking him in the groin. His hold loosened as he swore.*

*She ran through the dark woods. Branches scratched her face and arms. She ran blindly, unable to find the path back to campus. She ran until her muscles throbbed and her lungs threatened to burst open.*

*"Lily!" The man's voice boomed behind her.*

*She pressed on, her heart in her throat. Why hadn't she told Sarah where she was? Stupid, stupid, stupid. Tears pricked at her eyes. If only Ian hadn't let her go, she wouldn't be running from a strange man in the woods. Her chest heaved as she tried to catch her breath.*

*"Lily, don't run from me. We can be together."*

*She glanced behind her to see the light from his flashlight bobbing closer to her. He could see her, but she couldn't see him. She screamed as loud as she could.*

*"Someone help me, please!"*

*The frame of the new apartment building appeared through the trees. Lights lit the area. It was a skeleton of a building, but maybe it had places to hide. With a renewed burst of energy, she ran for it.*

*Hope blossomed in her chest when she saw a lone worker driving a nail into one of the frames.*

*"Help me! Please!"*

*He turned at her voice. Dark curls spilled out from under his hat. He dropped the hammer and ran to her.*

*"What is it?" he asked, his dark eyes filled with concern.*

*Lily tried to catch her breath. "Please, you've got to help me. This guy is chasing me."*

*The man looked over her shoulder. "What guy?"*

*"Paul, you really shouldn't be here at night." Lily's eyes widened when she saw the young professor standing behind the construction worker. He hit Paul in the back of the legs with a beam. Paul crumbled to the ground.*

*Lily screamed. Paul struggled to get up, but the professor hit him on the head with the beam. He was out cold.*

*Lily ran. The campus's lights poured through the trees. She was so close.*

*The man yanked her hair, pulling her to the ground. They rolled and tumbled into the open foundation.*

*"Oh, Lily, can't you see we're meant to be? Ian broke your heart, didn't he?" the man growled. Light glinted off his blond hair, making him look like a demented angel. He climbed on top of her. His big hands held down her shoulders. "He tossed you aside like tissue paper. He's already moved on to the next girl."*

*Lily struggled against him. Fear knotted in her stomach, her heart banging in her ears. His heft settled on her chest. Her breath came in shallow gasps as she pushed against him. She panted, begged for air. He was an immoveable rock. "You're lying. I don't even know who you are."*

*His eyes darkened. "But you do know who I am. We saw each other every day last year." He gritted his teeth. "You have to know me."*

*Tears streamed down her face. "I don't. Please, let me go."*

*He let go of one of her arms and slapped her. "If you'd love me, I wouldn't have to hurt you." Her cheek stung.*

*Lily bucked underneath him. She had to get away, get help. She heard a groan above her. Paul! He had to help. She breathed in, preparing to scream. She didn't get the chance. Big hands wrapped around her throat and squeezed.*

*Lily scratched and clawed at his hands, trying to get air. Her sight dimmed. Breathe! She had to breathe! Paul's head appeared at the edge of the foundation. He watched, not making a move to help her. She fought until she had no energy left. She needed energy to fight. She had to fight. The world went dark.*

"Breathe! Breathe, Tristan!" Cool hands touched his head. He fought against them, shoving against the weight on his chest. Blue eyes swam into view, but these weren't hard and full of anger. These eyes were soft and worried. McKenna, not Lily's killer. He wasn't Lily, and he wasn't dying.

Tristan panted as the vision broke apart. Sunlight, not a harsh artificial light, gave McKenna a soft halo. He blinked against the sudden illumination. The panic receded as he lay still. One deep breath, and another. He pictured his shields sliding back into place, pushing out Lily's past.

McKenna brushed damp curls off his forehead. "That's it, breathe. You're okay, Tristan. You're okay." The calm he felt came from her. He hung on to it until he was breathing normally again.

∼

McKenna closed her eyes and took a deep breath. She focused on staying relaxed, sending all that energy to Tristan. But a corner of her mind panicked. For a long moment, she almost couldn't pull him out of the vision. When he stopped breathing, she thought she had lost him.

Tristan seemed fine through most of the vision. He circled the edge of the clearing, the bow clutched in his hand. His jaw had clenched and his eyes darted back and forth under his eyelids. Almost as if he were dreaming. Suddenly, he had dropped to his knees, the bow flying away from him.

"No!" It was the first sound he made.

McKenna ran to his side in a flash. She crouched next to him and grabbed each shoulder. She shook him as hard as she could. "Tristan!" His eyes flew open, but he didn't see her. They were completely lost in whatever movie was playing out in his mind. She tried calling his name again. "Tristan!"

She forced down her panic and touched his head like she did last time. She calmed herself down before sending it to him. She held on through the thrashing. She wasn't going to lose him, not to this vision. When he finally saw her, she started to shake.

"What did you see?" she asked.

"I saw…" Tristan shook his head as he sat up. "I felt her die." He gripped her hands. "Her killer grabbed her throat and squeezed. His eyes were empty the whole time." He breathed in the sweet, cool air. "Paul, Mr. Martin, was there. He looked about my age. He tried to help her, but the killer knocked him out."

"Did you recognize her killer?"

Tristan scratched his chin. "I'm not sure. She didn't know his name, but I think I've seen him before." He tried to stand.

McKenna laid a hand on his arm. "Don't move. Give it a minute."

"Did I hurt you?" Worried green eyes cut through her heart.

"No. I'm fine. You held on this time."

"Help me up."

McKenna helped Tristan stand. She shouldered some of his weight while he found his balance. Tucking her hand in his, she followed him through the woods. "Where are we going?"

"I have to see something."

The midmorning sun warmed her face as leaves crunched under foot. Tristan's determination was light, but strong. McKenna reveled in it, enjoying this emotion better than the panic he had felt earlier.

Hidden Forest appeared through the trees, its large presence looming before them. They walked around behind it to the right back corner. Tristan crouched and touched the brick.

"Here," he mumbled. "She died here."

"No wonder she haunts the building." McKenna hunkered down next to him. She rested her hand on her heart, her throat closing up. "Tell me all of it, Tristan."

He did. He described how Lily thought she was meeting Dr. Cameron, her elation over the idea. He told her how that elation died when she realized the note was from a stranger, a man obsessed with her. She ran for her life, fought with everything she had inside, before she tumbled into the unfinished foundation of the building. He told her how it felt when Lily's life left her body.

McKenna's breath shuddered, warm tears streaking down her face. So many emotions filled her, the heaviest being pain for the girl who lost everything. The poor girl had tried to save herself. Even Mr. Martin had tried to help her. But she must have thought he hadn't done enough. She reached out for help. No wonder she pulled all the available energy she could.

Even though she had taken McKenna's brother from her, Lily wasn't the only monster in this situation. Someone had done this to her, killed her and left only rage behind.

"Lily blames all three of them. Dr. Cameron broke her heart, Mr. Martin stood helplessly by, and then there's her killer." She sat back on her heels digesting the information. "We have to let her finish."

"What?" Tristan's head whipped up.

"Seeing Dr. Cameron only made her angry, but I think if she can confront the man who killed her, she might be able to move on." She wiped the corner of her eyes. "God, I can't imagine being that terrified."

"I'll never forget it as long as I live."

She caught his arm. "How are you? Really?"

"My head is killing me, but I was able to hold it together longer. Thank you."

"No, thank you...for looking." She embraced him, pressing her lips to his.

His lips parted as he kissed her back. The forest around McKenna seemed to disappear. All she touched, saw, or heard was Tristan. Her heart fluttered, excitement building in her core. Tightening her hold, she melted into him.

Tristan broke the kiss. McKenna opened her eyes to see the weary look in his. She traced his jaw, stubble prickling her fingers.

"We should end the ghost before we do anything else." It was hard for her to say that with all of the energy coursing through her.

Tristan swallowed. "You're right." His voice was strained. "But I've got to rest first, maybe get a shower."

"I'll take you to my place."

He shook his head, his gaze going to the large brick building. "No, I need to reclaim my apartment."

She stepped back, but left her hands in his. "Okay. I'll go back to the hospital and check on Drew. Come by after you've rested."

"I will." He grinned.

They walked out of the woods together and parted in the parking lot. McKenna picked up on Tristan's concern and nervousness, but she let him go. He was trying to hold all of those emotions down and face whatever lay ahead. Watching him walk away hurt, especially since she wanted to protect him.

Once he was inside the building, she drove out of the parking lot. Her mind raced as she headed back to the hospital. All of the new information she had about Lily shook her to her core. Tristan had said he might know the killer, but he hadn't said who it could be. He hadn't even bothered describing the man to her. Maybe he was waiting to tell the whole group later. Tristan had been through a lot in the past two weeks; she needed to give him time.

When she reached the hospital, McKenna found Aaron sitting outside with a Styrofoam cup in his hand. He slumped forward on a bench, his elbows resting on his knees. He wasn't guarding his emotions and guilt poured out of him. Dark stubble covered his jaw, and dark circles were under his eyes. He looked lost, not like the usual confident man she knew.

Stuffing her hands in her pockets, she sat down next to him and filled him in on everything from Tristan's vision.

"How is he doing?" Aaron asked, his voice even. He sipped at the warm, black coffee in the cup. McKenna inhaled the scent and wished for her own cup of the caffeinated liquid.

"He's okay," McKenna answered, her mind back on Tristan. "He's frustrated that he couldn't name the killer, but he thinks he might know who it is."

Aaron took another sip. "Where is he right now? Looking for the guy?" He rested his elbows on his knees.

"He's at his apartment right now, probably sleeping. He said he'll meet us here later."

Aaron finished his coffee and tossed the cup into the nearest trash can. "I don't like the idea of him alone in that apartment." Worry spiked.

"I know, but he really does need the rest. He used a lot of energy reading Lily's hair bow."

Aaron stared down the walkway to the parking garage. The muscle in his jaw twitched, his mind probably going a mile a minute. McKenna stayed quiet, wondering what her boss was thinking about. In moments like this, she wished she could read minds instead of emotions.

When he didn't speak again, McKenna changed the subject. "How's Drew?"

Brown eyes turned back in her direction. "Resting. Tabby is sitting with him right now." He let out a long breath. "I should have been prepared. Should have studied this ghost better."

The guilt he bore made sense. "Aaron, it's not your fault. We all thought Dr. Cameron could calm her down and send her on." She laid a hand on his shoulder. Her heart broke for him.

"I'm the one who's worked with ghosts and psychics the longest. I should've taken more precautions. Hell, Tristan and Kayla shouldn't have been there in the first place. It wasn't safe." Aaron's features hardened. McKenna knew that look. He wanted to punch something. She wrapped her calm into a little mental ball and sent it his way. It bounced right off him. "Don't, Mac. Let me feel this."

"Okay." She dropped her hand into her lap. "Besides, that's a lot of should-haves. You're good, Aaron, but you can't see the future."

"There are days I wish I could." He climbed to his feet, stretched, and helped McKenna stand. He raked a hand through his short hair.

"Did Drew's mom make it down?"

"Yeah. She's with him now. His sister and her family live out west so she couldn't make it." Aaron's expression hardened. "The hospital couldn't find Drew's father."

McKenna blinked at the revelation. "I knew they weren't close, but I thought they'd be able to track him down." She sighed. "At least he's not alone."

Aaron started for the hospital door and McKenna fell into step beside him. "He's never been alone." Determination shoved all the other emotions aside. "He's got us."

rops of hot water pelted Tristan's back. He closed his eyes, the water running over his skin. The killer's face from his vision swam into view. He knew the man. Every instinct in his body said he had seen him before. Blue eyes, round face, stocky build. His eyes flew open. Dr. Smith's picture, the one that sat on his desk. The one that was taken years ago. But which one of the men in the picture was the killer. He had to see it again.

Tristan climbed out of the shower and got dressed. Picking up his phone, his hand hesitated over the call button. McKenna deserved to know. She wanted justice for her brother. But what if she got hurt like Drew had? He shoved the phone into his pocket.

He bit into an apple, his brain running through the plan he had already formed. He wasn't going back to the hospital to get the rest of the team. Too many people had gotten hurt because of him. He wasn't going to let that happen again. McKenna was going to be mad at him, but he decided he could live with that.

He grabbed his jacket and walked to the college.

The history building buzzed with students walking to their afternoon classes. He felt guilty not being there for his, but he had other things on his mind. He stopped by Dr. Cameron's office to find it locked. He didn't blame the head of the history department, not after last night. He made a mental note to call Cameron later and see how he was doing.

He stuffed his hands into his jacket pockets and continued on to Dr. Smith's office. No matter how crazy the whole thing sounded, he planned to tell the whole story to Smith. Maybe he remembered the professor and could help Tristan find him?

"Tristan!"

He jumped at the sound of his name. Jaime jogged over to him, her dark ponytail swinging behind her.

"Where have you been all morning?" she asked when she reached him. Her eyes widened when she saw his face. "Jesus, you're pale. What happened?"

He shrugged. "You wouldn't believe me."

"Like I wouldn't believe you're psychic?"

"Good point. I promise I'll explain later. Is Dr. Smith in his office?"

Jaime shook her head. "I think he left his door unlocked, though."

"Thanks." He walked away.

"I want to know everything when you get back!" she called after him.

He waved at her as he made his way to the office. Jaime was right, the door was unlocked. He slipped in and reached the desk in three strides. The picture sat on the edge, like it had the last time. He picked it up.

Scanning it, he found Dr. Cameron proudly holding his fish and Mr. Martin waving to the camera. Dr. Cameron's hair was indeed blondish-brown, matching with The White

Lady's first victim. Mr. Martin looked like he had in the vision with his unruly dark hair.

"No wonder you set your sights on me," he muttered to no one in particular.

In the left bottom corner, a familiar face with blue eyes and blond hair smiled for the camera. He was medium height, short compared to Dr. Cameron. His genuine enthusiasm for the trip showed through, meaning he wasn't Dr. Knight. No, Knight was in the back, scowling at the camera. Which one was Dr. Smith again?

"Can I do something for you, son?"

"Yes, sir." Tristan turned. His reply died on his lips. The blue eyes he'd been trying to match were staring right at him.

Dr. Smith stood next to him. "Well, son. What's your question?"

Tristan swallowed his nerves. He pointed to the man in the picture. "Who is that man, again?"

Smith chuckled. "That's me. I thought I told you that last time." He walked around his desk. "Did you really come in here to just look at that picture?"

Tristan set the picture down and took a step back from the desk. His palms were sweating. Dr. Smith was a killer? He tried to match the cold man he saw take Lily's life to the boisterous professor who loved to talk and constantly check up on Jaime and him. It didn't make any sense. He regretted not bringing McKenna.

Dr. Smith wrinkled his brow. "Mr. Johnson, are you all right?"

Tristan licked his dry lips. "I found out more about the hair bow."

"You did? Did it belong to that Lily girl?" Dr. Smith looked away.

"It did." Tristan paused. How was he going to get this man to his apartment? He hadn't believed him the last time he mentioned The White Lady. The door was open right behind him. He could leave, call the police. Call McKenna. And then what? He had no proof that Dr. Smith had killed anyone. All he had was a psychic vision in his head. No, it was up to Tristan to get the older man to Hidden Forest. He was the last piece. His presence would draw the ghost like Martin's and Cameron's had. He fisted his hands. "Her name was Lily Comer, and she was murdered in the woods behind my apartment building twenty years ago."

Smith stilled. He lifted his head. "Who killed her?" His voice was low.

"You did, sir." *Johnson, I hope you know what you're doing*, he thought.

"Close the door, Mr. Johnson." Smith stood. A drawer scraped open.

The door clicked closed. Tristan left his hand on the doorknob.

"Now." Smith walked around his desk, a small gun in his hand. "How do you know all this? And be careful how you answer. Accidents can happen." He kept the gun at his side, the muzzle pointed to the floor.

Tristan raised an eyebrow. *Who keeps a gun in their desk drawer?* He hadn't planned for that development. He gripped the knob. "I've got proof. At my apartment."

Smith cocked his head. "Then why are you telling me? Why not go to the police?"

"I didn't...I didn't want it to be true." Tristan thought fast. Lying had never been his specialty, but he had to bring Smith to The White Lady. It was the only way to finish this. He rubbed the back of his neck and tried to ignore the flutter in his gut. Sweat broke out along his brow. He fought to keep his voice steady. "I wanted you to tell me I was wrong."

"Well." Smith cradled his gun as he approached Tristan. "I

guess you made the wrong choice." He pressed the muzzle into Tristan's side. "Let's go get it."

~

"You know, you don't have to babysit me. I'll be fine." Drew pulled his gaze away from his computer game. "Besides, Mom'll be back soon." His color was better, not as pale. His hazel eyes were brighter. The rest overnight seemed to have done him a world of good.

McKenna glanced up from the notes she had been taking. "I'm not babysitting you. I'm keeping you company." She propped her chin with her hand. "Besides, Tristan will be here any minute."

She reached out to his emotions. His pain was a steady ache, but he was in good spirits. He was taking his aggression out on the evil assassins in the video game he played. McKenna breathed a sigh of relief.

The first time she had seen him after the attack, she found it hard to process what happened. His back was covered in cuts while his left side was black and blue. His arm was sprained, and he had needed stitches on his legs. He was in so much pain he was projecting it. McKenna had had to strengthen her shields in order to help get him and Tristan out of the apartment.

Drew nodded at the notebook. "What are you writing?"

"I'm trying to organize all the notes on this case." She tapped the end of her pen on her notebook. "If Tristan would get here already, we'd have the final piece of the puzzle."

Drew saved his game and closed the laptop. "What do you mean?"

"Tristan saw the killer."

"What?" He sucked in a breath when he jerked his side too fast. "Is he okay?"

"He's fine. He used the hair bow to hang on to the vision. He wanted to do it for you."

"Damn it, it's not his fault. It's not like he asked the ghost to drain him." He scowled as he snuggled deeper into his pillow. "He has the whole martyr thing down. You both do. Does that come with the whole psychic thing?"

"Maybe." McKenna turned back to her notes.

Quiet filled the room before Drew broke it. "I'm glad he met you."

McKenna met his eyes. "You are?"

"Yeah." Drew grinned. "I should have introduced you two sooner, but he didn't want anybody else to know he was psychic."

"He said you always knew."

He ran a hand over his laptop. "Yeah, I was there the first time he saw something. We were in class, and he went white as a sheet. His eyes glazed over. For a second, I thought he stopped breathing. And then he jumped up and started screaming. Scared the crap out of me."

"He said you stayed."

"I did. Hell, we'd been friends since fourth grade. He made me feel better every time my dad came home drunk. His parents gave me a place to stay. I wasn't going to bail." He rubbed the back of his neck. "I know his dad tried to help him control it, but…"

McKenna set her notebook and pen aside. Her heart ached for two boys who had no one but each other to rely on. "He wanted to ignore it."

"Yeah. I think his dad took him to past crime scenes to see if he could see anything. Tristan hated those."

"What about when Zack came into the mix?"

"Zack was the nicest guy in the world. Tristan didn't trust him, but I took to him pretty quick. Oh, Tristan got so pissed when we got into the whole ghost-hunting thing. Zack used

259

to do it with me. I don't blame him. Every time he walks into a building he's never been to before, he sees its past. I don't know how he deals. That would drive me nuts."

"It sounds like you two really trust each other."

"We do." Drew's eyes flickered to the clock on the wall. "Didn't you say he'd be here this afternoon?" He gestured at it with his thumb. "It's coming up on two o'clock."

"Yeah," McKenna's brow furrowed. "Maybe he's running late."

Drew arched an eyebrow. "Tristan rarely runs late." He nodded to her phone. "Call him."

She chewed on her bottom lip. Tristan had said he would be coming, but he hadn't given a specific time. She pulled up his name and hit the call button. The other end seemed to ring forever until the voice mail picked up. She disconnected. "If he's planning to meet us, he would answer the phone, right?"

"What's wrong?" Tabitha walked through the door with Aaron and Kayla right behind her. A fast food bag dangled from her hand.

"Tristan isn't answering his phone, and he's not here yet."

Drew winced as he struggled to sit. He closed his eyes for a minute, trying to catch his breath. "Tristan is the king of guilt. He thinks me getting hurt is his fault."

"Yeah," Aaron replied.

Realization dawned on Kayla's face. "He'd try to keep us out of this if he could." She wiped her face. "He'd try to find a way to stop the ghost on his own."

"What?" McKenna tightened her grip on the cell phone. "He said he thinks he knows who the killer is. That means he'd go after him alone."

Drew worked at the tape holding his IV in place. "We've got to go find him. Somebody help me up."

McKenna touched his arm. "You're not going anywhere. We can find him."

Drew groaned. "He's going to get his stupid ass killed. Let me help."

"You won't do any good in your condition." Tabitha shoved the bag of food at McKenna. "Eat fast, girl." She turned to Kayla. "Stay here and make sure this idiot doesn't get out of bed." She then set her sights on Aaron. He already had his car keys in his hand.

"Let's go," he said.

"That's it, son. Nice and slow."

Tristan's side hurt from the hard gun muzzle pressed into it. Smith kept it hidden under his coat, but his face never once betrayed it. He draped his free arm around Tristan's shoulder and informed anyone who asked that Mr. Johnson was a good man to help an old professor to his car. Anytime Tristan tried to deviate from the script, Smith pushed the gun harder into Tristan's ribs.

"You're quite the young actor," Smith commented as they crossed the street. "Maybe I'll keep you around. Depends on how I feel."

"Glad I could help," Tristan answered through clenched teeth.

They made their way across the parking lot and into Hidden Forest. The trek up the stairs was slow, but Tristan hoped it would be worth it. He hadn't planned his next move. He wasn't even sure The White Lady would appear. After all, it was close to two, and the earliest he had ever seen her was around six.

His phone rang in his pocket. His hand moved to pull it

out, but Smith jabbed him with the gun. "Keep walking." He did as he was told.

He opened the door to his apartment. Smith urged him forward and shut the door behind them. The older man dropped the pretense and his coat. The gun stayed where it was.

"All right, son. Where is this evidence?" Smith narrowed his eyes.

"I lied." Tristan kept his eyes forward, praying the ghost would somehow know her killer was here. "I don't have any evidence."

Smith cocked the gun. "Then why are we here?"

Tristan waited. "You can show up now," he muttered. Nothing. The room stayed warm. The electricity remained on. His heart beat in his ears. He was going to die, and nobody knew what he had done. His phone rang again.

"Blasted things." Smith yanked it out of Tristan's pocket. He tossed it to the floor and crushed it under his shoe. "You know, I think we should move out to the woods. Less chance of bothering your neighbors."

Tristan turned. "Don't you want to see her again?"

"What?"

"The legend. The White Lady of Hidden Forest. It's not a story students made up to explain the mysterious deaths. She's real, and she's Lily." Stall. He had to stall. If Lily was anywhere in this building and she still had the energy she had taken from him, she'd be there. For once, Tristan was ready for her to exact her revenge. And he was more than happy to help her do that.

Smith's grip tightened on the gun. "For twenty years nobody knew about Lily. She was my own secret." His shoulders sagged as his eyes appeared to soften.

Tristan didn't hide his surprise. "Did you know her spirit was haunting this building, killing people?"

Smith chuckled. "I didn't believe it at first. The White Lady, what a legend. But when that first boy died this year, I started to wonder." He looked at the ceiling. "I drove by one night and saw her in one of the windows. She was gorgeous. And I thought, she can be mine, like she always should have." His features hardened. "Then you started asking questions." The gun shook in his hand. "Well, no more."

"Dr. Smith, I don't have any proof. Who would I tell? Nobody would believe me. Let me go." Tristan walked backwards to his kitchen counter. He felt around for a knife, hoping he'd left one on the counter.

"Oh, where's the fun in that?" Smith pointed the gun at Tristan. "How else could I watch you die? You know, that was the best part about killing Lily, watching her die. It was the most amazing thing I had ever seen. In a way, I preserved a piece of history." He aimed. "She'll never grow old, and she'll stay here with us forever. Now." His voice dropped. "Let's take a walk."

The room became so cold that Tristan's breath puffed out in tiny white clouds. Goosebumps traveled along his arms, and the hair on the back of his neck stood. Female laughter filled the room. Lily formed right behind Smith, her terrible beauty glowing brightly. Smith glanced behind him.

"Came to watch, have you, dear?" he asked.

Screaming, she sailed towards him, only to pass right through. No! She touched everyone else, including him. Why couldn't she touch Smith? Tristan didn't have time to think about it. He dove for Smith. The gun went off.

The loud crack of a gun stopped McKenna in her tracks. "No. Oh, God, no." She pushed through all the emotions swarming the building – joy, sadness, frustration –

until she found the blackness of intense hate. She gasped, grabbing her right leg. Pain traveled along her thigh.

Tabitha dropped beside her. "What happened? Are you hurt?"

McKenna shook her head. "No, but I think Tristan is." She opened up, locking on the pain. He was there, and if he was shot in the leg, he was momentarily still alive.

Aaron took off up the stairs, his steps pounding and his long legs taking two at a time.

"Can you walk?" Tabitha's concern warred with the pain for McKenna's attention.

"I'll be fine. Right behind you."

She closed her eyes, willing herself to push past the pain and run. Tristan was here; he had to be. But how long would he stay alive?

The drive to the building was excruciating. McKenna had called one more time, only to be sent to voice mail. She shivered at the thought of Tristan facing Lily's killer on his own. Why would he do that? What was his plan? Did he even have a plan?

She ascended the stairs two at a time. The bitter cold on the third floor took her breath away. They weren't alone. Aaron rammed his shoulder into Tristan's door as she reached them.

"Locked?" she asked.

"I don't know." Aaron grit his teeth. "The knob won't turn."

"I think the ghost has the Do Not Disturb sign up," Tabitha said.

"No!" McKenna banged on the door. "Lily! Let us in! You have to let us help him!" Her leg throbbed. Her heart ached. No! She had just found him; she refused to lose him now. Her fists pounded the door. "Lily, please!"

The door remained closed.

❧

Tristan's leg throbbed with sharp pain. He sucked in air, stars popping up across his vision. Wet and sticky liquid bubbled out of the wound. Trying to ignore it, he pulled himself up. The gun had clattered to the floor, and his eyes searched for its landing spot. It rested near a book shelf on the other wall.

Tristan's tried to crawl to it, but Dr. Smith was faster. He leveled the gun. "I wanted to do this outside, but I guess we have no choice now, do we?"

Someone banged on his door. The wood rocked against the force. Quiet. Another bang. Voices argued. Then someone pounded on the door. "Lily! Let us in!" Tristan's eyes widened. McKenna! No! She wasn't supposed to be there.

Tristan crawled to the wall, waiting for Smith's bullet. His leg ached. Lily couldn't seem to touch Smith. His eyes darted to the glowing specter. Rage filled her face, her eyes glowing red. What had happened to the energy she had the night before? She had no problem taking out Mr. Martin and trying to take out Dr. Cameron? But neither one of them had actually taken her life. When she died, Lily had wanted more strength to fight off Dr. Smith.

That's what the psychic energy was for her—strength. Tristan raised his hand to Lily, and time seemed to slow down.

"Take it," he said. "Take all you need."

Lily darted passed Dr. Smith. She grabbed Tristan's head and pulled. Her touch was still cold, but it didn't feel like a bucket of ice. He fed her energy, and it flowed from him like a fountain. His body grew weaker while Lily glowed brighter, her body solidifying. The edges of his vision dimmed and his injury hurt. The wet blood ran through his jeans, soaking them. If he was going to die anyway, he might as well take Dr. Smith with him.

The door swung open. McKenna stumbled through. Her breath caught as she watched the scene in front of her.

Lily let go of Tristan's head. In a flash, she grabbed an older man's throat. His feet left the floor and his grip loosened on a gun. It rattled on the hardwood floor. He swung his legs, dangling like a fish from her grasp.

"Lily, I never meant to hurt you. I love you," he choked out.

Lily cocked her head to the side. "You have to pay." In the blink of an eye, she threw him through the sliding glass door. He sailed over the balcony, his screams echoing.

The ghost turned to McKenna and bowed her head. She floated to Tristan, resting her hand on his head. Her glow dimmed as Tristan began to stir. He gasped in a breath, his chest arching. When she released him, she held out her arms. Her glow brightened until she was engulfed in white light.

McKenna held up her hands, trying to block out the light. It brightened and was gone in an instant. She searched for any trace of the warm, peaceful emotion she had felt from the ghost, but there was nothing left.

She ran to Tristan while Tabitha and Aaron raced to the balcony.

"How are we going to explain this?" Tabitha asked.

"I'm going to need a drink," Aaron grumbled.

McKenna yanked off her jacket and wrapped it around Tristan's red-soaked leg. He coughed. A lazy grin spread across his pale face. He touched her cheek. "You're okay." He was tired, groggy, and in pain, but alive.

"Don't ever do that again, do you understand?" she

scowled as she dialed the emergency number. She had half a mind to kill him herself.

"Can't make any promises." He slid sideways. "I'm never living in an apartment again," he said as he laid his cheek on the cool floor.

## 26

Sunlight fell across Tristan's face, warming his skin. He smiled at McKenna, who held his hand tightly. He nodded encouragement to her. She released his hand and placed the bouquet of flowers on the fresh grave.

"Rest in peace, Lily," she whispered.

"I hope she doesn't come back," Drew said. "She packed a mean punch."

"Show some respect," Aaron said as he smacked the back of Drew's head.

Tabitha hit Aaron on the shoulder. "He hasn't been out of the hospital long. Be nice."

Tristan couldn't help but smile wider as he thought about the last week. None of them had any idea how to explain Dr. Smith's death. When the police and ambulance arrived, they all agreed to tell the truth, no matter what the police believed.

Detective Thompson swore when he saw who his witnesses were. "You? Again?" He glared at all of them. "You know, I think I'm on a first-name basis with all of you."

"Pleased to see you again, Detective Thompson." Tristan waved from the stretcher.

"Would someone like to tell us what happened?" Detective Morgan asked.

Tristan exchanged glances with McKenna, Tabitha, and Aaron. "You won't believe us," he said.

"Try us," Thompson ground out.

"It was a ghost." Aaron crossed the parking lot to meet the detectives. "The White Lady."

Thompson arched an eyebrow. "The one Ms. Collins was telling us about?"

"Yes, sir." Aaron pointed to the corpse. "She killed him like she killed the others." He patted the detective's shoulder. "Don't worry. We took care of her for you."

"You did?" Skepticism dripped from Thompson's voice.

Aaron slipped a card into his pocket. "Got a ghost problem? We've got your solution."

Morgan sighed. "How about we talk about this downtown?"

The EMTs started to roll Tristan towards the ambulance. "Wait!" he called. "Check under the building."

"What?" Detective Thompson's face turned as red as a tomato.

Morgan put a hand on his shoulder. "Calm down, Bill. Breathe."

Tristan raised up on his elbows. He winced as his leg throbbed. "My dad is Chief Matthew Johnson. He's retired now, but he worked with your department on a lot of missing cases."

Morgan nodded. "I remember him. Man could find just about anyone." He rubbed his chin. "Whispers around the precinct said he was psychic."

"He is," Tristan declared. "So am I."

A paramedic tried to push him down. "We need to get you into the ambulance, sir."

"Do me a favor and check under the building." Tired, he lay back down and let the paramedics put him in the ambulance.

A day later, McKenna filled him in on what happened. The police followed his advice and checked under the building. They found Lily's body right where Tristan had said it was. It took a while to dig it out from under the floor, but her family was finally able to bury her.

Detectives Thompson and Morgan showed up at the hospital. Tristan told them about the bow and about his vision, but neither cop appeared to fully believe him. They tried to find evidence that connected McKenna, Tabitha, or Aaron to Dr. Smith's death, but there was none. In the end, it remained a cold case.

When he finally got out of the hospital, Tristan wanted to see Lily's grave. In the end, they had helped each other find peace. He needed to pay his respects to her.

The grass behind him crunched. Jaime, carrying flowers, and a young girl made their way to the graveside. Tristan and McKenna moved aside.

"You came?" Tristan asked.

"I felt like it was the nice thing to do." Jaime set the flowers on the grave. "After you told me the whole story, my heart broke for her." She shook her head. "I can't believe Dr. Smith killed her. It's terrifying to think about." She took in all the other people. "Hi, I'm Jaime. I share an office with Tristan."

"We met." McKenna beamed. "Who is this?" She indicated the girl.

"This is Ella, my daughter." Ella waved at everyone, then stared at her shoes.

Tristan introduced Aaron and Tabitha, but Drew cut him off before he could introduce him.

He shook Jaime's hand. "Andrew Keane. I'm Tristan's smarter, better-looking friend."

Jaime chuckled. "Are you?"

Drew shrugged. "Everyone says so."

"Well, it's a good thing I'm not everyone." And, like that, the tension lifted.

As they walked away from the grave site, Tristan turned to Kayla. "What are you going to do now?"

Kayla smiled. "I'm staying here and finishing out the school year. I owe my students that much. Then I might head down to Charleston, spend some time with my brother. Give myself a chance to heal."

"Sounds like a good idea." McKenna patted her shoulder.

"Charleston's a great place," Jaime chimed in. "Thank you for letting us be a part of this. Tristan, I'll see you at work." With a wave, she and Ella headed back the way they came.

"Where have you been hiding her, man?" Drew watched her walk away as if he were in a trance.

Kayla nudged him. "Don't be creepy."

"I wasn't being creepy."

"That was so creepy."

Drew draped an arm around Kayla. "Come on, I'll give you a ride back to Angela's."

"Thank you." They waved good-bye and disappeared through the trees.

McKenna squeezed Tristan's hand as they approached his truck. "You planning on coming out as a psychic? Maybe help us out at the office? We could use someone who can see the past."

"Maybe. It felt good helping Lily move on and keeping my neighbors safe. I still have the world's worst control, though."

He stopped and wrapped his arms around her. She giggled as he lifted her into the air.

"We can work on your control, you know." She poked his chest.

"I'd rather work on something else." He lowered her to ground. Bending closer to her, he nibbled on her ear.

For the first time in his life, he had found someone who made him feel sane. And for that, he was grateful.

She pulled away, her eyes heavy-lidded. "How fast can you drive?"

He reached his apartment in record time. He opened the door, and for the first time since he moved in, everything was quiet. No shadows of the past pushed their way into his mind. No ghost sucked all of the warmth out of the room. McKenna was the only other person in his world.

Smiling, Tristan closed his door. He lifted McKenna into his arms and carried her into his bedroom.


The End

## ACKNOWLEDGMENTS

Like you do when you pretend to win an Oscar, I've been practicing my acknowledgments page for a while now. However, now that I'm actually writing one, I'm a bit overwhelmed. Bear with me. It's true that you can't write a book alone. Okay, you can do the actual writing alone, but all the encouragement and inspiration come from outside yourself.

Thank you to John Hartness and Falstaff for taking a chance on this quirky little book. When I started it all those years ago, I didn't know if it would ever see the light of day. Melissa Gilbert, I'm so glad I got an editor who could also be my friend. How many people can say that?

My two best friends in the whole world, Alexandra Christian and Susan Roddey, thank you for pushing me and telling me to finish this book already. And for liking my fanfiction all those years ago. It's true that you can meet your best friends while fangirling a movie musical.

Thank you to Rebecca Enzor and Tyffani Clark Kemp! I got so lucky when I found the best writer's group in Charleston. Our members may have changed throughout the months, but the three of us were a constant. You helped me shape this book into what it is now.

Thank you, Tina McSwain, for answering some ridiculous ghost hunting questions.

And thank you to Tally Johnson for imparting his ghost hunting wisdom, even when I didn't really ask for it. Seriously, though, may someone tie you down to the Devil's Tramping Ground one day and film it for all of our enjoyment. *Hey, Y'all, Hold My Beer* needs to happen. Bill Roddey, it's up to you!

Jonathan Phillips, little brother extraordinaire, thank you for looking at the first draft of this and saying, "You can do better than this." And I did better than that.

Love to all of my nieces and nephews – Genevieve, Annabelle, Fox, Mason, and Kit!

To my parents for patiently encouraging me, even when you weren't in the mood to read another story.

Finally, to my heart, Michael, who puts up with me every day. I didn't think I'd find someone whose weirdness matched my own. I love you! Still fifty more years to go!

FALSTAFF BOOKS

**Want to know what's new**
**And coming soon from**
**Falstaff Books?**

**Try This Free Ebook Sampler**

https://www.instafreebie.com/free/bsZnl

**Follow the link.**
**Download the file.**
**Transfer to your e-reader, phone, tablet, watch, computer,**
**whatever.**
**Enjoy.**

## ABOUT THE AUTHOR

Amy Ravenel has done a bit of everything – waitressing, customer service, teaching, librarianship. But writing has been the only thing she's ever wanted to do. She has a deep love for bookstores, the mountains, and all sorts of geeky things. A native North Carolinian, she grew up in the foothills near the inspiration for Mayberry. Today, she lives with her epically-bearded husband and her epically-furry cats.

THANK YOU FOR YOUR SUPPORT!

Thanks to the following awesome people for supporting
Falstaff Books on Patreon!
Dino Hicks
Staci-Leigh Santore
Sheryl R. Hayes
Scott Norris
Samuel Montgomery-Blinn